Whiskey River Runaway

Whiskey River Runaway

A Whiskey River Romance

Justine Davis

TULE
PUBLISHING

Whiskey River Runaway

Tule Publishing First Printing, March 2018

The Tule Publishing Group, LLC

ISBN: 978-1-948342-69-8

Chapter One

THE PLACE WAS a wreck.

There was no other way to describe it. This house on the outskirts of Whiskey River needed a lot of care. Truett Mahan was sorry to see it in such a state. There were a lot of memories here. Memories of good times and sad.

And the way Jamie Templeton was going, it just might become a fan shrine one of these days, since he'd first discovered his calling here. He grinned at the thought, remembering not the rock star but the quiet, kind of dorky kid from high school.

The kid whose world had shattered the same day his had.

"I should have thought about it sooner," True muttered, walking carefully given the rubble, a section of roof here, pieces of broken siding there as he headed for the back of the house. It wasn't really Jamie's fault. It wasn't like the guy had much time these days to come back to Whiskey River and see how his aunt's old place was doing. And after the way Millie Templeton had stepped up not just for Jamie but for him, and his sister as well, he should have stepped up himself.

He rounded the back corner of the house, skirting a large pile of debris, and glanced at the big picture window that looked out toward the river. Or had; it was broken now, the late afternoon sun highlighting a spider web of cracks overtaking nearly the entire expanse of glass, and he guessed one more good storm would take it out altogether. He'd have to board it up; he'd thought he might find problems like this so he'd brought out a couple of full sheets of plywood in his truck. The place had been well built originally, but no building could withstand total neglect for long.

Zee said old houses died of emptiness, a rather whimsical view for his practical little sister. Who had had a sizeable crush on Jamie, back when he'd just been that clever but withdrawn kid who spent most of his time up in a tree house with an old, battered guitar.

That thought made him glance toward the big post oak about halfway between the house and the river. And he laughed; the tree house Jamie had built was in better shape than the house itself. Which shouldn't surprise him, even as a kid the guy had been clever about how things went together. He—

He stopped dead in the act of turning back to the house. He'd seen. . .something. He was sure of it. Movement. Just inside that picture window. Quick. Almost furtive. Had some animal gotten in there? It certainly seemed possible, given the state of things.

He walked over to the back door, tried the knob. It, at least, was locked. He already knew the front door was as well. He might have to finish breaking this window to get in, which he could do since he had the materials to board it up.

He kept going around the house, mind already on offloading a full sheet of plywood, getting his drill out of the toolbox and digging out some wood screws long enough to hold it. He'd have to—

Again he stopped short. This time next to the only other exterior door on the house, the one that he knew led into the laundry room. The lower left corner of the glass pane had a fist-sized hole broken out. The corner that would give a person access to the door knob.

And suddenly that furtive movement he'd seen took on an entirely different feeling.

For an instant he thought of heading for his truck to grab his Winchester 94. Whiskey River was generally a quiet place when it came to serious crime, their very effective police department had a rep, but you never knew. Especially a trespasser with unknown motive. But the only living things he'd ever shot with the classic weapon he'd owned since childhood were rattlesnakes, and once a rabid skunk, and one of his life's goals was to keep it that way. So instead he backtracked to that pile of debris he'd passed, dug out a board about the length of a baseball bat. He hefted it; it seemed sturdy enough, and had a couple of good sized, treacherous looking nails sticking out at one end.

If I need more than this, then I'm in trouble anyway.

He went back to the door with the broken window. Tried the knob. A bit to his surprise, it didn't turn. Who would break into a place and then lock the door after them? Especially when it was obvious how they'd done it and anybody else could now do the same, thanks to the broken window?

Which he did, reaching through carefully to avoid the sharp edges of the broken glass with his hand and trusting his jacket to protect his wrist and arm. The inside knob turned easily. But of course the damn door squealed from disuse as he tried to open it quietly. *So much for stealth.* He shoved it the rest of the way and stepped inside, looking in all directions as quickly as he could.

Nothing. He scanned the floor. The layer of dust was fairly thick, although the tile floor beneath looked solid enough. And he could see it, thanks to the set of footprints that crossed it.

Small footprints.

A kid? Was the answer as simple as that, a kid exploring? For a moment he stood still, just listening for any sound of movement. Nothing. He looked at the size of that shoe print again. Lowered the board. Called out.

"It's okay, you can come out."

Still nothing.

"I know the place looks abandoned, so if you just wanted to explore, that's okay."

And again nothing.

He supposed the smart thing to do would be to call for the folks with the badges. But he kept thinking about the size of those feet and didn't do it. The police had better things to do anyway.

He followed the tracks into the hallway. Saw two sets of the same prints, one pointing toward the kitchen, one toward the den. The trail toward the kitchen seemed more traveled, as if whoever it was had been in there more. He knew the power to the house had been off while Jamie decided what he wanted to do, so it wasn't like anyone could get much practical use out of the place. And he was fairly sure any pest-attracting food had long ago been removed. Zee would have seen to that, even if she had been angry at Jamie.

"I just can't believe he doesn't care enough to come home to go through her things," she had said. "She's the one who so encouraged his music. I know he loved her."

True could empathize; it had been hell going through their parents' things after they'd been killed in the same accident that had left Jamie an orphan, and as the oldest, the task had fallen to him. As had taking care of his little sister. It had been an. . .interesting transition.

And good practice for your life later.

He snapped himself out of the thought with a shake of his head. Fine time to lapse into old, painful memories, standing in an abandoned house that had been broken into with the perpetrator likely still inside. He hefted the board, considered a half-second longer, then headed for the kitchen.

It appeared empty. The floor was less dusty here. Much less. In fact, it looked as if someone had made an effort to clean; the swirling marks looked like a dust mop. His brow furrowed. You didn't do that, did you, unless you were here a while? Or planned to be?

He turned to follow the other set of small tracks he'd seen, that led to the den on the other side of the house. Halfway there it struck him, what that room had that none of the others did.

A fireplace.

January in Texas would seem a paradise to many parts of the country, but it had been dropping into the mid-thirties at night lately, and he for one wouldn't want to be living rough in it. It was still chilly even now, shortly after sunrise. Somebody looking for something to steal was one thing. Somebody seeking shelter from the winter cold, with nowhere else to go, was something else again.

He nudged the door to the den open.

It was empty. It was also, he realized after a moment, warmer. The closed off room was definitely warmer than the rest of the empty house. After a glance around he walked over to the fireplace that looked as if it had been built from rock out of the river that ran by in the distance. He touched the rounded stones. Not hot, but noticeably warm. He had no doubt now, but bent slightly to test the temperature of the interior of the fireplace. Above the layer of ash and charred fragments of wood he felt an even stronger heat, and guessed one good stir would turn up some live embers. Recent, then.

The bare wood floor of the room was in the same state as the kitchen floor, looking as if it had been swirled over with a mop. And the space directly in front of the hearth was the cleanest of all. From someone sitting there? Perhaps sleeping there?

He walked back to the kitchen, considering. Stood in the middle of that room, looking around. And after a moment he walked over to a door in the far corner, which at one time had had a hand-painted sign above it that said "Millie's Pantry," a holdover from when she had run a small shop in town. He hefted the nailed board in his hand, just in case. He pulled the door open.

He'd found the trespasser.

And the mop.

And she hit him with it.

Chapter Two

SHE SHOULD HAVE known.

Hope Larson realized now that the moment she'd started to think she might be able to stay here a while should have been a clue that things were about to go sour on her. She should have expected she'd be found out, despite her care.

What she hadn't expected was Mister-Tall-Dark-and-Studly. And only belatedly did she realized the studly part could also apply to the board he was holding, with the wicked looking nails sticking out of one end. And once that realization hit, a stream of them hit. He must not have a gun. He hadn't hit her with that board, even when she'd hit him with the only thing she had, that worn out mop. He'd only let out one, succinct "Damn" when she'd connected. He was quick for a big guy; no matter which way she dodged he was there. And he was big. Tall anyway. Lean. Young. Or was he? There was a touch of gray at his temples. But his face was young. Not his eyes, though.

And if you're through cataloging his assets, perhaps you

might focus on getting away?

That inner voice of hers was getting snarkier by the day. And rightfully so; she had made an utter mess of her life. Pretty sad to be well down the road to ruin at twenty-three. When most women her age were starting careers, excitedly going places and doing things, exploring the world in their new adulthood, or getting married and producing children to grow up and break their hearts, here she was. . .going places and doing things she never would have imagined. Not excitedly, but with full blown terror that somehow, somewhere she would make a mistake that would end up getting her killed. Or worse, boomerang on those she loved, those she had left behind because it was the only way to protect them.

She hoped she hadn't just made that mistake.

She wanted to stay cowering in the corner of this tiny room, but she knew her only chance at escape was to somehow get past this guy. He was tall, if she went in low she might—

"Don't."

Her gaze snapped from his knees up to his face. Definitely young, she thought, never mind the bit of gray. And his voice was young. Strong.

"Just relax."

She almost laughed at that. She hadn't relaxed since the day she'd blown up her life by the simple act of being in the wrong place at the wrong time. Hopeless Larson, that was her. Back then, she never could have imagined how appropriate the moniker Kim had hung on her would become.

Hopeless, maybe. But she wasn't helpless. She'd been there once, too, and had sworn she would never, ever be in that position again. And if that meant she had to tackle this guy who had to be six-one at least, then so be it. She—

"Don't," he said again. "I don't want to hurt you."

"That's why the board with the killer spikes?"

"They're only ten penny nails."

"Looks like a buck's worth to me."

"Better than my Winchester."

Damn. He did have a gun. But not on him? She scanned him up and down from where she crouched up against the shelves at her back. Noticed the long legs, the jeans, the dark knit shirt tucked in over a flat belly, stretching across a broad chest. He could have a weapon beneath that worn denim jacket, but then why would he have picked up that fanged board? Besides, wasn't a Winchester a rifle? Like in a western movie?

"Look, kid," he said, "just take it easy."

Kid. Of course. She knew what she looked like, faded jeans with a hole in one knee, worn running shoes, and the ripped T-shirt with the logo of some club somewhere she'd never been or even heard of; she'd snagged the shirt out of a donation bin when no one was looking, along with the several sizes too big, stained but still warm jacket she was huddled in. Her makeup days were long behind her, and her hair was pulled in a long tail through the back of the Rangers cap on her head. She didn't like wearing hats, but it helped the image and even this small bit of coverage helped keep her warm. All in all, she knew she looked about fifteen, if that.

Which she had in the past used to her advantage, when she had to.

Her thoughts were racing. He was a big, strong guy. Chances were he wouldn't really use that thing on her if he thought she was just a kid.

"Look," she said, trying to sound young and scared. Not that it was an effort, it was how she felt. "I'll leave. I didn't hurt anything, really."

"I'm not sure the trespassing law requires that. Not to mention that broken window."

Her heart sank. A shiver went through her. If he called the cops. . .She tried to fight the chill that swept her.

"This is your place, then?" she asked.

"I'm responsible for it."

She couldn't help glancing around at the accumulated dust and general air of neglect. "Nice job." She winced inwardly. *That smart mouth of yours is going to get you in trouble again.*

But studly's mouth quirked as if he were suppressing a smile.

"I'm responsible as of yesterday," he amended.

"Oh."

He had a great voice, she thought. Deep, like you'd expect for his size, but not booming, not intimidating. No, something else entirely, she wasn't sure what, but it made her hyper-aware. Which made it hard to think. And she really needed to think.

"So," she said, "you weren't responsible when I broke in. So it's not your problem."

He drew back slightly. "You have an. . .interesting way of looking at things."

She sighed. "Yeah. It happens when. . ."

"You're cornered?" he suggested.

Reasonably sure now he wasn't going to just come after her with his spiky board, she sat in her corner, pulling her knees up and wrapping her arms around them. As if that could protect her somehow.

"Just let me go. You'll never see me again, I swear."

He didn't speak, but she saw he'd shifted his gaze. Focused on her left wrist. The tattoo. She doubted he would recognize the tribal style marking. No one outside of one L.A. neighborhood likely would. There, it was a sign of belonging to the group. Here, over a thousand miles away, it meant nothing. Unless you had an aversion to women with tattoos.

She couldn't read his expression. It didn't seem to change as he assessed her. And that's what he was doing, she was sure. She could only imagine what he was thinking. She was tired, hungry, dirty and she knew she looked it.

Even as she thought it his gaze narrowed. Sharpened.

"You're hurt."

She blinked. She'd been so focused on him she'd almost forgotten. But now that he'd said it, the ache slammed into her consciousness again. Instinctively she flexed her ankle, and couldn't keep herself from wincing.

"I noticed," she muttered.

That quickly he went from intimidating to concerned. He crouched before her, setting aside, she noticed, the menacing looking board with the nails.

"You're bleeding."

"I noticed that, too," she said dryly. Hard not to when the hem of her jeans was nearly saturated.

He reached toward her. She recoiled, as instinctively as she'd flexed that ankle. He froze. His gaze shot back to her face.

"I won't hurt you."

"Funny, that's what the guy who caused that said."

Something else sparked in his eyes then—something darker, hotter. It almost looked like anger.

"Some guy did this to you?"

"Indirectly," she said, back to full wariness after that look in his eyes. "It happened when I was getting away from him."

"Who?"

She shrugged. "No idea," she said. Which would have been her answer anyway, but in this case it happened to be the truth.

"Someone here? In Whiskey River?"

She heard anger and disbelief in equal measure in his voice. She wondered if he suspected someone, or if he was just angry at the thought it might be someone he knew, someone from his town. She had the sudden thought that if it was, they'd have him to deal with. It gave her a very strange feeling inside.

But it didn't matter, she needed to get away from this guy. And obviously she couldn't stay here any longer, so she might as well get back on the road. Too bad; this had been a nice little hideout, while it lasted. With the fire going, she'd been more comfortable than she had been since that lady in Tucson had taken pity on her and let her sleep in the room over her garage for a couple of nights.

"Who—"

"Look," she said before he could push harder, "I accepted a ride from the wrong guy, that's all. It's over."

"Except for the bleeding."

His tone was as dry as hers had been. And for some reason that sparked a trace of amusement in her. "Well, yes. That."

"You should see a doctor."

"No!"

It came out sharply, edged with panic, and she tried to control the instant leap her heart made. He leaned back on his heels—cowboy boots, she noticed; did everybody around here wear those things?—and studied her for a moment.

"Is it doctors you're afraid of, or just anybody?"

Everybody.

She made herself not say it. For some reason it was too much to admit to this man. She'd noticed that before; the more together, the more strong a person she met was, the more she hated admitting she needed help. And this guy looked well put together in more ways than one.

He was looking at her as if she'd said it. Or as if he'd read the answer in her expression. She supposed he thought it pitiful, to be afraid of everyone. And that rankled almost as much as the fear itself.

"Listen, cowboy," she began.

"I'm not a cowboy."

She blinked. He'd almost sounded defensive. "Sorry. The boots threw me."

"I wear them because they're comfortable, and practical on a job site."

"Job site?"

"Speaking of which, since I oversee a lot of construction projects, I'm semi-competent at first aid. Which you could use, if you won't see a doctor."

That didn't surprise her, that he was a boss of sorts. He had the air. And she was guessing first aid wasn't the only thing he was competent at. "You going to work on this place?"

"Maybe. The owner asked me to take a look."

"Owner must not care much," she said, with a glance

around. “Too bad. It’s a good house.”

Something else sparked in those blue eyes of his. Curiosity? She hoped not. The last thing she needed was a curious non-cowboy, or anyone else, poking into her business.

And it was the last thing he needed, even if he didn’t know it. Because the trouble she’d left behind could catch up with her at any moment.

Chapter Three

TRUE STUDIED THE kid for a silent moment. She appeared exhausted, her eyes much older than she looked. Worn, and not just her clothes. Although interestingly she was clean enough, even if her jeans could use a wash. So she made an effort. He wondered how; the power to everything was off here, including the well pump. But there might have been water left in the pressure tank. That would have given her enough for very basic needs for a few days, if she was careful. If she had any idea about wells, that is.

"What's your name?" he asked.

Again he saw fear flash in her eyes. Warm, cinnamon-brown eyes that matched the color of her hair.

"What should I call you?" he amended.

"Just not the cops," she muttered, so low he wasn't sure he was supposed to have heard it.

His mouth twisted at one corner as he wondered what he was about to get into. But somehow she reminded him of Zee back in the days after their parents had been killed; scared, worried, and with only him to trust.

"I'll make a deal with you," he said. "Come with me and get that leg seen to, get it bandaged up, and I won't call the cops." *Yet.*

She pulled back even further into that corner.

"I'll even throw in a hot shower," he said.

That registered. He saw the longing flicker in her eyes. And realized then those eyes had tiny specks of topaz gold, about the color of the birthstone ring Zee wore.

"And maybe a swing through somewhere for some takeout?"

He heard her stomach growl, so loudly she blushed. She looked pretty thin, and he wondered how long it had been since she'd eaten more than she could scrounge on the run. Because she was on the run, he had no doubts about that. As for what would put a kid like this in that position, he could think of several things, most of which he didn't much like.

"And then you call the cops?" she asked, her tone sour.

He looked at her for a long moment. "Did you do it?"

She blinked. Frowned. Glanced around as if looking for some damage in the room that he was referring to. And that that was what she thought he meant told him volumes. She'd answered him without saying a word.

"Come on, squatter," he said. "I can't leave you here."

Still she resisted. "You going to force me to go to a doctor?"

An old, familiar chill rolled over him. He fought it down with the ease of long practice. "I only facilitate. I don't force anyone to do anything."

Because I did force someone to a doctor once, and it didn't make any difference.

"Except trespassers to leave."

Well, she had him there. "Yes. I do draw the line at violations of the law that happen right in front of me."

She was already fair-skinned—he supposed it went with the reddish highlights in her hair—but he would swear she went even paler.

"Good for you," she muttered.

If her mood was as sour as her tone, as it appeared to be, he was likely letting himself in for an unpleasant time. But there had been more to it this time; there had been an undertone of something else. Fear? Sorrow? Anger? Something strong, anyway.

When she didn't move, he pulled his phone out of his pocket. She eyed it warily, then looked at his face. And suddenly he wondered just how old she really was, because no kid should have eyes like that: tired, world-weary, and scared.

"Don't make me call them," he said quietly. "Just come with me, get that injury seen to, have some food, a shower. Then you can decide what you're going to do."

She met his gaze then, almost challengingly. "And what's all that going to cost me?"

His brow furrowed, then cleared as he realized what she meant. The thought made him recoil inwardly. "I'll let that slide since you don't know me. And I'm glad to see you're suspicious."

"If I was suspicious enough, I wouldn't be bleeding."

He almost smiled at the self-directed sarcasm. But then it hit him he could be dealing with the victim of a much worse crime than trespassing. He tried to keep his voice steady when he asked, "What did he do to you?"

"He didn't get the chance, actually. When I realized what he had in mind, I bailed out of the car." He drew back slightly, looked her up and down for further injuries. She read the look. "I was lucky. He'd slowed down for a turn, and I managed to hit mostly grass. Except," she added with a grimace, "for the barbed wire fence."

"Ouch." Then, curiously, "He didn't come after you?"

She shrugged. "I guess he decided I wasn't worth it."

Something in the way she said it made him wonder if that was an assessment she'd heard more than once in her life.

He didn't ask why she hadn't gone to the police after she'd escaped that particular predator, because he thought he knew the answer; whoever had made her run in the first place was a bigger, badder predator.

It did occur to him to wonder if perhaps she wasn't a predator in her own right, using that innocent face to con unsuspecting, protective types into helping her. Maybe with an eye to what she could get, or steal later. But he discarded the idea, not because he didn't believe it but because it didn't make any difference in what he would do. His sister always said facilitator was just another name for fixer, and he had ever and always tried to fix things. And most times, did a creditable job.

Except when it mattered most.

He shook off the old refrain and stood up. "Your choice."

"I either come with you, or you call the cops?"

"That's the deal right now, yes," he said, thinking he might end up calling the police anyway, eventually. He just hoped it wasn't after she'd lifted anything of value she could stuff in that battered backpack of hers. Not that what he valued would be worth anything to anyone else. The most expensive things he owned were his tools, and could be replaced. But somehow he couldn't quite see her trying to fence a reciprocating saw.

"Why? Why are you doing this?"

She seemed genuinely puzzled. He wasn't sure he wasn't just as puzzled. And finally gave her the only answer he could. "Because the one who usually would have done it isn't here."

It made no sense to her, he could see that, but he hadn't expected it to. He wasn't sure it made any sense to him. But when he turned to leave the room, she followed him. He wasn't sure what he would have done if she hadn't.

He stepped outside, heard her footsteps falter behind him. He stopped, but didn't turn to look at her.

"If you run now, I won't chase you. But you'll miss out on that hot shower and food. And getting that leg seen to."

"No doctor?"

"I told you, I don't force anyone to do anything. I only help them do what they've already decided on."

"Unless it's illegal."

"Or harmful, yes."

He thought of Declan. He supposed helping Whiskey River's famous recluse stay a recluse might have been harmful. And eventually he might have tried to do something about that. But then Kelsey had come along and solved that problem neatly and thoroughly. Whiskey River's world-famous resident was a recluse no longer.

They made it to his truck. He opened the passenger door, standing by in case she needed help in with that leg; it was a four-wheel drive, and pretty high. And she was a good ten or more inches shorter than his own six-one. She led with the uninjured leg and almost managed it, he only had to grab her elbow when she wobbled. But she jerked it away, whipping around to look at him, and nearly slipped. He twisted so that his shoulder braced her.

"I was helping, not groping," he said.

She muttered something that might have been "sorry" if he could have heard it.

He walked around to the driver's side and reached behind the seat for the first aid kit fastened to the back. Saw that she was looking at his baseball cap on the console.

"Guess you really aren't a cowboy," she said.

"As much as anybody bred and raised in Whiskey River can not be."

He thought he saw the corners of her mouth twitch. He almost wished she would smile; he bet it would really change her face.

"Which means?" she asked.

"I know a bit about horses, a little less about cows. Enough to build them shelter or order feed if necessary, and I could saddle up in a pinch, but it's not my be all and end all."

He came back around with the box bearing the red cross symbol in his hands.

"Haven't been in here in a while," he said without looking at her, "but it should be pretty well stocked." He took out a packet that held a sterile antiseptic wipe, and a small tube of antibiotic cream. He'd wait on a bandage decision until he saw what was needed.

"Won't a shower waste all this?" she asked.

He gave a half shrug. "We'll redo it after. I think getting the antibiotic on it now is more important. You want to roll up your jeans?"

"No," she said, but her tone was so wry he wasn't surprised when she did it anyway. The wound was just above her right ankle, where her leg began to curve from that delicate slenderness into a shapely calf.

True froze, shocked into momentary immobility by his

own thoughts. *What is wrong with you, she's a scared kid!*

He didn't dare look at her face, and schooled his own to neutrality as he opened the wipe and began to clean away the blood that had already dried, then the cut itself. It was a couple of inches long, but thankfully not particularly deep except for the start point, where the barb had first dug in. A little fresh bleeding began in that spot as he cleaned it, but it stopped quickly with a little pressure.

"Two wide adhesive bandages, I think," he said, almost to himself. "Better than gauze that might rip the clot when you take it off."

"Thanks for the visual."

He glanced at her, saw she was joking by the quirk of her mouth. A very nice mouth, now that she wasn't glaring at him.

Whoa. Just. . .whoa.

It wasn't only that she was a kid, which made his thoughts beyond sordid, it was that he never reacted like this even to a grown woman. He felt nothing more than a vague flicker of interest, a hazy sort of reaction that seemed mostly to consist of "She'd be attractive, if I was looking." But he wasn't looking. Hadn't been, not for five years, three months and—he was calculating before he could stop himself—twenty-two days. He counted it progress that he no longer had it down to hours and minutes and seconds.

He finished as quickly as he could. "That should hold it for now. Just need to keep it clean and watch that one spot where the barb really dug in."

He closed the kit back up and latched it.

"Thank you."

She said it rather stiffly, and when he glanced at her face his brow furrowed at the visible tension. And again had the thought that maybe she wasn't quite as young as she looked. Telling himself that was wishful thinking since he was having this strange reaction to her, he asked, "Was I too rough with it? I didn't mean to make it hurt more."

"Too gentle, maybe," she said, very quietly, then looked as if she regretted it. "Thank you," she repeated, this time with a tone of finality.

He walked back around the truck, put the first aid kit back in its spot behind the driver's seat, and got in. He started the engine. Saw her gaze snap to his face when music poured out of the speakers. In this case, Mozart.

He raised one eyebrow at her. "Another preconception shattered?"

She shrugged. "You start playing opera, I'm out of here."

"Not before lunch." She just looked at him. "Kidding," he muttered.

"Thankful," she countered.

He smiled at that, glad she at least was able to joke now. Saw her eyes widen in the instant before she jerked her head back around to stare out the windshield.

"It helps me think," he said, not sure why he felt compelled to explain. "I save the contemporary stuff for the end of the day."

As they pulled out of the driveway she looked back toward the house. "I thought maybe you were one of those house flippers or something."

"I've done it," he said, "but I found I didn't like trying to predict what people will want. I'm more of a fulfilling a vision guy."

She repeated his own words back to him. "You facilitate."

"Exactly."

"Sounds like you work for a mob boss or something."

His mouth quirked. "Not that I know of. Not yet anyway."

"What do you have to know to do this. . .facilitating?"

"Jack of all trades, as they say. Enough to oversee a lot of different things." Including planning and building a pavilion overlooking the river for a wedding that would likely host most of Whiskey River and be news around the world. That was a new addition to his repertoire.

"And people pay you for it?"

He shrugged. "Lots of people have ideas but don't know how to make them real."

"And you do?"

"In many cases, yes. In others, I know where to send them."

"You go to college for that?"

He couldn't tell if there was sarcasm in her tone or not.

"Not something they teach."

"Maybe they should."

Okay, he was going for no sarcasm. "Might be too practical."

She made a noise that almost sounded like a laugh. She was asking all the questions when it should have been him, but she was talking, so for the moment he'd take it.

"You have enough. . .clients to make a living?"

"Believe it or not, I've got a bit of a knack with people. We're doing okay." *Sometimes one really big client is all you need to get started. Like world-famous Declan Bolt.* He smiled inwardly at the thought of the pen name of the man who had indirectly started Mahan Services by being one who needed a lot of stuff done and only trusted one person to do them.

"We?"

"My sister and I. I do the labor, she does the math and the paperwork." Lately, a truckload of paperwork and other formalities, stuff that drove him crazy. Zee was pretty good at keeping a handle on it, but it was starting to overwhelm even his efficient sister. And then there was that backlog of old stuff that she hadn't even had time to start on.

"Lucky her." Something in her tone made him glance at her as he drove. She hadn't been joking. She saw him look, then shrugged. "I like numbers. They mean what they mean, and they never change on you."

"Fair point," he agreed, wondering what had happened

to her to make her value that so much, and if it was the same thing that had her on the run.

They were approaching the edge of town before she spoke again. "Your sister. . .you're close?"

"Very."

"Because you work together."

"No. Because we're all we had for a long time."

"Did you—"

"Tell you what. I'll trade you. I answer a question, you answer a question."

That shut her up. He'd expected it would; he'd guessed she didn't want to answer any questions about herself so was trying to keep him talking. He was also surprised he'd told her as much as he had, and wondered why he had. Especially when he knew it was a trick of con artists to gather bits and pieces from people that they could later use on them. And even if she wasn't one of those, she was scared, and scared people did things they might not normally do.

He pulled to a halt at a stop sign, then turned his head to look at her.

"No?" He said it with mock surprise. "Well at least give me a name to call you. Or you'll end up being called Missy or Little Lady or some other patronizing thing you'd only tolerate from a grandparent."

She didn't laugh. In fact, a look of such anguish flashed across her face that it felt almost physical even to him. As did the sharp jab of remorse; he didn't like that his joking words had caused this. He wasn't someone who enjoyed causing anyone pain.

"I'd tolerate anything from my grandparents," she said, her voice barely above a whisper and full of that same stark, wounded emotion. "And my name, ironically, is Hope."

And suddenly his entire perception of her shifted. Maybe he was a fool, but he couldn't believe she was anything worse than a scared kid on the run.

He hoped he didn't pay too high a price for that assessment.

Chapter Four

HOPE SAT SILENTLY, staring at her hands, not even looking out the window as they approached the town square. She was embarrassed by how quickly she'd wolfed down that hamburger and fries he'd bought, and now wondering if the churning of her stomach meant she should have gone slower with the first full meal she'd had in a while.

Or maybe it just meant she was already starting to worry about how much she owed the man beside her.

She was startled when he suddenly spoke, in the tones of a semi-bored tour guide.

"And on your right is the distinctive fountain and the statue of the famous—and infamous—Ronan 'Booze' Kelly, who founded this place in the late 1800s. His descendents still live here, and are a vital part of life in Whiskey River."

She gave him a sideways, puzzled glance, wondering what he was up to now. He went on as if he had a busload of tourists behind him.

"Despite his fondness for the liquor, the name of the town—which was originally Kelly's Crossing—didn't stem from that, but rather an incident in 1900 when some of those barrels of whiskey tumbled into the river and broke when a bridge collapsed. To this day, Founder's Day is marked by, among other things, floating barrels down the river."

"With or without the whiskey?" she asked, almost against her will.

His head snapped around, startling her. But a smile curved his mouth, then became a grin. "I think most of it's been consumed by the time the barrels hit the water."

She couldn't help herself, she smiled back. It had to be because he had an honestly great grin. He was even better looking when he wasn't being so serious. And suddenly what he'd said about having a knack with people seemed obvious. She was here, wasn't she?

It felt odd to smile, she realized. Physically odd, as if the muscles weren't used to it any longer. Sad. She used to smile—and laugh—a lot. In her old life, that life she'd ruined by being young and idealistic and beyond stupid.

He started to whistle as he drove. Not loud, but light and cheerful, not a song she recognized but a meandering sort of tune that seemed made up as he went along yet was surprisingly intricate. She was glad. Not just because it was nice to listen to, but because it gave her an acceptable excuse to not talk.

When he made a turn that took them into what appeared to be a quiet, residential neighborhood, she did start to look around. This close to the center of town the houses were older, some looking like they might have been built when ol' Booze was still running wild. And they were big, set way back from the street, on large swathes of property. But with the occasional bike or basketball hoop in evidence, they looked like homes, not mansions. Although True had said Whiskey River had its share of those, as well.

When he pulled into a driveway at the end of the street, she turned to look at him. The whistling stopped.

"This facilitator thing of yours must pay pretty well."

"More importantly, it keeps me busy," he said. "This was our parents' house. We divided it. Zee lives in one half, I live in the other."

She looked at the big, two story house again. She noticed now that there were actually two front doors, both opening onto the same wide, expansive front porch. And a second driveway that ran up past the opposite side of the house. She could see a garage around back, and guessed there was a matching one on the other side.

"Zee?"

"My sister."

"And I thought my name was. . ." She trailed off, not sure what to say about someone whose name was just the last letter of the alphabet.

"Her name's really Zinnia, but she hates it. Mom had a thing for the flowers." He gestured at the bushes planted all around the foundation of the house. "It's pretty amazing in the summer."

"Oh." She wanted to ask where his parents were now, wanted to know how the house was divided into a duplex on the inside, and if he had done it, she wanted to ask why keeping busy was more important to him than making money, she wanted to ask a million things. That scared her, not just because it tacitly gave him the right to ask questions of her that she could not and would not answer, but because she hadn't been so curious about another human being in a very long time. But what scared her most of all was that before all that, she wanted to ask if anyone lived in his half with him. Like a wife or girlfriend.

She told herself that it was only because she wanted to be braced if there was a scene about him bringing home some strange woman. And she almost believed it.

HE STOOD AT the bathroom door, a set of clothing—a simple pair of black leggings, a T-shirt, and a pair of heavy socks—borrowed from his sister in his hands. Zee was taller than this girl, but he figured the stretchy pants would work. He set the items down on the floor.

"Clean clothes you can borrow just outside the door," he called out. "Then we'll get yours washed. And there's some shampoo and stuff here, too."

He heard a muffled answer that could have been thank

you or go away. Since she was in his bathroom—well not his personally, that was off the master bedroom—and had gone in eagerly, he chose to believe it had been thank you.

Zee had laughed at him when he'd asked for the clothes and any other girl stuff she might need. "Working with Kelsey must have infected you with the rescue virus. She's got the horses covered, so you went for runaway kids?"

"She's hurt and obviously scared," he said. "That's all."

"And once she's not scared and the hurt is tended, then what are you going to do with her?"

He hadn't had an answer for that then, and didn't have one now.

So instead, while the shower ran, he settled in at his desk to make some notes about his inspection of the outside of the house, and what little he'd gotten on the inside; he'd obviously have to go back again to do a detailed inspection. Good thing Jamie had said there was no hurry. He also made a couple of calls for current prices on some building materials; the last thing he'd done was Kelsey's house—although it seemed she wasn't ever going to live in it after all, he thought with a smile—and it had been a pre manufactured building.

He'd need to get going on that, too; they were going to convert the house into more of an office building, for the rescue and the youth outreach program Kelsey had started, with Deck's help. Too bad they weren't running another session until late spring, his squatter might be a candidate. But Kelsey wouldn't be doing much of anything except taking care of her rescue horses and planning the wedding for a while. He knew Declan wanted to pull out all the stops for her, and it seemed the whole town was getting involved in the plans.

Including him, he thought. Declan had surprised him, asking him to be his best man. *You're the only guy I could stand to have around enough to keep things running. I'd like you to stay around, but also as my friend.*

If he hadn't already known what a huge step that was for the once reclusive writer, Kelsey's smile would have told him. With Declan's history, he never thought he would ever say the guy was a lucky man, but just watching him blossom under Kelsey's tender care proved it. He—

"Thank you for the shower."

"You're—" He broke off in mid-sentence. Because he had swiveled his desk chair around and seen an entirely different person than the one in the stained jeans, torn T-shirt, and oversized jacket that had gone into the bathroom. "Welcome," he finished rather lamely, and after far too long.

For a moment she just stood there, looking at him. Dressed in Zee's leggings, which hugged slender legs above the heavy socks. He could see the outline of the bandaging, which she'd either redone or managed to keep dry. But then his gaze swept upward, and at first all he could see was the way what he'd thought was a plain T-shirt in some sort of shiny fabric clung to her in places, where her skin must still be damp. Clung to a contour he hadn't expected. Wisps of hair were also damp, curling around her face slightly, framing it along with the rather jaggedly cut bangs. The rest of her hair fell free now, in a long, smooth tumble down her back.

He took all of this in, but it was in a secondary sort of way. Because the first thing that had hit him with a thud that was almost palpable was a very simple and now obvious fact. This was no kid. And he must have been blind to think she was.

"Whose clothes are these?" she asked.

"My sister's. She lives in the other half."

"You mentioned."

He had. And he was still staring. Trying not to focus on the curves that T-shirt was doing nothing to disguise.

"Thank her for me."

He nodded, all he could seem to manage.

"It feels good."

Something entirely different than what she obviously meant slammed into his mind. He opened his mouth to answer, realized he was risking something entirely inappropriate coming out, and shut it again.

"Are you all right?"

That depends. "How old are you?"

Her expression changed, became shuttered. "Why? Does it matter?"

"I'm not sure." Nothing less than the truth. Except it might make him feel better if he knew he wasn't having this reaction to a kid.

"If I tell you I'm twenty-three, will it change your mind about how I can pay you back?"

Her tone was so bitter it quashed every earthy thought that had unexpectedly hit him. And it enabled him to get himself past the shock of realization and back in control of his power of speech.

"No. I offered, you didn't ask. That should never require payment. Are you?"

She looked as if she were considering whether to believe him, then finally said, "Yes."

That relieved him, in ways he didn't even want to delve into, although he felt even more foolish knowing he'd been off his guess on her age by years. Maybe he was just getting old. Didn't they say that's what happened, the older you got, the younger young people started looking?

She was moving now, walking around the room, scanning, taking in, and he had the feeling she wasn't missing much. "Where are you from?"

"Not Texas."

"Narrows it down a bit," he said dryly.

She did not, he noted, move like a kid either. If he'd seen that before, if she hadn't been huddled in that huge jacket he would have known instantly she was no kid. She stopped before the bookshelves on the wall beside the desk. He watched as she reached for the latest addition. Wondered how long she'd been on the run, and if she'd even heard of

Declan Bolt, although he was hard to miss. And adults as well as kids—himself included—read and enjoyed the Sam Smith tales. But it didn't seem like she'd have had much time for reading, at least not lately.

"My Gran reads these," she murmured. "She said there's as much for adults as for kids in them."

"She's right." The grandparents again. And she'd said it before with longing and now with love, so it was not them she was running from.

She tugged at the book, and it slid off into her hands. The bookmark was still in the front and as he'd half expected, she opened it. He knew what she'd see there on the title page, Declan's personalized, handwritten thank you.

She read it, glanced at him. "You know him?"

"I do."

He thought about telling her the world-famous author lived right here in Whiskey River, but did not. He didn't trust her that much. And everyone in town felt a little protective about the guy, especially after they'd gone through the media from around the world gathering like vultures when he'd done his first ever public book signing at Whiskey River Books last month at Christmas.

"I've. . .heard of him, but I haven't read them."

"You should. I think you could relate. So are you going to tell me where you're from, Hope?"

She gave a little start, as if she'd forgotten she'd told him her name. Which made him think she hadn't lied about that, at least."

"Is answering a bunch of questions a requirement?"

He studied her for a moment. Wondered if she was as smart as he was thinking she was. He leaned back in his chair—he'd been so dumbstruck by the realization of how wrong he'd been that he hadn't even stood up when she'd come in, a breach of manners his mother surely would have called him on—and crossed his arms over his chest.

"Why don't you just tell me what you're willing to, and we'll go from there?"

She turned her head to look at him then. "All right. If you'll answer one question first."

"I'm an open book," he said.

She pointed at the bookshelf. At the framed photograph.

"Who is this?"

He'd been bracing since the moment she'd put the book back and looked at the picture. Putting on the mental armor. So it was with a hard-earned steadiness that he answered her.

"My wife."

Chapter Five

THAT, HOPE THOUGHT, she hadn't expected. He wore no ring, and the clothes he'd given her had come from his sister, he'd said.

She studied the picture for another moment. Blonde. Pretty. Not model pretty but a sort of girl-next-door wholesomeness. A happy smile as she looked at the photographer. Him? Probably. She looked happy. No, more than happy. Much more.

It would be odd if she stared much longer, she told herself. But she couldn't help it, the strangest feeling was welling up in her, a sort of questioning, wondering what it would be like to look at a man the way this woman did, as if he held the sun in one hand and her heart in the other and she knew he would never drop either one. She couldn't even imagine that kind of feeling.

What kind of woman would draw a man like this? She wondered if there were children. She wondered how this woman would feel about him bringing home an injured stray.

Most of all, she wondered where this woman was.

On the next shelf was another photograph. Of a couple standing beside a river full of inner tubes with people sitting in them, drifting downstream on a beautiful sunny day. The water looked cool and inviting in the photograph, but at the moment the sun looked more appealing; she'd spent a chilly few nights until she'd found the house.

It was definitely the same woman. And the man looked like the younger brother of the man who sat just a few feet away. An identical but younger brother. She noticed a digital date imprinted in the lower corner of the photograph. Six years ago. Not so long. Not long enough to have put that touch of gray just over his ears, or the worry lines around his eyes. Although he was tan, like a man who worked outdoors, so that could be—

Abruptly she snapped herself out of the silly reverie. She was usually more aware of other things, like escape routes, and where to go next.

Yet still she asked, "Is she going to be mad you brought home a stray?"

"No."

He said it sharply, so sharply she couldn't help turning to look at him. "She's not allowed to get mad?"

The man who had brought her here seemed to vanish. In place of the mildly exasperated, faintly curious and sometimes amused guy who'd convinced her to come along stood a cold, shuttered, cut off stranger. And when he stood up slowly, he seemed to tower over her even more than the nearly a foot difference in their heights.

He is a stranger, you idiot, and you deserve this or worse for weakening and coming with him.

"She's dead." His voice was as flat as the land she'd crossed to end up here.

"Oh."

God, she sounded so completely stupid she couldn't believe it. She barely managed not to turn back and stare again at the picture of that happy couple. It was him, she guessed now, not some younger brother. And whatever had happened to this woman that man clearly loved, had probably been what had made those changes in him, that made him look a decade older than the man in that image.

She should say something, shouldn't she? Something that wouldn't make her seem like someone totally inept? Something comforting. Something sympathetic. *Damn, say* something!

"I'm—"

"Don't say you're sorry. You're not. You didn't even know her."

This time she heard the pain behind the flat tone. And it stabbed at her, in a way she hadn't felt in a very long time. Words tumbled out.

"You're right. I was going to say I'm sorry. For her, she was obviously young. But more for you. There's a lot of love in that picture, and it had to be hard to lose it."

He stared at her. She held his gaze as long as she could, but it was too intense, and as her own words echoed in her head they started to sound presumptuous. For just as she knew nothing about that kind of love between a man and woman, she knew nothing about losing it.

She did, however, know a great deal about loss.

Even as she thought it, he startled her by asking, "Who died on you?"

Caught off guard, she answered, "A friend."

"What about family?"

Surprising herself, she answered again. "They're alive. But they're as lost to me as if they had died."

He studied her for a moment, so intently she wished she hadn't said anything. And when he spoke again, the cold, flat tone was gone, replaced by something much, much kinder. "Your grandparents?"

He was too perceptive. And apparently didn't forget anything. She bit her lip fiercely.

When she didn't answer, he asked quietly, "There's no fixing it?"

Interesting—and she supposed to be expected—that his first thought was about fixing. She only wished it were that simple, a matter of going back, making what amends she could, and taking back the one good, clean part of her life.

"No."

"Your fault?" She stiffened. It was true, but that didn't mean she liked him saying so. Or being perceptive enough to realize it. At her stare, he shrugged. "If it was theirs, you wouldn't be missing them enough to call them lost to you with such pain."

That easily he'd cut to the heart of it. And understood.

I've got a bit of a knack with people. . .

Yes. Yes, he did.

She glanced once more around the comfortable room. Had he lived here with her, the woman who looked at him with such love? Or had the living arrangements with his sister happened after her death? Had some long, painful illness put that gray at his temples, or had it been the shock of instant loss?

He'd been born and raised in Texas. He had a life here in Whiskey River, clearly a solid one. There was no way he was connected to what she'd escaped. Just no way. Still, caution won out when she finally answered him.

"It is my fault. All of it. I had good intentions, but made some. . .bad decisions, choices. It's taken me a long time to get out from under some of them."

"And the rest?"

She couldn't. She just couldn't talk about the things she would never be out from under. "I'm still trying."

He smiled than, and he was once more the guy who'd been willing to help a stranger. "That's all we can do, isn't it? Keep trying."

"A little success now and then would be nice."

"It happens." He nodded toward the book she'd looked

at, the one signed with obvious feeling by the writer even she knew was world-famous. “By all rights, he should have been dead long ago. And yet he’s safe now, and very, very happy.”

The words sparked an emotion inside her that it took her a moment to recognize. Hope. That silly, foolish feeling she’d been named for. There would be no refuge for her, here or anywhere else. She didn’t dare risk it. Because if she did, someone else would pay the price. Again.

Chapter Six

"TRUE'S A GOOD guy," the solid, gray-haired checker in the drug store said. "Straight arrow as they come. Not to mention eligible. I think every woman in town has her eye on him."

Hardly a surprise, Hope thought. What was a surprise, to her at least, was that so far in this visit to downtown Whiskey River she'd been met with polite curiosity, but none of the wariness she'd gotten used to on her travels. Probably because she was dressed in normal clothes now, clean and hole-free.

The bigger surprise had been the ridiculous urge that had had her standing in the makeup section, actually considering spending some of her precious stash on something, anything, to make her feel more attractive. To make her not look like a kid.

To who? Him? What does it matter what you look like when you'll be gone in a few days?

The man behind her in line spoke. "Never mind that. If anything needs doing in Whiskey River, True's the man you call. He'll get it done."

A woman pondering the display of candy at the checkout turned her head to agree. "He's a man of his word, and as honest as the day is long."

Interesting, she thought, considering she hadn't asked. Apparently just being seen with True Mahan brought on this wave of endorsements.

They were all looking at her, and she felt oddly compelled to say something. Anything. "He seems. . .nice."

The woman with a candy bar now in her hand laughed. "He is, but honey, if that's all you see you need your eyes checked."

Hope felt her cheeks heat. She lowered her eyes to the box she held, which thankfully no one had even blinked at.

Candy bar lady was studying her now. "We all yearn after him, even us happily married types." The man behind her gave a snort, but with a smile. "Something about a man with that sadness in his eyes. . ."

When the checker spoke again, Hope didn't think she imagined the warning in her voice as she shifted her gaze to her. "It's nice to see him with someone after all this time, but no one in Whiskey River would like to see him hurt. That boy's been through enough."

With someone. She was a little stunned at how that assumption made her feel, and hastened to dispel the sensation. "Me? I'm just a. . .stray he picked up and helped. Next week it'll probably be a dog."

She escaped with her small shopping bag, and nearly ran into True coming in.

"Get what you need?" he asked, making a U-turn and exiting with her.

"Yes. Thank you." Her mouth twisted slightly. "I'll add the gas to the tab." She'd had enough for her purchase, but it would have been a long walk on a leg that still wasn't quite happy.

"I told you—"

"I know. No problem. You had to come to town anyway. Although I doubt normally to buy. . .these."

He glanced at the bag. She knew the label on the box of tampons was visible through the translucent plastic.

"Wouldn't be the first time," he said, easily enough. And not in the least embarrassed. But then, the man had been married. She wondered how long they'd had, that golden couple in the photo, before life reared up one of its uglier heads and destroyed them. She hastened to think of something else, anything else to ask before she let that question slip out; she seemed to have lost the governor on her curiosity since she'd met this man.

She glanced back into the store. "You have a lot of friends here."

He gave a half-shrug. "Lived here all my life."

"And apparently you mean what you say."

"I expect to be held to my words, yes."

"By who?"

"Me, if no one else."

She wondered if he realized how rare that was. A man who held himself to his own promises. Not needing the pressure of others, not needing a legal contract, just his word and his own. . .what? Code? Honor? Whatever it was, there hadn't been much of it among the males in her life except for her grandfather.

"I need to stop at the hardware store," he said as they neared his truck. "Anything else you need to pick up? There's a clothing store over on—"

"No," she said quickly, before the idea of some actual new clothes settled in her mind. "This is all I need. And my own clothes, when they're dry. Thank you."

She wondered if that had sounded as stiff and choppy to him as it had to her. And tried to remember the last time she'd ever thanked someone so much.

Because you haven't had much to thank anyone for?

That was probably true. But she had a great deal to thank this man for. Not the least of which was not being the kind of man who would expect the kind of payment many others did, sometimes for something as simple as giving someone a ride.

Which for some reason made her think of old Bill, the kindly, almost grandfatherly trucker who had picked her up outside of Flagstaff and given her a lift all the way to Albuquerque. He'd even let her rest in the sleeper portion of his cab while he drove. He was headed home after this run, he'd told her, and glad of it. He missed his Mary, he'd said.

Best woman I've ever known. I'd be nothing without her.

That he could say that after the forty years he said they'd been together had left Hope feeling a kind of awe. And when he'd let her off in New Mexico, he'd seemed honestly worried about her. So much that she worried about him; these days even picking up a woman could be dangerous. He'd laughed and told her he was a better judge of character than that. For instance, he'd known right away she was just in trouble, not a troublemaker.

She later found out how much he'd been worried—and how generous his soul—when she found a hundred dollars in twenties rolled up in her jacket pocket. That cash had gotten her to the Texas border.

So maybe she'd been a bit hasty about the men she'd encountered. Maybe that last one had soured her outlook a bit.

When they arrived at the hardware store, she went in with him. She wasn't even sure why. Maybe curious to see how he was received here, in what was probably a place very familiar with him. Or maybe because she wanted to see what he was like when focused on his work. Or maybe she had absolutely no idea.

He was hailed immediately by the man at the register and a woman in the blue shirt with the store's name and logo on the chest, and she heard his name called out even from a couple of customers. With liking from all.

She was looking with some longing at a warm looking

jacket—one that didn't smell like it had been used to wipe a barroom floor—when True came up behind her.

"They probably have one that would fit you better."

It didn't take much willpower to turn away from the rack; one glance at the price tag took care of that. "No point. It'll be too warm for it soon, and it'd be too heavy to lug around."

He didn't say much after that until he'd finished his business—ordering in some lumber, paint, and getting the number of a glazier for windows, so she guess this was related to the house she'd been in—and they were back in the truck.

"This is a nice town," he said as he started the engine. "Even fun sometimes."

"Floating whiskey barrels down the river?"

"Among other things. Maybe you should stick around for a while. Take a break from. . .your travels."

The burst of longing that shot through her at his words startled her. "I can't," she said, and the sudden tightness of her throat made it barely a whisper.

He was quiet for a moment, maneuvering out of the parking lot. Then he glanced at her.

"So you plan on hitting the road again right away?" His tone was so neutral she knew it was intentional.

"It's what I do," she said in the same kind of tone.

"But is it what you want?" She smothered a laugh. "So the idea of doing what you want is laughable?"

"Pretty much." *God, I sound bitter. I should get out of here before it rubs off on him.*

It hit her then that he had as much reason to be bitter as she had. He'd lost someone he'd obviously loved dearly. And yet he was not. His first instinct, when confronted with someone in trouble, was to help. Once, that might have been said of her, too—in fact it was what had gotten her into this mess—but for a very long time she'd thought of nothing but herself. Trying to survive, to keep moving and staying alive.

"Did you have a job?"

"Yes," she said, rather defiantly; she might be an idiot, and have made some really bad choices, but she wasn't a slacker.

"Doing what?"

She hesitated. "Office work," she finally said, figuring that was vague enough, and would give him no way to track down her grandfather's accounting business, where she had managed the office. And not quite sure why she was answering at all.

They pulled back into his driveway. He stopped the car, turned off the engine, then shifted in his seat to look at her.

"What happened to you?"

He said it quietly, and so gently the whole story bubbled up inside her, wanting to be spoken for the first time. She bit it back. She couldn't do it, no matter how much she might want to. He didn't know what he was asking, what might come down on him if he were to get sucked into her mess. And after everything she'd heard about him today, she did not want that to happen.

He just waited. Saying nothing, just looking at her with those eyes, that steady gaze, until the pressure was too much and she had to say something. And what came out was, in its shortest form, probably the whole story.

"A serious mix of foolishness and wrong place, wrong time."

"Did you break any laws?"

Her mouth twisted wryly. "Not unless they've made stupid illegal."

"In that case, I know an awful lot of people who should be in jail," he said in a tone that matched her expression. "Hurt anyone?"

She had to look away from him then. She stared at the dash of the truck, at the clipboard where he'd fastened the receipt from the hardware store. Finally she answered.

"Directly or physically, no."

"But someone got hurt. That friend?"

She let out a long, compressed breath. Tried to reassemble her armor of smart-assery. "If I'd known this ride was going to be so expensive I would have walked."

"This isn't for the ride."

She turned her head to look at him. He was still watching her in that way that seemed to unnerve her. "Then what's with the string of questions?"

His mouth quirked, and she could only describe his expression as rueful. "I think it's a job interview."

Chapter Seven

"IT WOULD ONLY be temporary."

Hope stared at him. The man was crazy. There was no other explanation.

"You okay with computers, scanners, that kind of thing? My sister wants to digitize our old records, but she hasn't had time."

"I. . .yes." It had been a while now, but she'd been reasonably literate, and she could learn quickly. That wasn't the problem. The problem was trying to figure out why she was even taking this seriously.

"Can't pay a ton, either, maybe five hundred a week for a couple of weeks' work, but. . .it might help."

It had been a very long time since she'd seen that kind of money, let alone had it in her pocket. She stared at him. "Why are you doing this?"

He shrugged. He did a lot of that, she'd noticed. Was it because nothing seriously bothered him, or because that's what he wanted people to think? As someone who'd now had a lot of practice in keeping up a front, she thought she recognized the signs.

"Seems like you need. . .running money," he finally said.

She didn't like the way that sounded. Or maybe it was the way he looked at her when he said it.

Stop it! What does it matter what this near-stranger thinks of you?

Except he didn't really feel like a stranger. And it wasn't just the annoying fact that she kept looking at his eyes, at the striking color of them, and the eyelashes that were, rather unfairly, longer and thicker than her own. Or that she felt a pang at the bits of gray hair at his temple, thinking they were like a badge of honor, hard-earned. Or that she liked just watching him move, with that easy, long-limbed grace.

Oh, no. You've got no room for that kind of thing.

But a thousand dollars would carry her a long, long way. Maybe even pay for a new identity, a prospect she'd been considering for some time now. She'd used different names in different places, but she'd never stayed long enough to find someone to fake papers for her, because that cost money and what she had went for just enough food to keep going.

"I'd need cash." She blinked, startled that she'd said it aloud.

"I figured," he said. "You can borrow my guest room, or maybe my sister's, but you'd have to take that up with her. I'll throw in a meal a day here," he added, "if you don't mind very basic."

For some reason that threw her even more than the idea

of staying under his roof. “You’d. . .cook?”

He laughed. “I don’t cook. I fix. Grill some meat, nuke some veggies, maybe toss a salad. That’s about the extent of my culinary repertoire.”

I fix.

She had the feeling those words were at the core of who this man was, from the livelihood he’d carved out to picking up strays. Strays he offered first aid, food, and a roof?

A sudden ripple of. . .something rolled over her. A longing, a wishing she’d thought she’d banished long ago.

Okay, you’re attracted to him. No reason to go all cow-eyed. Isn’t that what they’d say here in Texas? Be logical. You do need the money. And it sounds like something you could do. Unless his sister is an ogre.

“Have you even mentioned this to your sister?”

The look on his face gave her the answer. But then the shrug again. “She’ll be okay with it.”

She had a feeling there was a silent “eventually” attached to that one. “She’s used to you bringing home strays?”

His expression changed to something almost bemused. “No. No, she’s not. I don’t, as a rule. I mean, I see to them, but I don’t. . .bring them home.” Then he seemed to snap out of it. Gave her a pointed look. “But I’ve never come across a human one before.”

“Sorry I broke your record.”

“Are you always so. . .sarcastic?”

She hadn’t meant to be. Not this time. Not with the man who was offering a chance at some real breathing room.

She gave him a rueful grimace. "I prefer to think of it as smart-ass." She hesitated, then admitted, "It's a defense mechanism. When I'm nervous. Or scared."

"I figured."

"You figure a lot."

"Occupational hazard."

She couldn't help it, she smiled. After a second or two when he seemed stunned, he slowly smiled back. And it was a good one, warm, genuine, and it made that feeling of longing well up in her again. She wanted to run. The problem was, she didn't want to run away. And that scared her.

"Come on, try one of those meals. It might be enough to make up your mind." This time he grinned, and it nearly took her breath away. "One way or another."

And the next thing she knew she was out of his truck and following him inside.

✪

"TRUETT JOHN MAHAN, have you lost your mind?"

"Always a possibility." True said it with a shrug as his sister stared at him.

"You don't know who she is. You don't know where she's from. You don't know what she's done. You don't even know her last name!"

Zee was normally a very kind, generous and tolerant person. Except when it came to someone who might hurt those she cared about. Then she would protect with all the fierceness of a lioness.

"You're right, about all that," he said, pacing the den she had converted into an office in her side of the house. "What I do know is she's in trouble."

"And maybe rightfully so," Zee pointed out. Funny how she looked like their mother when she got upset, that worry line between her eyebrows, the concern in the big blue eyes that were also like their mother's.

"She says she didn't break the law. Didn't hurt anyone. In fact, I think she's on the run to protect someone."

"And you believe her? Just like that? Did you even do a search on her?"

He lifted a brow at her. "On the name Hope? Good luck with that."

"True—"

He held up a hand to stop her. "There's nothing you can say that I haven't already thought."

"Then why do you want to do this? Why is it so important for you to help this woman?"

He let out a long breath, because he wasn't sure he had an answer to that, not a full one. So he gave her what he did have. "I just keep wondering where Deck would be if someone hadn't helped him along the way."

That, as little else could, put an end to Zee's protestations. He knew she was a bit in awe of their most famous resident, and the client who was the cornerstone of this little business they'd carved out. They knew some of his history now—True doubted anyone but Kelsey knew it all—and even the bit they knew was enough to make them both shudder. And look at their own past in a different light.

"All right," she said with a sigh. "Just remember I'm the one who's going to be working in the same room with her. If she turns out to be a thief or worse—"

"I'll expect you to handle it like the Texan you are," he said with a grin. "Besides, you need the help, and if she can get all that stuff sorted and scanned, it won't be hanging over your head anymore."

She grimaced. "I should have been doing it all along. But who thought you'd end up making a career out of. . .facilitating?"

His grin widened. "We've got to think of a better name for it. Facilitating sounds a bit. . ."

"Unsavory? Faintly illicit?"

"Hope said it sounds like I work for a mob boss."

Zee's eyebrows rose, but she was smiling. "Okay, maybe I can work with her."

"It'll only be for a couple weeks."

"Then what?"

"Then I guess she'll be on her way."

"To where?"

True sighed. "I don't think even she knows that."

Chapter Eight

"YOU REALLY ARE tiny."

Hope blinked. That wasn't what she'd expected Zee Mahan's first words to her to be. But her next ones explained it. Sort of.

"Compared to him, who isn't short?" she asked.

"Point taken," Zee said, smiling for the first time since she'd come into the den turned office True had brought her to. "He is a tall drink of water, isn't he?"

Any answer she could come up with to that was going to get her in trouble, so she went the safer route. "You're no munchkin yourself."

True's sister looked surprised, then smiled. "No, but I see now why True thought you were just a kid in that jacket."

"I'm not a kid."

"No, you're not. And annoyingly, that shirt looks better on you."

"I doubt that," Hope said, meaning it; Zee was one of those tall—apparently it ran in the family—willowy sorts she'd always envied. Her short, slightly shaggy hair was as dark as True's, her eyes just as blue. Hope couldn't help noticing how True's easy, powerful way of moving translated to a smooth grace in his sister.

"There is one requirement if we're going to work together."

"Only one?"

"For now. I can't share my office with someone whose last name I don't know."

The way Zee was looking at her told Hope she meant it. Her first instinct was to lie, to give the first fake name she could think of. But there was something about this woman—and her brother—that made a bald lie very difficult. So, praying that her name was common enough to be overlooked, she told the truth.

"Larson."

For some reason Zee looked more relieved than anything. "Thank you."

"I'm sorry I've been. . .kind of foisted on you. I'm sure taking on a stranger wasn't your plan."

Zee shrugged. "This is True's circus, so he gets the say."

Hope glanced toward the doorway, where True stood just outside on his cell phone. "He has. . .quite a sense of responsibility."

Hope looked back at Zee just as she said, rather pointedly, "Lucky for you."

Hope didn't even try to deny it. Instead she tried to turn the conversation to the matter at hand. "What do you need me to do?"

"Long term, get all that—" Zee gestured to a large box full of papers that sat on a table beside the desk against the room's far wall "—sorted by date and project, then scanned and into some sort of logical filing system on my computer. Short term, you can go to the office supply store in town and pick up a box of file folders to hold it all in the mean time."

"All right. Of course." She shifted her weight, testing her leg. She felt a twinge from the bandaged cut, but if the store was in the downtown they'd come through, she thought she could make it.

Even as she thought it, True was back in the room and saying, "I've got to get out to the Mitchell site so Hope, you can ride with me. Save you walking on that leg."

"Is it bothering you?" Zee asked, with every evidence of genuine concern.

"It's much better, thanks," Hope said quickly. Odd how apparently real caring made her nervous.

"Not what I asked, but all right. Get yourself oriented and set up today, and we'll start digging in tomorrow."

Hope saw her exchange a glance with her brother. Wondered just how crazy Zee thought he was, for doing this. But clearly she'd meant what she said, True got the say in this. Because. . .it was his circus.

Hope wondered if she was the wild creature to be tamed, or merely one of the clowns.

WHISKEY RIVER, HOPE thought, was a different sort of town. It wasn't so small that everybody could actually know everybody else, but it sure seemed as if they recognized most of the locals in passing. At least, judging by how they reacted to her unfamiliarity.

Of course, that only lasted until she mentioned she would be doing some work for True Mahan. His name was like the magic password in this place with the colorful past and unique present. It had become predictable and almost laughable, how everyone she met was cautious, until True's name came up. Then suddenly she was treated like a welcome guest.

He had told her to take her time—and his truck, after he'd gotten out at the work site—picking up the supplies Zee needed and get to know her way around a bit, because they might need her to run another errand now and then. She had been reluctant. Her license from back there—she never dared think of it as home—was still valid, at least until her birthday this year. But she hadn't driven in a while, and never anything that big. He'd laughed and said he kept the old thing precisely because he didn't have to worry about the occasional ding, and handed her the keys. She wasn't sure which affected her more, that laugh or his easy trust of a virtual stranger, watching her drive off a big chunk of his livelihood, especially if you counted all the tools in back.

But she did as he'd suggested. Although once in town she'd parked in a spot with no one else parked close by, and done her reconnoitering on foot. And she learned many things in the process. She already knew he was held in high esteem around town, from the way people accepted her simply because True had trusted her enough—God knows why—to hire her.

But she was also learning exactly what he meant by facilitator. The riverfront park that had languished half-finished until True had stepped in to ramrod it through to become the gathering place it now was. Repairs to the famous bridge, the site of the Founder's Day barrel float, which had dragged on seemingly endlessly until True took on overseeing the project and got everybody to stop arguing and get the job done. And that year when they'd had the big flood, it had been True who had coordinated both the salvage efforts and most of the rebuilding. Quite a record for a guy who hadn't quite hit the big three-oh yet.

She also now knew that he'd actually been born in San Antonio, although nobody in Whiskey River held that against him since his parents had only been there for the weekend at the time. Also that he'd been born early, and so had been a small baby. That one she'd nearly laughed at, thinking of his six-foot-one height and muscular build. The clerk in the office supply section of the rather quaint general store, who wore a name tag with Martha printed on it, had actually laughed, sharing the moment.

"Made up for that in a hurry, didn't he? He's a sweetheart," the woman had said. "And he manned up when he had to, took care of his little sister when their parents were killed."

That had stopped her in her tracks. "Killed?"

"Awful, it was. One of those multi-car pileups. Both their parents and the Templetons. It was a shock to all of us. True was off at college, only eighteen and just starting, but he came right back. Went to court and got custody of Zinnia, and stayed home to raise her."

"He. . .quit school?"

"Not many these days who'd do that," Martha said as she handed her the bag and receipt. "He was always going to go back, I think, but by the time his sister graduated high school he already had his own business going. And there," the woman said with a widening smile, "is the woman who can tell you just how good True is at it."

Hope turned to see a woman with long, blonde hair pulled back in a jaunty ponytail, sunglasses pushed up above her forehead, wearing faded jeans, cowboy boots that looked like they were used for their original purpose, and a snug, dark blue T-shirt with a logo for something called Whiskey River Rescue.

"Kelsey, this is—I'm sorry, honey, I didn't catch your name?"

"I. . ." She couldn't see a way out of it. Wished now she hadn't given True and Zee her real name. "Hope," she said, leaving it at that and hoping no one would press for more.

"This is Hope," Martha said. "She's new here, doing some office work for True."

The blonde's smile was instant and genuine. "Welcome to Whiskey River."

"I. . .thank you."

"Kelsey here's our horse rescuer," Martha said.

"Hence the shirt," Kelsey said with a laugh.

"She's also engaged to our most famous resident," Martha barreled on.

"Once known as Crazy Joe around here," Kelsey said, cutting the woman off smoothly. Martha colored slightly, and Hope wondered what that was about.

"I'll get that cartridge for you," Martha said, and bustled off as if glad for the excuse.

"She's a bit of a gossip," Kelsey said with a wry expression, "and sometimes it's better to head her off at the pass, as it were."

Hope couldn't help herself. "Crazy Joe?"

Kelsey smiled, clearly taking no offense. "Joseph is his first name. Whiskey River's a pretty open town, and he was a complete recluse. He was going through a very rough patch for a while."

"I understand that," Hope said, surprising herself with how much empathy she let into her voice.

The other woman studied her for a moment. "I think maybe you do."

Hope felt awkward. It had been a very long time since she'd been in a position to simply talk with anyone, and it was more of a strain than she would have expected.

"She said you know True Mahan?"

Kelsey laughed. "Indeed I do. He got Deck through a very rough patch. But the poor man, first time I saw him I screamed at him. Went off half-cocked, as he says."

She tried to picture this smiling, laughing woman being that angry. She couldn't. "What on earth did he do?"

"He was bulldozing my house at the time."

Hope drew back. "What?"

"He was working for my fiancé."

Hope blinked. Frowned. "Wait. . .you mean those two things are connected?"

"Yep. That's how I met Deck. AKA Crazy Joe. Since True was only following his orders, I went after his boss. Still in high dudgeon, I might add."

"And now. . .you're engaged?"

Kelsey nodded, her smile saying everything about how crazy in love she was. Hope felt a jab of pain, tried to stifle a longing for something she would never have. She didn't think it showed, she'd gotten very good at masking her emotions. Or at least she thought she had, until she'd met True Mahan.

Martha was back with the toner cartridge Kelsey had apparently come to pick up. The clerk bagged it and handed it over.

"Speaking of True," Kelsey said as they both walked toward the door, "we're keeping him a bit busy right now, or he'd be doing this. That Crazy Joe guy wants a wedding pavilion designed and built by spring."

Hope didn't know which to react to, the woman's obvious joy was almost overwhelming. So she said only "It sounds wonderful. Congratulations."

They were outside now. The sky was grayer than it had been when she'd gone inside.

"Looks like we might actually get that rain they were predicting," Kelsey said with a practiced look. "I'd better get back, I've got to make sure the hay that was just delivered is under cover."

Hope's gaze flicked to the logo on her T-shirt. "I never really thought about horses needing rescuing."

"Wish I didn't have to," Kelsey said. "My greatest goal is my own obsolescence." Hope smiled at that. "Come by sometime, I'll introduce you to the crew. Do you ride?"

Hope was sure she probably looked a bit alarmed. "Um. . .no. Horses are beautiful, but. . ."

"Never too late to learn," Kelsey said blithely.

She left with a cheerful wave. Hope watched her go. Strange, how much she had enjoyed that simple act, chatting with someone nice, with no ulterior motive, no real fear.

She started down the block she had yet to cover in her walking around the town square. As she walked she glanced over at the park, at the statue of the town's founder, the

Kelly it had originally been named for. She found it fascinating that his direct descendents still lived here, were as important in this town as he had been in this place that had once been called Kelly's Crossing.

She reached a real estate office, thinking she'd turn at the church up on the corner and head back to the truck. With that in the forefront of her mind she idly glanced in the window of the bookstore as she passed. Saw the latest Declan Bolt book on display, and a sign noting they still had a few signed copies.

It hit her then, belatedly. The image of what she'd seen in True's copy of this very book.

True—

Never was a man more aptly named. With eternal thanks,

Deck

The pieces tumbled together. She turned, stared back in the direction Kelsey Blaine had gone. Declan Bolt? Here?

He got Deck through a very rough patch.

And now he was getting married. Hope felt an odd tightening in her throat at the thought that at least one person had found refuge here.

Whiskey River was indeed an interesting place.

Chapter Nine

HOPE LABELED THE next folder, then slid the stack of documents into it. This one was for a clean up he'd arranged for a small ranch outside of town that was about to go on the market; apparently the ranch house and outbuildings were in okay shape, but a lot of clean up, painting, and weed clear out had been needed. The papers before that had been expanding a garage apparently for a horse trailer at someplace called *Kelly's Champs.* And before that had been resurfacing a driveway at a place called, amusingly, the Hell's Half Acre B & B. She was beginning to see what True had meant about jack of all trades.

No wonder he'd rolled out at the crack of dawn this morning. She'd been awake anyway, unable to quite accept that she could simply let go and sleep, in a real bed for the first time in recent memory, so she'd heard him leave. And lay there long after, still a little amazed that the man had simply left her here, in his home, apparently without a second thought. What was to stop her from finding a bunch of easily hawkable stuff and taking off?

She wouldn't, of course, ever, but he didn't know that.

Scruples are too heavy to carry on the run, girl.

The bit of hard-earned wisdom echoed in her mind as she wondered, not for the first time, how Brittany was doing. She'd met the young runaway—who had assumed Hope was not much older than her own sixteen—her first night in Texas, and the girl had shared what she'd learned as if Hope were much younger. Which, in the ways of being a runaway, she supposed she was. As it happened, she'd been a little flush at that moment, still carrying some of the money Bill had snuck to her, and with some idea of passing it on, she tucked a twenty into Britt's pocket before they parted ways. It wasn't much, but it was twenty more than the girl had had, and Hope didn't want to think what she might do for a meal otherwise.

She shook off the memory and refocused on the table before her. She'd managed to get a year's worth of assorted receipts, estimates and other notes separated into piles, although she'd had to set a couple aside because she had no idea what they went with.

"You'll have to ask True," Zee told her when she asked. "He's finally gotten pretty good about writing the job name on everything, but it took a while."

Hope looked at the small paper on top, full of various numbers in different configurations. Dimensions of something, Hope thought. A lot of somethings. "Will he remember what this is?"

Zee grimaced. "He'd better. I keep telling him most of us can't look at something like that and instantly know what it relates to."

"But he can?"

"He knows how things work. And how they go together. If you gave him a list of a hundred separate parts for something, he could tell you what they'd be if you put them together, and what size it would be down to the inch."

There had been nothing short of pure pride in Zee's voice.

"You love him very much, don't you?" Hope said softly.

"He saved me," Zee said simply. "I would love him for that alone, but he's become quite a man, my big brother."

Hope could not argue with any facet of that statement. "I. . .someone in town told me about your parents."

Zee expression was exasperated but resigned, and there was an unmistakable affection in her voice when she spoke. "Welcome to Whiskey River. There's always somebody who feels compelled to share."

"And they all seem to think the world of your brother."

"He's earned that," Zee said. "Having his trust will get you in any door in this town."

"So I've noticed. I've never had total strangers be so. . .accepting."

"You're reaping what True has sown. And he takes that very seriously. He knows people trust his judgment. It's a responsibility to him, to be careful."

There was no tone of warning in her voice this time, but still Hope hesitated. Asking what was on her mind could destroy the tentative ease they had reached. But she couldn't seem to stop herself.

"I saw. . .the picture of his wife. What happened to her?"

Zee went very still. There was something about Zee's expression. . . Protective. That was it. Very, very protective. As hard as it might seem to think of a man like True needing protection, he apparently had it. Which made her wonder all the more just how horrible his loss had been.

"Given how little you've shared with him, I'm not sure that's any of your business," Zee said stiffly.

"Fair enough," Hope admitted. "I just didn't want to inadvertently cause him pain because I didn't know."

Zee seemed to consider that. Finally, she answered. "Cancer. It was ugly. And he was there with her every step of the way. He earned that bit of gray that happened practically overnight."

Hope sucked in a breath. She almost said "I'm sorry," but it seemed so inadequate. And "Thank you," seemed inappropriate.

"Then it's even more amazing he's. . .who he is," she said, stumbling over all the things she was beginning to think True Mahan was.

Zee softened at that. "Yes. Yes, it is. He is." Her love for her brother was clear and shining in her face.

Hope went back to her task, and tried not to feel envious.

TRUE HANDED THE receipts from the hardware store over to his sister, who had come over from the office. Took one back when he realized he hadn't put the job name on it, wrote it in the upper right corner they'd agreed on, and handed it to her again.

"Good," Zee said. "I'll get these entered. When does the stuff come in?"

"Tomorrow, Charlie said. But maybe afternoon, so don't schedule it until Wednesday."

"All right." She turned to head back to her side of the house and the office.

"Zee." She stopped, turned back, and suddenly he couldn't find the words. Finally he blurted out, "Maybe she should stay on your side."

His sister arched a delicate dark eyebrow at him. "Problem?"

"No, it's just. . .I thought. . . She's working there anyway, and she has to go out one side and in the other. . ." He trailed off.

"She making too much noise in the morning, disturbing your beauty sleep?"

He gave her a sour look. "No. She's so quiet it's like she's tiptoeing around."

"Something else bothering you?"

"No. I just thought it would be easier."

"Tired of cooking extra already, after one day?"

"Never mind," True muttered, wishing now he'd never started this.

"She getting to you, big brother?"

"No!"

"Then why is her staying there a problem?"

He glared at her then. "Have I mentioned lately what a pain in the backside you can be?"

She grinned. "Wondered if you'd forgotten," she said, and he knew she'd been deliberately provoking him.

He shook his head in brotherly exasperation. "I'm out of here. I have to go talk to Kelsey, before I make the final materials order. At least she's nice to me."

Zee stuck her tongue out at him. But when he headed back out toward his truck, he was smiling.

"SHE REMINDS ME of Shadow," Kelsey said, nodding at her latest rescue. The raggedy looking black gelding who at first had seemed afraid of his own shadow, hence the name Kelsey had given him, was now standing peacefully as his rescuer groomed him.

True glanced at the little horse, who seemed to be enjoying—no, luxuriating—in the steady strokes of the brush. His head lowered a little the longer she brushed, as if he were about to doze off.

"You picked up on that?" he asked, returning to the subject of Hope; after she'd told him they'd settled on the final design, Kelsey had mentioned her encounter with her at the store.

"I've had a little practice dealing with people who carry their nightmares with them all the time," Kelsey said.

True's gaze shot back to her face. "Yes. Yes, you have."

"He still has times when it. . .tries to grab him. But now he fights it. We fight it." She smiled, a small yet potently contented smile.

"If I haven't said, I'm really happy for you. Both of you."

"We know," she said, her smile widening. "Otherwise you wouldn't be building that pavilion thing for us."

True grinned. "It's going to be something."

"Deck's thinking it might be used for something else someday. Like some kind of gathering for kids. . .like he was. They could play, swim, and he'd talk to them. Maybe read Sam to them. Just a few, who are on the edge, to maybe keep them going another day."

True stared at her. "My God," he said softly, "what a distance he's come."

Kelsey's smile was glorious this time. "I knew you'd get it."

"That would tie in nicely with your horse camp, wouldn't it?"

"What we were thinking," she said with a nod.

He gave a slow, wondering shake of his head. "Kelsey Blaine soon to be Kilcoyne, I'm honored to know you. Both of you."

Her smile became a grin. "Good. Because we're going to need a facilitator to get it all set up and running."

"That would be my pleasure."

He was still smiling when he got home. The house—his half, anyway—was empty. And locked. He had the sudden thought that Hope had no way to get back in, he hadn't thought to give her a key this morning.

Give her a key.

He gave a sharp shake of his head.

What you should be doing is rethinking this whole having her live here thing.

He clamped down on that voice in his head. He wasn't about to go another round with his sister and her teasing. And it was only for two weeks, after all. He could deal with anything for two weeks. And he'd meant it when he'd said she hardly made a sound, even though she had to go out his front door and over to Zee's.

He supposed the door in the common wall was an option, although by mutual agreement he and Zee never used it without calling or at least knocking first. Brother/sister closeness was fine, they'd decided, but they needed separate lives. But he doubted Zee would have shared that information with Hope; his sister might be younger than he, but she'd been ferociously protective of him ever since Amanda had died. And—

A knock on the front door spun him around. Glad of the interruption to his chaotic thoughts, he went and pulled it open. And was face to face with the subject of those thoughts.

"Hi," she said, seeming rather embarrassed. "I saw you pull in."

"Oh." *Brilliant, Mahan.*

"Do you always work so late?"

"I had some catching up to do."

She looked instantly contrite. "My fault, I'm sure. I'm sorry."

He waved off the apology. "It's always something," he said. Realized that sounded a bit dismissive, but was afraid if he tried to fix that it would only get worse. So instead he just unlocked the door and stood aside to let her in.

"Did you find everything you needed?" he asked.

She nodded as he closed the door behind them. And suddenly his usually spacious living room seemed smaller. "I'm afraid I used the last two slices of bread this morning, for toast."

Memory sparked. "Damn." He pulled his keys off the rack he'd just hung them on.

"I'm sorry," she said again, "but you said to—"

"Help yourself, I know," he said. "That wasn't aimed at you. I just forgot I picked up some stuff at the market, but it's still out in the truck." Only when she relaxed did he realize how tense she'd gotten at his muttered oath. "What did you think, that I was going to yell at you for a couple of pieces of bread?"

"Sorry," she said, avoiding his eyes. "It was sort of a thing with. . .a guy I was seeing. Using the last of anything."

It was the first time she'd volunteered anything of her past. Keys in hand, he studied her for a moment. "Is he who you're running from, Hope?"

Her gaze snapped to his face as she exclaimed, "No!" She looked appalled enough that he believed her.

"Then what? Who?" he asked.

"You never give up, do you?"

She sounded tired now. And a night's sleep—assuming she'd gotten more than he had, which wouldn't take much—hadn't taken the weariness out of her eyes. He doubted a simple night's sleep ever would. That bone-deep exhaustion had more than just a physical source. He knew that all too well from the times he'd looked in the mirror and seen that same expression.

"Not even when it's a losing battle," he said with a grimace.

He pulled open the door and headed back to the truck, conscious of her gaze upon him every step of the way.

Chapter Ten

SHE SHOULD GO. Tonight. Now, even.

He'd come too close. He saw too much. And if she didn't get out of here, away from him, she was going to bring it all down on him. And he deserved better than to have his life destroyed because he'd been foolish enough to help someone who had a knack for bad decisions.

Is he who you're running from, Hope?

Oh, no. Cagan wasn't someone who'd chase down his own game. He'd send someone, one or both of the mindless ones, as she'd always called the duo who served as Cagan's bodyguards, enforcers, and attack dogs. She'd seen what they could do, and the thought of True up against those two-legged grizzly bears made her heart slam in her chest.

She fought for calm, afraid he would ask again, try to pry more out of her. And the more time she spent around him, the less she was confident that she could keep hidden what she had to. He was such a. . . Her thoughts trailed away. She had no words for the kind of man True Mahan was. Good, solid, caring, and a man of his word clearly all applied. As did hard-working, respected, responsible, and God help her, even noble. Enough that just his approval was enough to get her accepted all over Whiskey River.

You're just thinking that to avoid the rest. The hot, gorgeous, sexy part. The tall drink of cool water in the middle of the desert part. The part that makes you almost wish he would want payback in that very basic of ways.

In all her time on the road she'd managed to avoid that. She'd learned the hard way that appearance counted for nothing, that it was safer to assume everyone was out for themselves, and that everything came with a price. There was the occasional Bill, but they were rare.

Besides, looking at sweet, old Bill was hardly the same as looking at True. She remembered her first, flashing thought when he'd opened that pantry door. Tall, dark and studly. It had been half joking, an acknowledgment that she was now in Texas, the land of cowboys and horses.

I'm not a cowboy.

Oh, but he could sure pass for one, those boots, the jeans that emphasize the length of his legs, and hugged a backside that made her want to slip her hands into those back pockets.

She shivered, feeling swamped with unfamiliar feelings. She wrapped her arms around herself, as if that could keep her from simply flying apart. And then she heard his steps on the front porch as he returned.

And she ran. Coward that she was, she ran. Darted down the hall to vanish into the guest room he'd given her.

She sat on the edge of the bed, the bed that was the most comfortable place she'd had to sleep in weeks. She hadn't unpacked what little she had in her backpack last night, except to take out that dog-eared picture and look at it. Unpacking would have been a decision to stay, and she hadn't made that yet. At least she hadn't last night. But now? She'd actually enjoyed the day. Enjoyed having something to think about, something to do, that didn't have to do with where to run next, how to survive. The sorting, the organizing, the preparing all the papers for scanning had taken just enough of her concentration to allow her mind to let go of the fear for a while. Zee went about her own business quietly; thankfully she didn't seem to be one who needed to fill the air with chatter and was content listening to the music that played at mid-volume from a system she set her phone in.

So the part of Hope's mind now free had flitted about until it had solved the mystery of why True was doing this, why he would help a total stranger who had trespassed on property he was responsible—that word again—for. It was the only thing that made sense to her. He saw her as one of his rehab projects. She was like that house, abandoned, broken here and there, neglected, but for the moment still standing.

And how he would laugh if he knew what lascivious thoughts his new rehab project was having about him.

But there, in the businesslike atmosphere of Zee's office,

she had been able to figure it all out. Two weeks of some routine work for a grand in running money? She would be crazy to turn that down. She would do it, do it as well as she possibly could. She would be helpful, she wouldn't irritate Zee, and most of all she would stop having these ridiculous thoughts about Zee's brother. There, that was it, she would think of him as Zee's brother, put that one step back between them. Not to mention it would remind her of how protective Zee was of him, remind her the woman would likely take her head off if she messed with him.

. . .he was off at college, only eighteen and just starting, but he came right back. Went to court and got custody of Zinnia, and stayed home to raise her.

And suddenly she was curled up on the bed, her face buried in the pillow to muffle her sobs. She didn't think she still had it in her, to cry. She thought she'd hardened herself against that kind of breakdown, but she guessed it proved her point. When True Mahan set out to help someone, he got it done. When she tried, all she did was make it worse. He had had such tragedy in his life, his parents, his wife, and yet he was all the things they said he was. She had let her life spiral out of control, until she'd had no choice but to cut ties and run.

There was only one explanation. Her parents had been right. She was weak, useless, and stupid into the bargain. Gran and Gramps had been wrong, they were just too sweet, too generous to see the truth about their wayward, deficient granddaughter. The only thing she had to be thankful about now was that they couldn't see now what a mess she'd made of her life.

And that she'd done the only thing she could do to protect them.

No, whatever it took to go on the way True had, she didn't have it. In the same way he was good, and strong to the core, she was weak, cowardly.

She could not bear it if she brought the shambles that was her life down on the Mahans. So she would take this unexpected windfall, because it would enable her to do what she must.

She would keep running.

"YOU LOOK LIKE hell, brother mine."

Zee set the mug of coffee in front of him. He hadn't asked for it, but he supposed she'd taken one look at his eyes and assumed.

"Thanks," he muttered, and let her decide if it was for the coffee or the assessment.

"What happened? And don't bother to say nothing, because I've seen her and I've seen you."

He let out a long breath. Zee had called while he was standing rather blankly in the kitchen, thinking there was something he should do but unable to get his fuzzy brain to remember what. She hadn't asked to come over, she'd merely announced that she was, and moments later the adjoining door opened and she'd swept through into his kitchen, coffee in hand, and ordered him to sit down.

He took a swallow from the mug. Blinked. Usually his sister went for a milder brew, but this stuff would strip paint.

"Just drink it," she said before he could comment. "I want you awake enough to tell me what the heck is going on."

He took another swallow, thinking if this didn't wake up his brain he was in trouble. He took a third for good measure, then set down the mug. A bit warily, half-afraid the stuff was going to eat through the ceramic and perhaps the table.

"Ready?" Zee asked, her tone saying he'd better be.

"Is she. . .messing up?"

"Hardly. She showed up two seconds after I turned on the lights. I'd swear she'd been waiting outside. She's working like a woman driven. She's going to do that two weeks' worth of work in three days at this rate." Zee's gaze narrowed as she looked at him. "And she's got the shakes."

"I don't think she had breakfast. And I know she didn't have dinner."

"Why? I thought you were feeding her as part of the deal?"

"I. . .yes." He rubbed a hand over his eyes. Felt a shudder ripple through him. And suddenly the inquisitor was gone and his loving sister was crouching beside him. Her voice was gentle now, coaxing.

"What is it, True?"

He gave in, for he knew she would be relentless now. Gentle, but relentless. "She. . .cried. Half the night. Locked up in her room."

"Why?"

"I don't know." He glanced at her. "I know, I'm a stupid man, I should know what set her off."

"You've only known her two days. You're not a mind reader."

"Not what you used to say."

"Stop it, True. You were married to Amanda, and you'd loved her for years. That's different, you—" She stopped suddenly. Stared at him. "She cried half the night," she said slowly.

He stared into the mug of dark, potent coffee. Contemplated taking another swig. Decided against it. Stood up. Meant to leave. But suddenly Zee's arms were around him in a ferocious hug.

"It must have been like a. . .a flashback. I'm sorry, True. So sorry."

He let her. She was probably the only one who really understood, because she'd been there for him every step of the way as the vibrant, lively woman who had loved him and he had loved since they were fifteen slipped away from him. It had been years, and yet sometimes it felt like yesterday.

And it helped. Somehow it helped, and the tight knot in

his throat that had made him decide against that last swig eased. And finally he hugged her back.

"You have to know," she said, her voice tight, "it's not your fault you couldn't fix her."

He drew back slightly. Stared at this woman who had once been the bane of his teenage existence, but was now one of the wisest people he knew. He had never realized she knew how he'd felt.

Zee looked up at him, held his gaze. "She's the one thing you weren't able to fix. You've been trying to make up for it ever since by fixing everything you can for everyone else."

"I. . ."

His voice trailed off because he couldn't think of a thing to say to this woman who had just turned a completely different light on the last five years of his life. He'd never made that connection before, that he was a fixer *because* he hadn't been able to fix Amanda.

"You know I'm right."

He let out a long, slow breath. Couldn't deny it. Hugged her again, gently this time. "Thanks, Sis," he whispered.

"I love you."

"I know. Sometimes too much."

"No such thing."

When he finally headed out to his truck, he was feeling better. Drained, but better.

Chapter Eleven

SHE HADN'T MEANT to eavesdrop, but she'd gone to refill her mug with the extra strong coffee Zee had made this morning. She'd needed the jolt, and Zee had told her to help herself. And she had just happened to be passing by the door that was still ajar, the door that she only now realized was a direct connection between the two halves of what had once been their family home.

She's the one thing you weren't able to fix. You've been trying to make up for it ever since by fixing everything you can for everyone else.

Hope froze. The words had been spoken so gently, with such love, it almost took her breath away. And then the love itself had been spoken.

I love you.

I know. Sometimes too much.

No such thing.

She heard Zee's footsteps as she came back toward the door. Hope moved quickly back toward the office and her work table, wiping at eyes that had teared up at the sheer love expressed between this brother and sister, something she had never known. She felt a little as if she had witnessed something miraculous, or sacred maybe, and it made her feel. . .unworthy was the only word she could think of. Her entire view of the brisk, efficient Zee Mahan had changed. She wasn't just smart, quick and beautiful, she was capable of great love and gentle perceptiveness.

The fresh tears stung. It surprised her that she had any left, after last night. But what she'd overheard had solidified her choice. She would finish this work, take the money she'd earned because she needed it, and then she would leave, taking herself and her problems away from this town and these people. They'd already had enough tragedy in their lives, they didn't need her garbage spilling over onto them.

She dug into the next pile with determination. It was a few minutes before Zee came back to the office, and Hope wondered if perhaps she'd had to regain her own composure. But when she did come back she had not just her coffee mug but a plate that held two slices of toast spread generously with peanut butter going about the process of melting on the crisp, warm bread.

It smelled heavenly.

"Eat," Zee ordered. "It's not fancy but it will keep you going." Hope looked from the plate to the woman who put it down on her table. Zee shrugged. "I can't concentrate with your stomach growling."

Hope ate, and her stomach calmed. She had to admit, with the food she was better able to concentrate. She had made a nice dent in the box of papers, and thought she would have them all sorted soon. Then she could start scanning them. And be closer to collecting her earnings and hitting the road.

The thought didn't cheer her much.

"Here."

Zee was holding out an envelope now. Hope wiped her hands free of the peanut butter that had escaped before taking it.

"What's this?" she asked.

"True said to give you an advance."

She blinked. Opened the envelope. There was a small stack of twenty-dollar bills inside. Something turned over in her chest as she looked up at Zee.

"He said to give me this?"

Zee nodded, watching her assessingly. "He said you needed to buy some things, clothes and such."

"I—" She broke off, not knowing what to say.

"And he seems to think you won't just take it and run."

Hope drew herself up. "I've done things I'm not proud of, but I would never steal from someone helping me out."

"Good to know," Zee said, and the woman's smile made Hope feel as if she'd passed some sort of test. Maybe she had.

After 9AM Zee began making phone calls, apparently asking for prices on a long list of materials; Hope saw the estimate form was filled out in True's bold hand. She wondered what this fix-it job was.

. . .fixing everything you can for everyone else.

She gave a sharp shake of her head and kept sorting. But it was getting slower the further down she got in the box; apparently the realization that the papers needed to be labeled had been a late arrival. The papers she was dealing with now were from over four years ago.

"You're frowning," Zee said.

Hope almost jumped, she hadn't even heard her get up, let alone come to stand at her shoulder.

"I. . .yes. No labels on these."

Zee looked at the papers she held. Nodded. "Those are from when it was just True, before I started helping. He had it all in his head and knew with a glance what was what, so he didn't need to identify each one. And there weren't as many, when he was starting out."

"But there are now."

She nodded. "He's as busy as he wants to be. Word got around quick that he's good, reliable, and knows a little bit about everything and a lot about some things. Although Whiskey River folks already knew that."

"He's carved out an interesting niche for himself. And you."

Zee was looking at her steadily. "He never intended this to be his career. He was going to be an architect."

And he gave that up to come home and take care of his little sister. "I'll bet he would have been a good one."

"Yes. He would have." Zee let out a sigh, and for a moment something darker, something sad, flickered in her eyes. "It's lucky for me he truly loves what he does, or I'd feel horribly guilty."

Hope was surprised at the admission. "I can understand that." Guilt was something she understood all too well. "Does he. . .I mean is there enough new work here in Whiskey River to keep him busy long term?"

Zee looked surprised. "I got the idea you weren't much on long term thinking."

Hope's mouth twisted ruefully. "Not unless long term is next week." *Because there's no point. It would all have to change anyway.*

Zee didn't respond to that, but did answer her original question. "Like I said, word gets around. People recommend him, and his job radius has expanded. He did a job over in Fredericksburg a couple of months ago, and when he started out he did one all the way up in Waco. Doubt he'll do that again, though, it was a big, complex thing and he didn't like being that far away that long. He only did it because back then he wanted to be busy 24/7."

She could guess why. She could have told him avoidance only worked for so long, eventually you had to face the truth.

Since Zee seemed unusually chatty, she risked another question. "So how long has he been doing this now?" Zee's gaze narrowed, and Hope quickly gestured at the papers left in the bottom part of the box. "Just curious if there's another box after this one."

"Oh." Her expression cleared, and Hope felt a twinge of guilt, because she had the feeling Zee had thought—accurately—that she wanted to know how long it had been since he'd wanted to be busy around the clock. And asking this had seemed more tactful than flat out asking how long his wife had been dead, since it was really none of her business. "No, that's it. My brother's idea of filing. Which is weird, since he's so meticulous about the work itself. He—"

The doorbell cut her off, and Hope felt her heart give that little jump again. It couldn't be True, she knew that. Which was an embarrassing admission in itself, that he could do that to her.

She stayed where she was as Zee answered the door. Trying to regain the relative calm that had been startled out of her. She thought she'd gotten past flinching at every unexpected sound or person, but apparently not.

Zee came back with a small box and a frown on her face. "You haven't even opened it yet, and you're frowning?"

"Oh, I know what it is. The samples for Kelsey and Declan, for the wedding. I'm just trying to figure out how I can finish these calls and—" Zee interrupted herself with a roll of her eyes. "Hello, I have help now. You can take these out to Kelsey at the rescue."

"I can?"

Zee walked over to her desk, opened a drawer and took out a set of keys. "Take my car. I'll let her know you're coming. Got a map program on your phone?"

"Um. . .no phone."

Zee blinked, but recovered quickly. And thankfully didn't ask why. Hope assumed it was because she thought she couldn't afford it. And while that was the truth, there were other, more important reasons that kept her from being tethered to a device that knew—and could betray—too much. They'd almost gotten her once, before she'd decided she really had to run. She knew they had a couple of good hackers, and in case that was how they'd done it she'd dumped her phone and gotten on the next bus.

"Okay, from the town square, just head out on the main road, with Booze at your back." Hope smiled at that, wondering if everyone in Whiskey River referred to the statue that way. Since there were no tricky turns in the rest of the directions, she thought she could find the place all right.

"What if she's not there?"

"Then she'll be at the house. Which is the next driveway on the right." Zee smiled then. "If I were you, I'd hope for that. It's quite a place."

It wasn't until she was on the road, heading out of town that Hope put together exactly what Zee had meant; the house was likely Deck's place. And she couldn't help but do exactly what Zee had said, and hope for that. Where would someone like Declan Bolt, world-famous author, live?

But she knew it wasn't to be when she saw the pretty blonde in a corral with a small black horse that looked a bit careworn even to her uninformed eyes. A man sat on the top rail of the fence, watching her as she ran her hands over the horse. Hope noticed the small house off to one side. It looked new, as did the barn and the lean-to that sheltered the hay Kelsey had mentioned the day she had met her.

She drove in slowly; she didn't know much about horses, but racing in across gravel that could spray didn't seem like a good idea. As she came to a halt at what she hoped was a safe distance, the man turned his head and glanced at the car, waved—at the driver he no doubt assumed was Zee, she thought—but went back to watching the woman in the corral. Who was starting again at the horse's head and working her way to his tail, rubbing, patting, and she could see now, talking. The animal seemed to be loving it.

She got out with the small box in her hands. She walked toward the corral. Before she had taken three steps the little horse's head came up sharply, turning in her direction. She didn't know much about horses, but he also looked suddenly tense. And this was a rescue, perhaps he'd been abused? She stopped in her tracks, not sure what to do.

She could hear a low murmuring, Kelsey still talking to the animal. After a moment the murmuring changed to an almost normal tone. "Take a few more steps, then stop."

Kelsey hadn't looked her way, but obviously this was meant for her. She did as instructed. The horse watched her warily. As instructed she repeated the few steps and pause until she was almost at the fence. Then Kelsey spoke to the man sitting on the fence.

"Got a little encouragement for him?"

"Always," he said.

He swung his legs around and dropped to the ground. He walked over to her, one hand digging into the front pocket of his jeans. He pulled out a couple of sugar cubes.

Hope couldn't help smiling. "Bribery, huh?"

"I'm not above it," he said with a laugh as he handed them to her. "Here, I'll take the box. What is it, anyway?"

"Zee Mahan sent me over with it for Kelsey," she explained as she surrendered the package and took the sugar. "It's. . .samples or something."

He grimaced. "And I thought it was going to be so easy. Just put up a pavilion, add lots of flowers, some chairs, and done."

"Keep talking," Kelsey called out, "he's relaxing."

Hope wondered if it was because she was talking to someone the horse clearly already knew. And then it hit her, the way he'd said that he'd thought it was going to be easy.

"You're. . .Declan?"

"And you must be Hope," he said as he set the box on a stone next to the fence. "Kels mentioned you were helping True out."

She wasn't sure quite how to act; the man was so famous even she couldn't miss having heard about him. Around Christmas, it seemed the newest Sam Smith adventure had been front and center in every bookstore she'd seen. Not to mention in the hands of more people than she could count, and not all of them children. And those were just the physical copies, who knew how many more electronic copies were out there in the ether?

"I'm embarrassed I haven't read your books."

He smiled. "Millions haven't."

She managed a smile back. "But millions have."

To her surprise he was the one now who looked embarrassed. He gave a slow shake of his head as he said, "Never fails to amaze me."

She could see he meant it. It did amaze him. But the way he looked at Kelsey made her think what he'd found there just might amaze him even more. And right now he seemed concerned about nothing more than making sure the horse Kelsey was working with didn't get upset.

"Shadow just came in, so he's still pretty nervous. The more people he meets who don't hurt him, the better."

Hope's breath caught. "So he has been abused?"

"Yes. But that's over now. Kelsey has him, and he's safe."

There was something in the way he said those last words that made her think there was more than one layer to them. It had to be quite a story, how the famous kids' author and the horse rescuer had ended up together.

"Will he ever really feel safe again?" she asked, looking at the animal who was still watching her, but not with the tense awareness she'd noticed at first. Kelsey continued to murmur to him, still running her hands all over him.

"Kels will see to it. She's had lots of practice with skittish creatures." She glanced at him then, and there was no mistaking the wry smile that curved his mouth. That he meant himself was unmistakable. "I get the feeling you know how that feels."

Startled, she tensed much as the horse had, realized the animal must have been readying himself to run, because that was what she wanted to do. And something she saw in this man's eyes told her he knew that. Because he'd been there.

"I owe my life to three people," he said softly. "Kelsey. The cop who stood up for me, back when I was in hell. And True Mahan."

She stared at him, running forgotten. "True?"

"I have trusted him with my life. He never, ever let me down."

Hope couldn't speak. Her throat was so tight, she could barely breathe. She'd known this, but to have this man say it, in such a way, nearly shut her down completely. To think that the simple fact that True had trusted her enough to hire her had made her acceptable in this place. . .

For the first time in a very long time, the urge to run was almost matched by the desire to stay.

Chapter Twelve

KELSEY LEFT THE horse and walked over to the fence. She crossed her arms on the top rail and after a glance at Declan that was almost palpably warm, she looked at Hope. But Hope noticed she was also angled so that she could see the horse out of the corner of her eye. The animal took a couple of tentative steps toward them.

"Just keep talking," Kelsey said in a conversational tone.

"I. . .um. . .when's the wedding?" she blurted out, unable to think of anything else.

"May," Kelsey said.

"Too far away," Deck muttered.

Kelsey laughed, and the horse took a few more cautious steps. "You're the one who wanted the big deal, or we could have eloped."

Declan flushed slightly, but there was nothing but love in his gray eyes as he looked at his fiancée. "Haven't quite discarded that possibility. We could do it again in the spring."

"Uh-uh. You got Mom involved now. And you know

how she is."

Declan grinned suddenly. "A force of nature."

He said that with love as well. There obviously weren't going to be any in-law problems in this marriage.

And then the horse was there, nudging Kelsey's arm, still keeping a wary eye on Hope. Hope couldn't help smiling. "He wants more of your rubdown."

"I know just how he feels," Declan said, and it was Kelsey's turn to blush.

"Try the sugar now," she told Hope. "Just move slowly."

She'd never done this before, was a little frightened at the prospect of holding her hand out to the horse who suddenly seemed a lot bigger than she'd thought.

"Just put it on your palm, keep your hand flat and hold it out," Declan said.

She did so, moving so slowly she had time to realize she was unconsciously holding her breath. The horse's ears flicked, nearly making her jump.

"And keep talking," Kelsey said, "because he needs to know there's nothing wrong."

Hope had no idea what to say. But then she looked at the horse, and something about his guarded demeanor registered. He was just scared. And she knew what that was like.

"It's all right," she said softly, raising her hand slowly. "Shadow, isn't it? Well, Shadow, I would never hurt you. I know you don't know that, but it's true. Your trust won't be misplaced this time. You're safe here, they can't reach you, can't get to you."

The horse stretched his neck, sniffing. Instinctively she stopped moving, letting him make the next move.

"That's it. Yes, there's a bribe involved, but it's not a lure with a hook, just a gift, no strings. And I'll bet you can smell your friend Declan on it, can't you? So you know it must be all right, and—"

She stopped as she felt a soft, tickling swipe across her palm. No teeth, not even a touch of them, just the gentle brush of lips and the sugar was gone.

It was all she could do not to laugh out loud. "That didn't feel anything like I expected!"

Kelsey and Declan were looking at her, Kelsey with warmth and approval, Declan with a knowledge and understanding that hit her low and deep. Whatever his life had been, he hadn't been kidding when he'd said he'd been in hell. And he'd seen it in her, too, a sort of like recognizing like that shook her.

And she suddenly realized how much she had betrayed in her words to the horse, although she doubted anyone who hadn't been through something like that would have picked up on it. But Declan obviously had.

Embarrassed now, she focused on the horse, who was nudging her hand. Not having any more of the treats, she glanced at Kelsey.

"I think you can pet him now, if you want. Start with his

neck, though, and work your way to his head. And keep talking, he's very responsive to a gentle tone, as you saw."

She did as instructed, amazed at the feelings bubbling up within her at the animal's acceptance of her touch. She stroked his neck, then his strong jaw, then down to his soft, velvety nose.

"Thank you," she said to him, not even caring that she was crooning now. Or that what she was saying would only verify what Declan had already guessed. "Thank you for trusting me, sweet boy, enough to get even this close. I know how hard it is, when trust has been betrayed, to give it again. You're wonderful, so strong to be able to do it."

She lowered her head, afraid the moisture building in her eyes was going to spill over. And when Shadow nudged her with that soft, velvet nose, as if he were returning the caress, it did.

TRUE WALKED SLOWLY, carefully, taking in the scene before him. Kelsey, Deck, the new rescue horse. . .and Hope. She'd told him she knew nothing about horses, but she was nose to nose with this one.

He'd slowed the truck when he'd seen Zee's green sedan parked between the road and the corral, then pulled in when he saw Kelsey in the corral. He hadn't been surprised to see Deck there; the guy stuck to his writing schedule like glue, but whatever breaks he took were spent with Kelsey.

But Hope. . .he hadn't expected her.

Deck spotted him, and started his way. They met about twenty feet from the fence.

"What's that all about?" he asked with a nod toward Hope.

"Getting over being scared?" Deck suggested.

"Shadow looks like he's much better already."

"I wasn't," Deck said, "talking about the horse."

True's gaze shot back to his friend's face. Eyes that had once been as dark, as haunted as Hope's but were now alive and bright looked back at him.

"She's been through some hell," Deck said.

"I. . .thought so."

"Good thing you're very good at handling that."

"Not so good in this case."

Deck lifted a brow at him. "Why?"

"I don't know. She won't. . .she just. . .she's. . ." He gave up flailing for words he didn't have.

"Yeah," Deck said solemnly. "She is." Then he glanced over his shoulder. "What's her trouble?"

True's gaze shifted to Hope as well. She'd turned her head slightly to lay a cheek to the horse's head.

A cheek that was damp. She'd been crying. She wasn't now, but she had been. He tried not to think about that night when she'd wept half the night. Tried to focus on answering Deck.

"I don't know. Except that a friend died, and she had to leave people she loved behind. And I'm only inferring that from a couple of things she said."

Deck looked thoughtful. After a moment he said, "Trying to think of anything that could get me to leave Kels."

"Nuclear obliteration?" True suggested, only half kidding.

"Nope, not enough." And Deck wasn't kidding at all. "Only one thing could make me even think about it. If it was to protect her."

True's gaze shifted to Hope, who was now rubbing Shadow under his jaw, in that spot so many horses seemed to like. The animal had clearly surrendered. *Can't blame him.*

He gave himself a mental shake. He had to stop thinking like that. "She said she hadn't broken the law. She was foolish and in the wrong place at the wrong time. That's all I know for sure."

"You do a search on her?"

"Zee did," True answered, a little too embarrassed to admit that it hadn't even occurred to him. "Got a few hits but nothing she could verify was this Hope Larson. And nothing bad."

"Maybe you ought to call Ducane."

True blinked. That hadn't occurred to him either. Jack Ducane was the brother of True's childhood friend who had lived across the street. He was also a Texas Ranger, and True had once hooked Deck up with him for some book research.

True knew he'd gone back to work a couple of weeks ago, albeit only light duty at a desk, after a gunshot wound he'd acquired taking down a kidnapper who had grabbed and terrorized a little boy.

"I'm not sure she'd like that much," True said.

"I didn't like it much when he dug into me, either."

True's gaze snapped back to Deck. "You knew?"

He nodded. "He told me. But I got over it, once I realized he was doing it for your sake, to make sure you weren't signing on to work for a serial killer or something. He also said you suddenly told him to stop." Deck cocked his head slightly. "I always wondered why."

"Because by then I'd read your first book."

Deck looked startled. Then, slowly, he nodded in understanding. "Thanks." His mouth quirked up at one corner. "For all of it."

It wasn't until he was headed home, Hope following him in Zee's car, that he replayed Deck's words in his head.

But I got over it.

Would Hope, if he started digging into her past?

He left his truck in front of the house, since he'd be heading back out as soon as he grabbed some lunch. Hope pulled Zee's car carefully into the house's other driveway. Before he even realized what he was doing he was walking toward her. He got there just as she was getting out of the little coupe.

"Why were you crying?" he asked bluntly. He hadn't

asked her after the night she'd spent weeping, he'd been too raw himself with awful memories.

She stared at him. "What?"

"Out at Kelsey's, with the horse, you'd been crying. Why?"

For a moment he thought she wasn't going to answer. And when she finally did, her voice was a harsh, bitter thing.

"Because it was hard to realize that even a horse, a poor, abused animal, is braver than I am."

She turned on her heel and walked away, up onto the porch, and went into Zee's office and shutting—not slamming, but shutting carefully and quietly—the door behind her.

Of all the things he'd thought she might say, that hadn't even been on the list.

Chapter Thirteen

SHE HEARD THE shower start. Tried to rein in her riotous thoughts. What was she doing, just sitting here letting her imagination run? It was bad enough she practically hyperventilated every time she saw him, did she have to start picturing him naked in the shower?

Whatever he'd done the rest of the day, he obviously hadn't left the hard work to others. He'd come home late, dirty, still a bit sweaty, and obviously tired. And looking sexy as hell, with his shirt sleeves rolled up over muscled forearms, and the top three snaps—she'd noticed that earlier, that it was snaps instead of buttons for this Texan—undone, baring a narrow V of his broad chest.

And suddenly two weeks seemed like a lifetime.

He'd stopped dead in the entryway, staring at her as she sat on the couch, Declan Bolt's first book in her lap. She'd just found it on the shelf above where the new, autographed one sat.

"I hope you don't mind," she'd said with a gesture at the book, "but after meeting him I wanted to read it."

"Fine."

It was short, clipped, and matched his expression. And without another word he had vanished up the stairs. And only then did it occur to her that perhaps he'd been shocked to find her making herself at home in his living room. They had never discussed the parameters of her staying here, perhaps he'd expected her to just stay up in the guest room while she was here.

She thought about retreating there now, but the sound of the shower would only be louder, more taunting up there than here, so she stayed.

She turned to the book, looking first not at the dramatic cover with the title *Escape* in a bold font, but rather the back flap and the very short, uninformative author bio. Interesting, she thought, that the word "escape" was there, too. She opened the front cover then, paged through to the title page, then beyond. When she reached chapter one, she started to read.

✪

"SORRY TO INTERRUPT, but dinner's almost ready."

She never even lifted her eyes from the page. She'd gotten about halfway through in the time it had taken him to clean himself up and get the meal organized, so she read fast.

For a moment he just stood there, looking at her. Something about the way she was so intent, the way she'd curled her legs up on the couch, the shine of her long, cinnamon colored hair in the light from the reading lamp. . .he liked the scene before him.

Something hot kicked through him, low and deep. Something he hadn't felt in so long it took him a moment to recognize it. A sudden, sharp reaction to the curve of her hips as she sat there, the way that shirt licked over her breasts. Something much hotter than that vague sense of awareness and response he'd felt at first.

Damn.

He fought it down. Something he hadn't had to do in so long he'd almost forgotten how. On some level his mind was wondering why her, and why now, but he knew it was only to keep from acting on the sudden, fierce response.

It was a moment longer before he trusted his voice to speak. "Hope?"

"Hmm?"

She said it vaguely, still clearly rapt. And it made him smile, even as an echo of that unexpected heat lingered. He walked over and picked up the bookmark she'd set aside on the adjacent couch cushion. She still didn't look up. He leaned over and stuck the bookmark between the pages. She jumped.

"Oh!" She stared up at him, clearly completely startled.

"Haven't heard a thing, have you?"

Color flooded her cheeks. "I. . .no. I'm sorry. Were you talking?"

He laughed, he couldn't help it. "Don't apologize. I was the same way, reading those."

She smiled. "May I ask. . .why did you?"

"Because they're supposedly children's books?"

She nodded. He hesitated, then gave her an honest but incomplete answer. "Zee made me read that one, the first one. As a distraction from. . .things. After that I was hooked. He's a hell of a writer."

"Yes. It's amazing. Even the awful parts that make you want to cry for Sam. He makes it all so. . .real."

He sat down on the coffee table before the couch. "That's because it was."

She blinked. "What?"

"I doubt anyone but Kelsey knows the whole truth, but he lived a lot of that crap."

She stared down at the book in her hands. "How could anyone live through that and. . .keep going? Especially a child?"

"Sam's a tough kid," he said. "And so was Deck. Scarred, closed off, and spookier than any horse Kelsey ever came across, but tough as he had to be to survive."

Her expression changed, and even though she wasn't looking at him he had the strongest feeling she was comparing herself to both Deck and his creation, and finding herself lacking. He saw her jaw tighten, sensed she was fighting for. . .something. He wasn't sure what. And when she spoke again, still staring at the book, he wasn't sure if she'd won that inner battle, or lost it.

"So. . .Declan Bolt helped you just as you helped him."

He drew back slightly. Pondered. "I never thought of it that way. But you're right. He did. I'll have to tell him."

"Do. It will mean a lot to him."

He wondered how she could be so sure of that, having only met the man this afternoon. And then she answered without him having to ask.

"Just ask Sam. It means a lot to anyone who's felt helpless to know they somehow managed to help someone else."

His gut was telling him she was speaking from experience. And he had the feeling she remembered the helpless feeling a lot better than the good feeling of helping.

A timer dinged from the kitchen. He welcomed the interruption.

"Come on. It's some of Zee's lasagna, so you're in for a treat."

She rose, putting the book down on the couch with great care. "Zee cooks, too?"

"Too?"

"In addition to running a business, being razor sharp, and beautiful."

He smiled as they headed for the kitchen. "She is all that, isn't she?"

"Seems to run in the family."

"That," he said, lifting an eyebrow at her, "was perilously close to a compliment, Ms. Larson."

She stopped in the doorway. "Have I ever said anything to indicate I didn't admire both of you, for your looks least of all, mostly for what you've survived, and what you've built?"

"Uh. . ." He swallowed, he hadn't expected that powerful response to his simple teasing.

She gave him a wry smile. "But I guess I've not said it, either. But I do. Admire you, I mean. Both of you," she added hastily.

Had she been afraid he'd think she admired him, personally? That niggled at him, and he was glad when she busied herself getting plates and silverware; he'd shown her where things were yesterday and told her to use what she needed.

He cut into the steaming pasta dish while she opened the foil-wrapped loaf of garlic bread. Steam rose from it, sending the luscious smell into the room. Their stomachs growled in unison. Loudly. Both startled, their gazes locked. Then he grinned. She grinned back, and it was like a slam into that protesting stomach. For the first time he'd had a glimpse of what a happy, carefree Hope would look like, and he couldn't beat down the urge to see her that way all the time.

They had eaten enough to quiet the growling before she spoke again. "Thank you for the advance. I'll buy some things so Zee can have hers back."

He just nodded. "Zee said you'll earn it, you're making good headway. And you're quiet."

She smiled as if pleased. "She's really into the music playing in the office, so I try not to bother her too much with questions while she's working. I save them up till the end of the day."

"In that case," he said rather glumly, poking at that last bite of lasagna, "you should probably bring them to me. It's my mess, after all."

"It's not really a mess, just disorganized."

"It's a mess," he repeated. "In the beginning, I didn't pay much attention, because all I was trying to do was. . ."

"Keep busy?"

He picked up the slice of garlic bread. Put it down again. Finally, he looked at her. Saw he didn't have to explain, she had already put together the timing. Zee had probably told her.

"Yes."

"You must have loved her very much."

"I did. We were together since ninth grade."

Her eyes widened. "Real high school sweethearts?"

"I know, corny. But Amanda was the one. It was like finding the other half of myself. Half the time she knew what I was thinking before I did. We just always knew we would be together. And when my folks were killed, she was the one who stepped in and handled everything, took care of Zee, until I could get here."

He wished he hadn't blurted all that out. He was usually able to keep the old memories barricaded in his mind. She didn't say anything, just looked at him. Somehow that was worse than the chattering he sometimes got, when people didn't know what to say. Apparently when Hope didn't know what to say, she didn't say anything. But then, he'd already snapped at her when she'd been about to use the usual "I'm sorry," response.

And then she turned it around on you, digging into territory you haven't visited in a very long time.

Finally, she spoke. Quietly, staring down at her plate. "I've seen bonds like that, but I can't imagine having it, so I can't even come close to imagining the pain of losing it."

Perhaps we met so young because this was all we were ever going to have.

Amanda's words, spoken from the hospital bed that had been set up by the hospice group in their apartment living room, the day before she had finally lost her valiant, painful battle.

"I hope you never do," he said, his voice harsh with the memory that hadn't been so vivid in some time.

"And yet you built something out of it. Something successful, helpful, and unique."

And then he was in the unexpected position of being the one who felt like chattering. Anything to push that memory back into its cage. "I never expected this to turn into anything. That's why everything from back in the beginning is disorganized, because I didn't think it was going to become what it did. Some friends needed stuff done, didn't have time to organize it, so I did. I kept the paperwork because it seemed like the thing to do, but I just tossed it in a box. A shoebox, at the time."

She smiled. Damn, those real, genuine smiles of hers were something. "So when did you realize you were gonna need a bigger box?"

He found himself smiling back, the difficult moments past now. "Those friends told other people, who told people, and it just sort of grew from there."

"Shows you how valuable—and rare—someone with those skills, and a knack with people can be. And who is also utterly trustworthy."

He'd been told that, or variations of it, before. But somehow it seemed different coming from her. Perhaps because of her emphasis on the trustworthy part, as if they were some fabled species she hadn't quite believed really existed.

"You already got the job," he said lightly. "You don't have to flatter the boss."

"It's not flattery if it's truth," she said with a shrug. And then, so straight faced he wasn't certain if she was serious or not, she added, "Besides, Zee says she's the boss."

His brows shot up. "She does, does she?"

For a long moment she just looked at him. And then he saw the corners of her mouth twitch. And then she was laughing. And it was the most beautiful sound he'd heard in longer than he could remember.

"She told me to say that to you, I swear she did."

"I'll just bet she did." He was grinning at her now.

"She said really you're partners, and she'd hate to ever have to work with anyone else. And that she's very, very proud of you."

He blinked. "Zee said that? My sister, Zinnia Rose Mahan said that?"

"Zinnia Rose?"

"Damn, don't tell her I told you that. She hates her full name."

"I think it's lovely. Different."

"Too different for her," he said as he rose and gathered up his plate and utensils. "She doesn't like to stand out."

Hope did the same. "Doesn't want to stand out? Or wants to blend in?"

He looked over his shoulder at her as he headed for the dishwasher. "Isn't that the same thing?" he asked as he put the dishes in the rack.

"Not necessarily," she said. He reached out for her plate, and when she handed it to him he slid it into the next spot in the rack. She dumped her own silverware in the bin for it before she went on. "But it would be nearly impossible for a woman who looks like your sister not to stand out. She's so beautiful. Those Mahan genes, I guess."

He straightened, stared at her. "Flattery again?"

She held his gaze for a silent moment. "You have to have heard it before."

In fact, on occasion, he had. It was just that most of the time he never paid any attention. The part of his life where it might matter what he looked like—other than the occasional business contact he cleaned up for—was over. The part where it might matter in that male and female way. And yet. . .

"Not something I aspire to," he muttered, turning away, putting his back to her before he said something stupid.

"Of course not." She said it as matter-of-factly as if she were commenting on the dishwasher she now closed. "If you did you wouldn't be nearly as attractive."

What the hell was she saying? He spun back. She'd moved, and they collided. Instinctively he grabbed her as she wobbled, knocked off balance. Her hands came up, her fingers curled around his arms. Squeezed, but not trying to push him away. She stared up at him, and he saw once more how warm those cinnamon colored eyes were, saw the golden specks that seemed to sparkle.

Her lips parted, and for a moment he imagined she was leaning in, trying to get closer to him. Then he realized it was not imagination, because she moved, took that last crucial step that separated them. And then she was there, so near, so close that he could feel her heat, and it stirred him in a way he'd utterly forgotten was possible. He was surprised his body didn't snap audibly as it woke up, reminding him that while his heart might be done, the rest of him was not. After those moments when he'd watched her reading, he wasn't surprised that it woke up to her. And then there was the way he'd responded when he'd thought her just a kid.

And how relieved he'd been when he realized she wasn't.

He just hadn't expected it. He hadn't ever expected it, not since the day they put Amanda in the ground.

"True," she whispered, and he had no idea if she meant his name or what had sparked to life between them. He sucked in the air that seemed to suddenly be in short supply. But air didn't seem to matter. The only thing that mattered were those eyes, that mouth. . .

He leaned down, wanting to feel that mouth more than get that breath of air. She reached up to him, moving her hands to his shoulders now, urging him on. He lowered his head and—

He stopped. Something had caught the corner of his vision. The tattoo on her left wrist, that band of sharp edged curves with a tribal look. It reminded him sharply of everything he didn't know about her, of everything she'd left behind. . .and that she was afraid was still after her.

Afraid.

If I tell you I'm twenty-three, will it change your mind about how I can pay you back?

He released her suddenly, backed away, hands up as if that would help him keep them off of her. He wasn't sure it would be enough.

It had to be enough.

"True—"

"Stop." His voice was colder than he'd meant it to be, but it was the only way he could beat down the fire she'd so unexpectedly kindled in him. “You don’t mean this. You’re just feeling. . .obligated.”

“Is that what I’m feeling?”

He countered with a question of his own, still unanswered. “What are you running from?”

She didn’t answer, but he saw the heat fade from her eyes, felt it as if the chill had swept him as well.

“If you don’t trust me enough to tell me that, you sure as hell shouldn’t be trusting me with. . .anything more.”

For a long moment she just stared at him. So long he felt his pulse begin to hammer again, felt his body’s signal that it was more than agreeable to resuming what he’d so abruptly ended. No matter how wrong it was.

And then she turned away, and without another word left the room. A moment later he heard her footsteps on the stairway. In sudden need of support he reached for the counter, closing his eyes, grabbing the edge of the cold stone and holding on.

To stop himself from going after her.

Chapter Fourteen

HOPE DIDN'T MAKE it to the bedroom. Instead she dove into the bathroom, because it was closer. And had cold water. Which she needed, after what the man downstairs had fired in her.

She pulled the door closed, turned the lock. Knowing him—oh, God, knowing him—he could probably open it with a couple of toothpicks, but it gave her sense of security anyway.

If you don't trust me enough to tell me that, you sure as hell shouldn't be trusting me with anything more.

And then she realized that yes, he could likely unlock this door, but he wouldn't. Because, outside of an emergency, he wasn't the kind of man who would ignore such obvious signals. And he would honor them. Because that's who he was.

Her back against the door, she slid down to the floor, shaking. She tried to think of him ever running from what she'd left behind. The images wouldn't form in her mind, because she knew he never would. No, honorable, strong

True Mahan would never have run. He would have stood up to them, he would have found a way to do it, and to keep everyone safe. She'd been wrong when she thought he couldn't match them.

Oh, yeah, that's what she needed, a tall, dark, studly Texan, maybe with that rifle in the back of his truck, barreling in and taking charge. Cagan and the rest wouldn't know what hit them.

That it was so easy to imagine, that he could and would, just made the differences between them seem even starker.

And insurmountable.

She didn't know how long she'd been sitting there, her arms wrapped around her knees, when she heard the tap on the door. She didn't even jump; she was too weary of it all. And she'd known he'd come anyway.

A silent moment passed. Then, "Hope, say something."

That seemed an odd enough request that her head came up.

"Say anything. Tell me to go to hell. Just so I know you're. . .alive in there."

Faintly, as if from a long distance, something sparked inside her. "Go to hell," she said, as instructed. A moment later she heard footsteps retreating down the hall.

When it was quiet again she thought about that spark. Realized it was because he'd been afraid she had come in here and. . .what? Committed suicide? She nearly laughed. If she'd had his kind of nerve, maybe she would have back then. It would have put an end to it, for sure. But she hadn't had the nerve then, or now. She wasn't like strong, solid True Mahan who had gone through seven kinds of hell and not broken. True Mahan, who would take a stand and protect those he loved. But she didn't have that strength, so to keep those she loved safe, she had run. It was the only thing she knew how to do.

Well, that and nearly ravish the man in his own kitchen. Apparently she knew how to do that.

She wondered what would have happened had he been a different kind of man. The kind who would take what she'd obviously been offering. And probably more, whether she offered it or not.

Images rippled through her mind, images like those that had taunted her as she listened to the shower running, imagining him with rivulets of water running over his naked body. Images of being in his arms, feeling his strength and solid goodness, of that tall, lean body taking hers to heights she'd never felt before. Giving her what she'd never known.

And she would take it. Because that's what she did. That's who she was.

Nowhere near good enough for the likes of Truett Mahan.

✪

FOR AT LEAST the third time in the last hour, True picked up his phone, stared at it as if it held the answer, then put it down on the desk again. Once he'd gotten as far as pulling up the number, but hadn't called.

When he picked it up again he made a call, but not the one he'd been pondering.

Deck's cell phone was a relatively new addition, acceded to only because he didn't want to be out of touch with Kelsey. "Besides her, you're the only one who has the number," Deck had said warily when he'd first gotten it. "Well, and Mom."

True knew he meant Kelsey's mother, from whom Kelsey got her heart, her strength, and her beauty. The creature who had biologically produced Deck wasn't worthy of the name.

Mindful of Deck's trust, this was the first time he'd initiated a call on it; usually he called the house phone and left a message there, which Deck would eventually answer one way or another, usually a way that didn't involve actual speaking. Although that, too, had changed since Kelsey.

Surprisingly, he answered on the first ring. Not surprisingly, he didn't bother with hello.

"If you need more decisions, I'm fresh out."

True laughed, felt better about calling. "Not going well?"

"Sam," Deck said sourly, "can be a real jerk sometimes."

"Can't we all?" True said, meaning it on levels he could never explain right now. "But no, no decisions. Not even wedding decisions. Just a question."

"Shoot."

"Just how pissed were you when you found out I'd had Ducane check you out?"

"Really. If you hadn't told him to stop when and where you did, we wouldn't be here now. I didn't. . .forgive easily back then."

"But you did."

"Eventually." There was a moment of silence, but True didn't speak. He knew this whole friendship thing was new to Deck, and he did best with time to process. And finally he went on. "I think part of the reason I was so angry was that. . .I really liked it here. I didn't want to have to move on again."

"But if I'd pushed too hard," True began.

"I'd have been gone."

True thought of Kelsey. "Then I'm really, really glad I didn't. For lots of reasons."

"Me, too. So, you going to dig into what your girl's running from?"

He tried to ignore the flash of. . .whatever that was that shot through him at the words "your girl."

"Would you?"

"If it was Kelsey in trouble, I'd dig down to the core, and damn the consequences."

After they'd ended the call, True tapped the phone against his palm. He wasn't really any further along than he had been. Because there was one major, irrefutable difference in their situations. Deck would have every right with Kelsey. He loved her to distraction, and she knew it, and loved him right back just as hard.

What Hope Larson felt was nothing like love, but a debt to someone who had helped her. And that was something a man simply did not cash in on. Not if he wanted to live with himself. And he felt nothing of the sort for Hope either. What he felt was merely concern for a person in trouble. Nothing more.

Those flashes of heat and sexual awareness were just. . .reminders he was still breathing. And if what he'd felt when they'd almost kissed nibbled away at that certainty, he ignored it.

He pulled up that first number again, and this time he hit the button.

HOPE WAS FEELING quite relieved this morning. True was already gone when she got up, and when she arrived at the office next door, Zee mentioned casually that she'd be providing the promised meals for the rest of the week. She seemed upbeat about it, so Hope guessed she wasn't being ordered to by her brother, at least.

And she guessed her brother hadn't told her why. That he didn't want to be around in case his house guest/temporary employee tried to jump him again. Hope supposed it was a measure of the distance she'd gained from her old life that that now seemed like the stupidest thing she'd done in recent memory.

But Lord, she'd wanted that kiss. And she couldn't ever remember feeling like that before.

She realized Zee was talking and snapped back to reality, hoping she hadn't missed much.

"—the music festival this spring. He'd love to get a foot in there, it's a huge deal and they always need this built or that organized."

"I'm sorry, where?"

Thankfully, Zee only laughed. "The Kerrville folk festival. I keep forgetting not everyone outside of Texas has heard of it. Bet you've heard of some of the names that have came out of there, though."

"It's a big thing?"

"About thirty thousand people show up. About two and half weeks of a big campout with music, crafts, a ton of food vendors. And," she added, "one of their usual staff who builds and maintains the stages, booths, and other structures just crashed on his motorcycle. They called us to see if True could help out until he's back on his feet."

Hope nearly laughed out loud at herself. So much for thinking True's absence had anything at all to do with her, or what had happened last night.

When did you start having delusions of grandeur? As if True Mahan would run rather than face you. As if he'd run rather than face anyone, or anything. It just wasn't in the man.

Belatedly something occurred to her. "When will he be back?"

"No idea, maybe a couple of days, maybe not until the weekend. Definitely not tonight, at least." Zee eyed her curiously. "Does it matter?"

Yes! Hope bit back the exclamation and managed to say fairly levelly, "Only if I want to get back into the room he's letting me use. I didn't know so I locked the door when I came over."

Zee frowned. "He didn't give you a key?"

Hope blinked. "Why would he? I'm a stranger, I could steal him blind."

Zee gave her a smile that was achingly said. "He doesn't worry about theft much. He's already lost the most important thing he ever had."

His wife. Hope didn't know what to say. After a moment Zee went on briskly.

"I'm sure he meant to. He must have forgotten, when this call came in. It is kind of a big deal, and if he helps out now they'll keep him in mind for the future. Anyway, I've got a key. Or heck, use the inside door."

Hope hesitated, then shook her head. "That's. . .yours. Between you two. He explained how it works."

"Did he now? That's interesting."

Hope had no idea why a simple explanation of respecting boundaries would be so interesting, but Zee seemed to think it was.

On the other hand, she knew exactly why she was breathing easier now. And it had nothing to do with knowing she could get back into her room. And everything to do with know there would be some breathing space between her and True Mahan, at least for a while.

Chapter Fifteen

ONLY ONCE HE was gone did Hope realize how much of her attention and awareness True seemed to automatically draw. She didn't feel relaxed, exactly, more. . .at loose ends. Or in limbo. A holding pattern, as if everything was hovering, waiting until the center of gravity returned and everything went back to normal.

She spent a quiet night in his house, mostly reading. It was a pleasure she'd not often had, and she tried her best to savor it. She'd finished the first Sam Smith book and moved on to the second, eager to see what happened next even as she ached inside for the brave boy who had become as real to her as any living, breathing one.

She went to bed early, and for a while lay there thinking how odd it was that she should be more relaxed in a strange, empty house than when its owner was present. But then she pictured that owner, and sleepily decided it made perfect sense after all.

The next day went much the same, and she made great progress on the big box of papers. This time at the end of the day she declined Zee's hurried offer of a meal, realizing the woman was getting ready to go out somewhere. Wondered idly what kind of man would risk taking on her protective big brother.

And only found out when Zee paused to look at her consideringly that it wasn't a date at all.

"You know, Kelsey wouldn't mind at all if you came with me."

Hope blinked. "What?"

"She really liked how you were with her new horse the other day. She said it was clear you were a little afraid, but that you recognized Shadow was more scared than you."

"I. . .it was fun," Hope said. "I've never been that close to a horse before."

"Welcome to Texas," Zee said with a grin that reminded Hope of her brother. "Anyway, it's a bridal shower for Kelsey. Sort of."

"Sort of?"

"It's not for the usual stuff. It's for stuff for the rescue. Equipment they need, gift cards for feed, that kind of thing."

Hope had only met Kelsey briefly, but she already knew how much her work meant to her. "What a great idea!"

"It was Declan's. He knows his woman." The grin flashed again. "I'm giving her True."

Hope blinked. "What?"

"She needs a new corral. Others are giving her the materials, I'm giving her him to build it."

Hope couldn't help laughing. "Does he know this?"

"Not yet. I'll spring it on him when it's done and he can't back out. Not that he would. He'd never let Kelsey—or Declan—down."

"I think," Hope said seriously, "he'd never let anyone down."

Zee gave her a long, assessing look. "No, he wouldn't. If you have him on your side, he'll go down with you before he'll let you crash."

Hope told herself there hadn't been any pointed message for her particularly in that. And she was tempted, seriously tempted, to accept Zee's offer. Spending an evening among people honoring a friend, someone she barely knew but already liked, was something she hadn't experienced in a long time. But deep down she knew it would only give this place a greater hold on her, and it was already tugging at her with useless hopes and silly dreams.

And so she spent another night alone in True Mahan's home. And this time, before settling in with her book, she spent some time looking around, not in a nosy, taking advantage of him being gone sort of way, but in a trying to understand the man way. And she told herself it was not prurient interest that had her peeking into the master bedroom, merely curiosity.

It both surprised her and confirmed what she'd expected, in those weak moments when she allowed herself to wonder; it was like the rest of his home, masculine, but not harshly so. Also like the rest, the colors were light and bright, almost cheerful. The floor was a subtle shade of gray wood, polished and smooth and sleek looking. No flower prints here, but long blue and white striped drapes at the windows. One tall chest of drawers beside a door that was probably a closet. One nightstand. Only one, she noted, with a couple of books, a lamp, and a small wood tray with a slightly off kilter dog carved into the side.

And the bed.

The heavy four-poster in wood that had the same gray tones as the flooring seemed huge to her, but as the image of True hovered in her mind, as it was wont to do, she realized he would need a bed that size. Even if he did sleep alone, as the one nightstand seemed to indicate.

She stared at the tossed bedding; he hadn't bothered with making it when he'd needed to get rolling early. The cover was a blue and white plaid that blended well with the drapes. She stifled the urge to tidy it, because then when he got back she'd have to explain not only why she'd done it, but why she'd been in his room to begin with.

Yet the itch to touch, to see if a trace of his warmth lingered, was almost overwhelming. Had he picked the furnishings himself, or had Zee had a hand in it?

Or. . .Amanda?

She backed out of the room abruptly, calling herself several choice names for poking her nose where it didn't belong and getting it singed. And for letting her mind wander down paths she wasn't free to walk.

She put it—and him—out of her mind as she went back to work the next morning. Zee was still yawning, her usually stylishly tousled hair looking a bit flat this morning.

"Good party?" she asked.

Zee smiled. "A bit too good. And late. If I'm cranky, I apologize in advance."

"Accepted in advance." She wanted to ask if she'd heard from her brother, if he was on his way home. But she didn't. Even if it was a natural question.

A while later she was down to where she could actually see the bottom of the large box. She might even have this done today, if True got home in time to explain this last batch of random receipts from the bottom of the box. She sorted them as best she could, by date, matching purchase receipts with delivery receipts, and where she could matching up the addresses with job sites Zee knew. But there were many where he'd had the materials delivered here, and apparently taken them to the job himself, and those would have to wait in the hopes he'd remember what went where.

"Oh," Zee said at one point when she was passing by with a coffee refill and glanced at what Hope was holding, "pull those out. Those are for this place."

"This place? Oh, you mean when you divided it?"

She nodded. "Didn't make much sense to me to each keep renting our own place when we owned this outright. True was doing the upkeep anyway, when we had it rented out. And it was big enough, with room to expand where necessary. So I talked to True and he agreed, and came up with the plan to divide it. Took some rearranging of space, building a second kitchen and adding a couple of bathrooms, but it's worked out perfectly for us."

"Helps that you get along," Hope said, all the while her mind racing as she looked at the dates on the paperwork she was holding. Realized what it meant. They had done this, moved into this house, after his wife had died.

Amanda Mahan had never lived under that roof. She felt a spurt of relief, followed immediately by a stab of guilt; it was a horrible thing to be glad about. Not to mention it was none of her business. She fought to listen to Zee.

"Yes. Although we didn't always. When he had on the parent hat instead of the brother one."

"That must have been. . .hard. For both of you."

"We clashed, inevitably. I'm just forever glad my brother had the fortitude to do it. I don't know where I'd be without him. And I like having him close." Zee laughed then, waving at the wall that separated the two halves. "But not too close."

"You'd never know it wasn't originally this way."

"That's True," Zee said. "And if we ever want to sell it, he'll just wall up that door."

"As long as that's the only reason he'd do it."

"True? No, he's the original slow burn. That's why he tolerates my quick temper so well." She smiled. "Besides, he loves me. He'd never do that no matter how mad he got."

Hope had nothing to say to that. She went back to work on the last of the papers. More evidence of True's versatility. Everything from building wheelchair ramps to repairing the sign announcing you were entering Whiskey River. A sudden image flashed through her mind, of a couple of old cowboys standing there pondering a truck crashed into that sign, one of them rubbing his chin, the other drawling "Better call True." And it wouldn't surprise her in the least to find out that would be the reaction anytime anything needed fixing in Whiskey River.

She set the papers dealing with the wheelchair ramps aside until she found the labor estimate that should go with them. On top of them went another page without that charge listed, and she wondered if perhaps these, being fairly early on, he'd been paid in cash for. And then she read the details on the page she'd just set down.

"You're laughing," Zee said, and Hope realized indeed she was.

"Did he really," she asked, holding up one of the last sheets of paper, "install a fairy fountain?"

"Yes, he did," Zee said, but she wasn't laughing in turn. At all. "For the Avila's little girl, Lucy. Outside her bedroom window, where she could see it. And he went by every week to make sure it was working. She adored him for it."

Now she felt a rush of something other than laughter, that sort of warmth she'd felt more often since being here than she could remember since her grandparents.

"Of course she did. That's sweet," she said. Then Zee's last words registered. Past tense. "Adored?"

"Yes. She died eight months after he put it in. Leukemia."

"Oh." It all made a very sad sort of sense now. "That's awful." Not sure what to do or say, she just stared down at the page. And suddenly realized there wasn't really anything missing.

"He didn't charge them, did he? For installing it."

"No. He wouldn't." Zee sighed. "It was the only time I've seen my brother cry except when Amanda died."

Somehow that made it worse. Made her feel worse. Made her wish she'd never said anything, or seen the page at all. How on earth had he dealt with so much loss and stayed sane? Let alone become the kind, generous man he was?

Because he's much, much stronger than you are.

It was a long, silent moment before she was able to meet Zee's eyes and ask, "Why did you tell me that?"

"So you would know," Zee said, in a tone that was nothing less than ominous, "why I would do anything to keep my brother from being hurt again."

As warnings went, that one was too blunt to be mistaken. "I would never hurt him. He's been too good to me." She meant every word of it.

"I believe you wouldn't mean to," Zee said. "I don't think you're going to rip him off, or slit his throat in the middle of the night, but you're not telling him the truth, either. Not all of it, anyway."

She couldn't deny that, at least not believably. "I. . .can't. It's for the best, it really is."

"Finding out he misjudged you would hurt him. But he'd get over that. But if you bring whatever it is you're running from down on him, I promise you I will not get over it."

Hope met True's fierce little sister's gaze, saw the truth of her words there. Wondered what it must be like to have a sibling like that. Didn't wonder what it took to inspire such loyalty and love, for hadn't she been dealing with the walking, breathing inspiration for five days now?

Only five days. Had it really been? She felt as if her entire life had shifted, changed irrevocably. And the last time that had happened, it had sent her on this mad run.

She had a sudden vision of exactly that, of what she was running from crashing in on True. How could she possibly be so certain what this man she'd only know five days would do? But she was. He would stand. True Mahan would always stand.

"I'll be gone when this is done, as agreed," she promised.

"Finish it early, and I'll see you're paid as agreed," Zee said.

Hope nodded, even as some hidden part of her protested, as if she'd had her heart set on at least that promised two weeks in this place—with this man—who drew her so.

"Good," Zee said briskly. "Now to that end, I need you

to go into town again. The dedicated scanner I ordered for this has come in, go pick it up, please."

"All right."

"Keys are on the rack."

"Your car?"

Zee gave her a wry smile. "It's big. I didn't expect you to carry it back walking."

Hope's head came up. "If you did, I would try."

Zee studied her for a moment, oddly as if she'd just noticed something. "Yes," she said slowly, "I believe you would."

Hope had the car keys in hand and the door open when Zee spoke again.

"And more than anything, Hope?" She turned back. "Do not make my brother fall in love with you, not when you're just going to leave."

Hope stared, speechless for a moment. Then the old bitterness rose up in her, a bitterness born of the immutable knowledge that she had brought all this on herself with her own at best misguided at worst downright stupid actions.

She finally found her voice. "Oh, I'm sure he's much, much too smart for that."

But as she got in the car and headed toward town, she couldn't help wondering what had made Zee think that was even a distant possibility.

Chapter Sixteen

HOPE STOOD LOOKING up at the statue above the fountain, then at the colorful pamphlet in her hand. Ronan "Booze" Kelly. What a name. She wondered if there was a written history of the guy somewhere, the story of how he'd seized an opportunity, supplied what he saw as a necessity—as in the Texas of that day it might well have been, and for that matter might still be—started a town, and today stood guard over his creation.

And then she laughed at herself, standing here in this strange—well, not so strange now—place reading a tourist brochure and looking at a statue of the town's founder. But odder still was simply standing out here in the open like this, instead of hiding. But the general knowledge that she was working for True Mahan was like a protective dome around her, it seemed.

She leaned over, trailed her fingers through the water of the fountain. It wasn't hot out—that, she'd been assured, would come soon, this was Texas after all—but the cool water still felt good, soothing somehow.

"Watch out for the sharks!"

She managed not to jump. The young voice that called out to her belonged to a small, towheaded boy peeking at her from the other side of the statue. She smiled at his mischievous grin. She looked down at the water consideringly.

"Little shallow for sharks," she said, her expression serious.

He leaned around further. "Alligators, then."

"Piranha maybe?"

The boy's grin widened. He came out from behind the statue. He looked about ten or twelve to her, not that she was any judge.

"It would keep the tourists away," the boy said.

"You don't like tourists?"

He shrugged. "Depends. Are you one?"

I've never been a tourist anywhere. "No. I'm working here for a while."

He considered that for a moment as he looked her over. She saw his gaze snag on her left wrist. The tattoo.

"I know you," the boy declared. "You're the lady helping out Mr. True."

She hadn't been called a lady in a while, but she wasn't about to quibble with a kid over it. So instead she focused on the rest. "Mr. True?"

The boy grimaced. "He says I can call him True, but my mom says I have to call him mister because he's a grown-up."

"Sounds like you found a equitable solution."

The boy frowned. "What's that mean?"

"That it works for everyone."

"Oh. Yeah." He seemed to like this, and finally came all the way around the edge of the fountain. Apparently True held sway even with the shorter set in Whiskey River. The boy climbed up on the edge of the fountain, which put him much closer to eye level with her. "My name's Adam."

No last name, she noticed. Was that because kids didn't think it important, or because he didn't want her to know? *Stop it. Not everybody's hiding who they are like you. Especially not a little kid.*

"Nice to meet you, Adam," she said, and when, to her surprise, the boy held out his hand, she shook it. "I'm Hope."

"I know." She must have looked startled because he shrugged. "Everybody knows everything around here. News goes faster'n greased lightning, my gramma says." He eyed her wrist again. "I like your tattoo. I want to get one."

Liked it, or that she had it? she wondered. "I don't, anymore."

He blinked. "What?"

"I thought it was cool when I got it, but things change and it can't."

"It can't? And why don't you like it anymore?"

She wasn't quite sure why she was standing here having this conversation with a little boy, but it didn't seem right to just walk away. Not to mention that she was beginning to wonder what he was doing here in the middle of the day on a Friday, instead of being in school.

"It's from a time when I was different," she began, but saw by his furrowed brow this was not registering. "If you were to get a tattoo, would it be of your first baby rattle?"

He looked horrified. "No!"

"Why? Back then, it was probably the most important thing in your life."

"But I'm not a baby anymore."

"Exactly. And just like that rattle, what's important to you now might not be later. But that tatt's there forever."

"Oh." He looked thoughtful now. "That makes sense."

"Thank you. It happens." She grinned at him, and he laughed.

"I like you," he declared, and she felt as if she'd won some kind of battle. "Most grownups'd be pestering me about why I'm not in school today."

Even though she had wondered, she put her hands on her hips and glared at him in mock outrage. "Do I look like a truant officer to you?"

Adam laughed. "Nope."

"And you're not a baby, so I figured you know where you're supposed to be, and a stranger telling you otherwise isn't going to matter. And shouldn't."

He was looking at her curiously. "You're different."

"Been told that before." She was a little surprised herself at the weariness that had crept into her voice.

"Uh-oh." Adam was looking over her shoulder now, and slowly backing away.

"Let me guess, the real truant officer?"

"As good as," the boy said. "Ol' Mr. Reid. Mom says he's the worst stick in the mud in town. That means he doesn't believe in fun. See ya."

As quickly as that the boy had darted back toward Booze's statue. Somehow she thought the guy would understand.

Down the street a truck turned onto Main Street, heading briskly toward the square. Other than that nothing was moving, and that alone was a novelty to her. She turned around and started walking in the direction the boy had been looking. Saw not the crotchety old man she'd expected but a younger one, rather portly and with a beard she guessed he thought masked that somehow. She turned her head just enough to see, out of the corner of one eye, Adam taking to his heels from behind Booze Kelly toward the street.

She wondered if she could engage the man in a conversation long enough to let him get away. Perhaps she shouldn't, maybe the boy should be in school, but she didn't want to betray the kid.

She could just ask for directions, she thought. He probably knew everyone, and would know she was new here, so that should work. She could—

A warning honk from behind her ripped through her mental planning. Instinctively she whirled around.

Adam had darted right into the path of that rapidly moving truck.

She didn't think. Didn't hesitate. She ran. Dove. Into the street. Hand outstretched.

She felt the fabric of the boy's shirt. Swore she could feel the heat of the truck's engine.

Then it was all sound.

Brakes squealing. A thud. And a scream.

✪

"REMEMBER THAT OLD joke Millie Templeton used to make, about opening a can of worms and finding scorpions on top?"

Uh-oh.

True grimaced as he edged over to the side of the road in the first turnout spot he came to. He'd almost made it home in blissful ignorance, he'd topped the last rise and could see the river from here. But he put the truck in park and his flashers on; he had a feeling this phone call was going to need his full attention.

"Since Jamie turned it into his band's name, yeah, I remember," he said. "I gather you found something?"

"Eventually," Jack Ducane said. "That is if this is your girl. Pic incoming. It's from seven years ago, so keep that in mind."

Seven years ago. She would have been sixteen. His phone

signaled a text coming in. He almost didn't want to look. Then had the thought that maybe it wasn't really Hope, so he did.

It was her.

Or rather, a variation of her. He stared at the photograph, having to search to find the Hope he knew beneath the dark, heavy makeup, the raggedy hair that masked half her face, and the tough expression. But there, buried under all that, were her eyes. Her nose.

And if he'd had any doubts left, there was the tattoo.

Yes. Younger, but yes.

He let out a breath. "It is. She looks nothing like that now, but it's her. What did you find?"

"Had to expand the search quite a bit. But what else have I got to do, with active duty still a month away?"

"At least it's coming," True said, knowing the man would be shattered if he couldn't do what he'd been born to do. "And I told you she wasn't from Texas."

"But you didn't mention I was going to get to sift through all the crap L.A. manages to produce."

"California?" True asked, surprised.

"Didn't mean Louisiana."

"Damn. She's a long way from home."

"If you want to call it that." There was a note in Jack's voice that told True he wasn't just expressing an opinion of Los Angeles. A string of questions rose in his mind, and it took him a moment to decide what to ask first. Finally he chose the one that seemed to matter most.

"Does she have reason to have run so far, and be so scared?"

He heard Jack let out a long breath before answering. When he did, his voice was flat, definite.

"Yes."

Before he could work out what to ask or even the nerve to ask it, his phone signaled another call coming in. He glanced at the screen, ready to swipe it away. Then he saw who it was. A reaction he thought he'd beaten swept him full force, as if it had been only yesterday. Or as if it still mattered. But he hadn't gotten a call that mattered from the Whiskey River medical clinic in years. To be exact, the day they'd told him Amanda's case was worse than they could handle and she needed to go to Austin.

"True?" Jack said, his voice a bit distant since True was still staring at the screen.

"Sorry." The signaling stopped. "Another call."

"Okay, I'll make this quick. You've got trouble on your hands."

"Believe it or not, I knew that already," True said, still fighting for calm. He couldn't quite believe a call from a medical facility years after Amanda's death could rattle him so much.

"For what it's worth, she herself doesn't seem to be lethal."

The hell she doesn't. "Is she in trouble, or is she the trouble?"

"Depends where you stand."

Jack always had had the knack of seeing from all sides. Sometimes sides no one else saw. It wasn't that he empathized or felt sympathy for a proven bad guy, but he could put his head where they were and often figure out what they'd do next. Of course that had earned him some ragging now and then, about seeing sides that weren't there, but he took it with equanimity. He saw what he saw and he stood where he stood, and you could take it or leave it. And being able to think from a suspect's point of view had helped him break some pretty major cases.

True's phone beeped that a voice mail had been left. So it hadn't been a wrong number. So much for that hope. He pulled himself together on a deep breath.

"Jack, that call was from the Whiskey River medical clinic. I need to check it, it could be Zee. Can you hang on a sec?"

"Hate those calls. Go ahead." At the assent, he switched over to voice mail, listened.

"True? It's Sharon, at the clinic, emergency side. Can you get here? It's not Zee, but there's been an accident."

He breathed a little better, thankful to Sharon for getting that out first: not Zee. They must train them to do that when leaving a message. Everybody in town knew she was all he had left of family. But if it wasn't Zee, why were they calling him? Damn, maybe it was Deck. Or Kelsey, or—

It hit him then, belatedly, probably because he'd been so rattled.

Hope.

Chapter Seventeen

HE'D BEEN SO close to home he didn't call back, he just laid on the accelerator and hoped if he got stopped it was a local who'd let him get there first and deal with his lawbreaking later. But he ripped into town and up Boots Lane without interference. There was an ambulance parked near the entrance to the emergency side of the small clinic, but no sign of anyone around.

He parked kind of cockeyed in the only spot available and hit the automatic doors at a run. He had to catch himself when they didn't open in as big a hurry as he was in. And then he was inside. He headed for the counter, then something caught his peripheral vision. He turned his head as he kept moving. And then he stopped dead.

Hope. Huddled on one of the plastic chairs against the far wall.

And bloody.

His breath jammed up in his throat. There was blood all over her. His stomach roiled, and he felt panic creeping in around the edges of his mind. The sounds, the smells of this place hammered at him. Medical sounds, smells. His mind screamed at him to get out, get away. To be gone before the bad, awful, unchangeable news came.

But someplace else, some deep, hidden place in his chest, urged him forward.

Practically before he was aware of moving he was at her side, crouched down before the chair. He had to remember how to breathe before he could speak.

"Hope, what happened?" She lifted her head then, and the turmoil in her eyes was vividly clear. He tried to gentle his voice as much as he could but wasn't sure it had much effect, he was too wound up. "Why the hell are you out here and not in a treatment room? You can't be that stubborn, you need—"

"True, she's all right." Sharon was there then, and she sat on the chair next to Hope. "She wasn't actually hurt in the accident."

It took him a moment to process, given all the blood.

"I didn't ask them to call you," Hope said. She sounded as shaky as if she had been hurt, and he frowned. And what did that have to do with anything?

"She didn't," Sharon confirmed. "But once I realized she worked for you, of course I did."

"Of course," Hope echoed, "because you're True freaking Mahan and everybody in this town thinks you walk on water."

Sharon looked startled. True thought he might have felt

stung if not for how she'd sounded. He couldn't even put a name to everything that had echoed in Hope's voice. But he shelved that question in order to ask the more obviously crucial one.

"All that blood—"

"Is that her?" A rather piercing voice called out across the room. True recognized it immediately, and the churning in his stomach reactivated. Ginevra Hawkins, one of the social mavens of Whiskey River, second only to Paloma Kelly, who claimed the top spot by virtue of being one of the founding Kelly family.

Mrs. Hawkins was what his grandfather used to call a civilizing woman, meaning everyone around her had to conform to her standards or never hear the end of it. But she was also the founder of several genuinely helpful charities, and worked tirelessly for them, so they all gave her the benefit of the doubt. When they couldn't avoid her altogether.

She was striding across the room with an energy that belied her nearly seventy years. Dear God, what had Hope done?

She doesn't seem to be lethal. . .

And then Mrs. Hawkins was there, bending over Hope. Reaching, taking up her hands, seemingly oblivious that they were covered in blood. "Thank you, you wonderful girl."

True blinked. Drew back slightly; he'd never heard such a tone from this woman in the entire time he'd known her, which was most of his life. Hope herself looked startled.

"Adam is her grandson," Sharon explained to Hope.

"Adam?" True asked, sharply. He liked the clever, live-wire boy with the fascination for how things worked. And so did everyone else in Whiskey River.

"He collided with a delivery truck, out on Main," Sharon said.

"And this young woman," Mrs. Hawkins declared, "saved his life. Pulled him clear."

"She did," Sharon said. "He would have been crushed. As it is, the bumper of the truck tore an artery. But she got in there and stopped the bleed. Kept pressure on it until EMS got there and could take over."

"And she's so modest about it," Adam's grandmother exclaimed. "Didn't even want credit, wanted to just fade into the crowd without even leaving her name."

A whole new kind of storm whirled up in his gut. Because now he knew. He'd gone back to Jack on the phone, mainly as a way to tamp down his panic as he raced for town. But as the man talked, True had finally begun to understand the scope of what Hope was running from. And why she feared what she'd left behind could reach her even here.

He would get her side of it. Soon. But right now he just wanted her out of here.

There was some more bustle, soothing words from Sharon saying Adam was going to be fine, loud, appreciative ones from Ginevra Hawkins, but True only half-heard most of it, because Hope was just sitting there looking pole axed. Sad. Scared. Upset. All the things he'd heard in her voice.

As if the world had just caved in on her.

"Can I take her home now?" he asked Sharon.

Hope didn't even react, which told him how rattled she was.

"I think the police are through with her," the nurse said.

Damn. He should have realized they'd have been involved. A kid didn't get hit on the main streets of Whiskey River without them being all over it. And now that he knew. . .what he knew, it was no wonder she was so shaken.

"Come on," he said, reaching out to take one of her bloodstained hands. "Now, while Mrs. Hawkins is on stage over there," he added, gesturing with his other had to where the woman seemed to be holding court with anybody willing to listen. But since she was again loudly crediting Hope with saving her grandson's life, he cut her some slack.

Silently Hope stood up. True realized her clothes were nearly as bloody as her hands. Sharon, who had pulled out her phone when it had chimed, suddenly looked up, grinning. "You're already a star, girl! Somebody posted a photo of your heroics."

Hope made a tiny sound he doubted anyone else could have heard. True looked at the woman clad in the blue scrubs. "Sharon, please. . .if anyone asks, especially media, you don't know who she is."

"But she's—"

"You don't know her name. Please."

Sharon frowned. "But the police know who she is."

"I'm hoping that will take time to get out. Just give us time to get home."

Sharon looked from him to Hope and back. A look of speculation came into her eyes. "All right, True. For you I'll stall as long as I can. Good luck."

Hope didn't say a word all the way back to the house. She seemed almost numb. The moment he pulled into the driveway the front door of Zee's place swung open and his sister came belting out, crossing the distance between them quickly with her long, leggy stride.

"Hey, Bro, welcome back! Cops didn't chase you home, did they? I heard all kinds of sirens this—"

He put up a hand and shook his head. Zee frowned, but she fell quiet as he walked around to open the passenger door. Hope just sat there, as if she barely realized where she was.

Zee gasped when she saw the bloodstains. "Oh my God, Hope, are you all right?"

That seemed to get through to Hope, who frowned as she looked at her.

"She's not hurt," True said. *Physically.*

"Your car," Hope began, then stopped as if she couldn't think of the rest of the words she wanted to say.

"We'll get Zee's car later," True said, taking her elbow to

urge her out of the vehicle. "For now let's get you cleaned up."

She looked down at herself, then at her own hands. "Again," she murmured, and he guessed she was thinking of the first time he'd helped her clean up blood.

"True," Zee whispered. "What—?"

"Long story," he said. "Bottom line is she saved Adam Hawkins's life."

Zee, usually unflappable, gaped at him. Then she looked at Hope. "Well, girlfriend, seems you rattle cages wherever you go."

For the first time Hope seemed to focus. But she wasn't looking at Zee, she was looking at him.

"I didn't want to," she said, her voice barely a whisper. "I didn't want to get involved, I knew they'd want my name, I couldn't lie because they'd know, or they'd just ask you, I liked it here and I didn't want to run, I should have but. . .I saw the blood, pumping, knew it was bad, I couldn't just leave him to die in the street when I knew what to do."

It came out in one long tumble, and True felt a tightness in his chest he'd not felt in a very long time.

Hope Larson had finally broken.

Chapter Eighteen

THE RAP ON the door gave her a start, but she didn't stop. She didn't dare stop what she was doing, or she'd chicken out. She didn't want to do it, and how much she didn't want it stunned her. She'd been in Whiskey River less than ten days, she'd only known True six of those, and yet with every item she slipped into her battered backpack her heart screamed at leaving.

How had she come to treasure these days, the normalcy of them, so much so fast? How had she allowed this man to assume such a huge stature in her life, in such a short time, that the thought of never seeing him again ripped at her as surely as that truck had ripped at little Adam just hours ago? How could she leave?

But she had to. For his sake.

She pulled out the photograph to steady herself. To remind her that she had to leave him for the same reasons she'd left them.

"Hope."

His voice came through the door when she didn't respond to his knock. She didn't answer. She tried to focus on her task. She would wear her old clothes, for the road. The new ones—the ones that weren't bloodstained anyway, although True had, with his usual efficiency, dumped them in the washing machine as soon as she was out of the shower—she would pack, keeping them clean in case she needed to look more presentable. . .wherever she ended up. Crazy, she had begun this in bloody clothes, from the cut on her leg that was nearly healed over now, and now it would end the same way.

"Hope, we need to talk."

She couldn't. If she talked to him she'd weaken, start looking for a way for this not to happen. For a way not to leave this place.

For a way to stay with him.

She told herself it was simply because this was the first taste she'd had of a normal life since the night she'd run. It wasn't him, not specifically, it was what he represented.

Yeah, right.

The nights she spent thinking about him put the lie to that. And the dreams, oh, yes, the dreams proved in every possible way that she was kidding herself when she claimed he had nothing to do with her reluctance to leave.

She swiped at her eyes. She was not crying. She would not cry. Crying only made things worse. Made you weak. Or showed you were weak. It was like blood in the water to the kind of shark that was after her. And she was so weak to begin with, too weak to fight off that kind of predator.

"Not going away," he announced through the door.

No, he wouldn't. If True Mahan set his mind to something, it got done. But that was in a normal world. What she brought with her was something else again. She—

"I know about L.A., Hope."

She froze. She couldn't have heard that right. She was still in shock, after the accident, after being terrified that clever child with the adorable grin was going to die before her eyes. She was projecting, mixing up her roiling thoughts with his voice. Easy enough to do, given how much she thought about that voice, that deep, lovely voice that could be soft or stern, gentle or booming by turns. That voice that softened her days and tormented her nights.

"You can come out, or I'm coming in. Your choice."

Her choice. She nearly laughed. If she had, she knew it would have come out crazy, like some maniacal madwoman in a horror flick. She hadn't had a choice. Not since the night—

She cut that thought off with the speed of long, long practice. And then she heard the sound of the doorknob being turned, as if he were making sure she'd locked it.

She had, she'd made sure of that. But if she'd really thought she'd have realized the idea of him letting a little thing like that stop him if he was determined was absurd. And he clearly was; this was not like the time she'd locked herself in the bathroom, this was the crisis that bent the rules for him.

She had no doubt that jack of all trades tag included lock picking, if necessary; she was sure not every abandoned building he took on had every door left conveniently open for him. He could probably get past much more complicated locks than the simple one on this door in his own house.

And she was obsessing about locks to avoid facing the fact that he really had said he knew about L.A.

He couldn't. Could he?

Of course he could. Hadn't she seen that every person in Whiskey River would do whatever he wanted, tell him anything he wanted to know? Why shouldn't that extend beyond his home town? He was just the kind of guy people trusted. With anything.

Never was a man more aptly named.

If he could get the famous recluse to let him in, he could charm anybody.

He'd certainly come close to charming her.

Another sound from the doorknob warned her. And suddenly it seemed crucially important that she be the one to open the door. As if that somehow gave her some tiny bit of control. She shoved the photo back into its pocket and went quickly across the room.

She pulled the door open. He was standing there, but not with lock picks as she'd half expected. No, the ever-practical True was there with a simple screwdriver in his hand. He hadn't been going to pick the lock, he was going for the much quicker path of simply taking apart the doorknob. If she hadn't been so churned up she might have laughed. She should have known.

"Sorry," he said, not sounding it at all as he shoved the screwdriver into his back pocket. "I needed to be sure you were all right."

She held up her arms, turned around, to indicate she was intact. "It's Adam you should be worried about."

He stepped into the room. She backed up instinctively as he closed on her. He was so damned tall. And no boundaries just now, it seemed. Then again, it was his house.

She saw his gaze sweep over the end of the bed, where her pack was. It was obvious what she'd been doing, but he said nothing, stuck to the subject.

"I called the hospital. He's going to be fine. His roaming will be curtailed for a while. Until he's thirty if his mother gets her way."

His voice held that gentle tone that seemed to turn her to jelly. She tried to smile. Couldn't make it. Sat on the edge of the bed. "He was scared. Maybe it will take."

"It didn't with you. You just roamed further."

Her gaze shot to his face. She studied every bit of it, his forehead creased with concern, those incredible eyes troubled, his jaw set, and his mouth. . .God, that mouth. . .

"Tell me what happened," he said.

She lowered her eyes, she couldn't bear to look at him anymore. "I thought you said you knew."

She couldn't help the bitter tinge to her voice. It just felt like she'd been running for so long, like some prey creature trying to dodge the inevitable, like the impala who still fought even as the cheetah struck. But right now, sitting here, she didn't feel like she could take another step. She'd planned to, been getting ready to, but now that he was here, standing before her, she couldn't summon the strength to even stand, let alone run.

He grabbed the chair from the small desk in the corner of the room. Reversed it and sat down, his arms resting atop the back. She stared at the rug on the floor beneath her feet, felt the strangest urge to trace the muted geometric pattern with her toe.

"I know their side, Hope. The official side. What's yours?"

Her head snapped up. "What?"

He gave a half shrug, as if it was of no import. "I have a friend who's a Texas Ranger."

Of course he did. Of course he would.

"You. . .called him? And he. . .what, called them? In L.A.?"

She heard her voice rising, wasn't sure herself if it was in anger or panic. What had he done?

"He just—"

She leapt to her feet. It was worse than she'd feared. "I have to get out of here now. Right now."

She grabbed at her pack, finished stuffing the clothes into it.

"Hope, stop."

She spun around then. "Don't you get it? You must, if you know what happened in L.A. You must know it's not safe if I stay. For anyone."

"Jack Ducane is the height of discretion when necessary. And he has a cousin who works at LAPD. They're the ones who want you back, aren't they?"

"Yes." She tried to steady herself. "But not because I broke any law."

"I know. You told me."

For a moment she just continued to stare. "And you believe me? Just because I said so?"

"Yes."

"Then why did you do this?" It burst from her, she couldn't stop the words or the panic that was again edging into her voice. "Why did you have to go poking around?"

"Because you wouldn't tell me."

"For your own good!" She sank down wearily on the edge of the bed again. "You just couldn't leave it alone, could you? In another week I would have been out of here, moved on, and you would have been fine. There would have been no reason for them to come after you, you would have been safe."

"Even if the police had come all the way here, I—"

"You still don't get it, do you?"

"Then explain!" It seemed she'd finally reached the end

of his considerable patience.

"It's not the cops I'm worried about. They'd just want to take me back."

He waited, silently. But she knew as well as she'd ever known anything that he was also immovable, planted there in that chair.

"True," she said, hating how desperate she sounded.

"You think you owe me? So this is the price. The truth."

She couldn't fight him any longer. He would never give up. He was too strong and she. . .wasn't. She thought of all the explanations she could give him, all the justifications and good intentions, but when it came down to it all she could manage was the truth he wanted, condensed to the bottom line.

"I saw a murder. And the killer knows it."

Chapter Nineteen

A MURDER.

Damn.

True sucked in a breath. Jack had only confirmed she was not wanted for a crime, but as a witness to a felony, and that he'd sworn his cousin to silence until they got it straightened out on this end.

"Tell me," he said, his voice made harsh by his thoughts. "What more is there?"

He'd never anticipated what she would sound like if she ever did finally break. Now that she had, he knew that even if he had anticipated he could never have guessed how it would make him feel. She was staring down at that rug on the floor as if the random pattern held the answer to all the world's mysteries.

"Start," he suggested, "at the beginning."

She laughed, but it was a harsh, bitter sound. "The beginning? That would make for a long, stupid story."

"You're not stupid, Hope."

"I just make stupid decisions." He didn't think he was

mistaking the self-loathing in her tone, but he didn't want to derail this now that she was finally talking by trying to convince her otherwise.

"What decision started this?"

"I thought I could save someone."

"Who?"

"Kim. My best friend." She grimaced. "Or at least, she had been. Since elementary school."

"She changed?"

"After we graduated high school, she started hanging out with people I didn't like or trust. And after a while I did, too, because I was afraid if I didn't I'd lose her."

"But you were right about her new friends?" He wanted her to keep going, although he was fairly sure of the answer.

She nodded. "It took me a while to realize they were. . .essentially a drug ring. And I didn't know it, but I'd already lost her."

"She was using."

Hope nodded, and every slumped line of her body screamed her sorrow. It made him ache inside in a way he hadn't felt for a long time.

"I tried to get her away from them, but she just got mad. And so did they."

"They were her source. She didn't dare alienate them."

Her head came up then. "That's what I finally figured out. But I was young, full of being a brand new adult. I thought I could still convince her, to get away, to get clean, so I stuck it out. For nearly a year."

He noticed she was running a finger over the tattoo on her wrist. "Is that when you got that?" he asked, nodding at the circlet of markings.

She grimaced. "They made me, before they'd let me even talk to her. On my eighteenth birthday. Kim already had one. They all had them. Said I had to prove I belonged."

"And it marked you as one of them, to everyone else."

Her gaze flicked to his face, then away, as if she found it too hard to look at him and keep talking. "Yes. I didn't realize that then. Like I said, stupid."

"Naïve, maybe."

She let out a harsh laugh. "To the point of—Never mind. All that matters is Kim wouldn't listen. Then I thought about going to the police, telling them what I knew. By then I'd seen some stuff, knew some of the dealers, some of the stash locations."

"Seems they'd be interested."

"If they'd even believe me. Nobody turned on those guys." She held up her wrist. "And I was marked as theirs, so why would they believe me? Besides, I was afraid Kim would get hurt, if she was with them and the police came charging in."

She let out a deep breath.

"Rock and a hard place," True said quietly.

"More like a silly rabbit in a lion's den," she said. "By then I knew they were connected to one of the biggest cartels out of Mexico, who killed people without a second thought. Which was why I was so desperate to get Kim out of there. So I decided—this is the crowning stupidity—to give it one last try with her, before I gave up. That's when it happened."

"What?"

"I called Kim. Asked her to meet me. She agreed, but it had to be at one of their hangouts. I tried to talk her into leaving again, but she wasn't listening. Wasn't making any sense. I finally realized she was high, along with most of the rest of them who were there. And then Cagan arrived. The leader. Kingpin. Whatever they call them."

It was coming out jumbled, but she'd never told it before and she couldn't help it.

"He came in with one of the kids who hung around, ran errands and made drops. Apparently he'd blabbed something about them."

Her hands were knotted together in her lap now, and as she spoke her knuckles got whiter. True wanted to go to her, to offer support, but he wanted even more to make her let it all out before it poisoned her any further, and if he moved now it could derail everything.

"The kid was hysterical. Screaming about them hurting his mother. They beat her up, badly, to get her to tell them where he was. That was the way they worked, attack the family. And Cagan had a gun, so I grabbed Kim and hid."

He'd guessed what was coming, but he resisted the urge to make it easier for her by saying it for her. She needed to get this out, like the venom from a snake bite. Her fingers tightened even more, and she slammed her intertwined fists on her knee a couple of times. And then, finally, the rest of it came out in a rush.

"He killed that kid. He was maybe fourteen. Shot him, practically in front of us." He saw a shudder go through her. "Kim screamed and he spun around. Saw her. Grabbed her. I. . .froze, still hiding. I was terrified. Then he yelled out my name like he'd known I was there all along. He said this was on me, and he. . .shot Kim. In the head. Her brains. . .the blood. . ." She took a gulping breath. "He killed her, because of me. I freaked out, gave myself away."

It took all the restraint he had to keep his voice even. "So he threatened you with the same?"

"No threat. He just started shooting at me. I ran. I'm still not sure how he didn't hit me. But I kept running. I had to." She took a shuddering breath. "He knew I worked in my grandfather's office. And he knew where my grandparents live."

I'd tolerate anything from my grandparents. . .

Her words from that first day echoed in his head.

"So you ran to protect them, too."

She nodded. She fell silent, staring down at her hands, that fierce grip easing now. As if she'd said it all. As if there truly were no more words.

"Did it work?"

Her gaze shot up to his face. And for the first time he

saw a hint of ease there in her eyes. "Yes."

"You're sure?"

"After I was far enough away, I called. And I still do, when I can. I don't talk, they can't know where I am. But. . .they answer."

She lowered her head again, and he saw her make a quick swipe at her eyes.

"They reported you missing," he said.

Her head came up again. She wasn't surprised at the news, he guessed, only that he knew. "I knew they would."

"You didn't tell them?"

"I couldn't. They had to be able to say believably they didn't know where I was. So Cagan wouldn't try to get it out of them. I hated that they'd think I'd turned out badly, after all they did for me. But better that than. . ."

"At least they'd be alive to think it?"

She nodded.

"And if you're not there, and they don't know where you are, there's no use in threatening them."

Again the nod. She lowered her head again, and he thought he saw her shiver. No wonder, after what she'd been through.

"So it's been four years? When have you run far enough?"

"Never." The bitterness in her voice ate at him. "The cartel has connections everywhere, not just L.A. I probably should have left the country, but I'm not that brave."

"You abandon your entire life to protect your grandparents, and you think you're not brave?"

"I never would have had to if I hadn't been stupid in the first place."

"So you think your stupid decision was to try and help a friend?"

"Who couldn't be and didn't want to be helped."

"But that doesn't mean you don't try."

This time she met his gaze and held it. "You would, wouldn't you? The difference is, you'd get it done."

"Hope, you were barely more than a kid yourself. And innocent about such things, I'm guessing. You were in way over your head."

She let out a harsh laugh. "Tell me something I don't know."

"That it's a testament to your ingenuity and resilience that you got away, and that you've survived on the run this long."

She stared at him, as if she'd never considered that. Perhaps she'd never slowed down long enough to consider it.

"What's the but?" she said.

"What?"

"There's a 'but' coming after that. I can feel it."

"Not really. Just wondering how long you think you can keep this up."

"As long as it takes."

"As long as it takes for what?"

"For my grandparents to not be in danger."

Belatedly it occurred to him that there was an element of life she had never mentioned. Wondered if it was for a reason all too familiar to him. If it was, he knew too well it would cause her pain to ask. But she was already in pain, and he wanted to know.

"Where are your parents in all this?"

Something flashed in her eyes then, something dark, but it wasn't pain. At least not the pain of loss. "What parents?" she said with a sour grimace.

She got to her feet suddenly. Her arms were still wrapped around herself, her hands clasping her own shoulders as if she could protect herself that way.

"Hope," he said gently as she walked over to the window and stood, her back to him. He had the feeling she wasn't seeing anything outside.

"My parents," she said, and there was an undertone in the words he couldn't even begin to name, "decided when I was twelve that they didn't want to be my parents anymore."

"What?" It came out sharply, but she didn't turn around.

"All my life they told me that I'd been a mistake, a stupid, weak, useless burden. That they'd done their best all those years, but I was a lost cause they couldn't deal with anymore. So they dropped me off at my grandparents' one day and never came back."

True's breath jammed up in his throat. So much had just become clear to him. The emotional abuse, then abandonment. . .

He got up from the chair, reaching for her before he even got to her. She went stock still, he felt her rigidity, but somewhat to his surprise she didn't throw a punch at him. He pulled her into his arms and held her. He didn't say anything, certain whatever he'd come up with would be wrong, until he felt some of the stiffness leave her. Then he whispered to her.

"My God, Hope. How have you managed to stay sane at all?"

"Some would say I didn't. I. . .acted out, more than a little, after they dumped me." He heard her sigh. "I got in trouble a couple of times as a teenager, another reason I knew the cops wouldn't believe me. I don't know why my grandparents stuck it out."

"Because they love you."

He felt her tremble slightly. "They do, despite it all. They're the best."

And so you saved them, the best way you knew how. The thought of what courage that had taken, to give up her life, everything she knew, to go on the run to keep the only family she had safe. . .

"I thought Zee and I losing our parents was the worst that could happen. But having them walk out on you by choice, when you were just a child. . ."

"Sucks."

"In a word," he said, tightening the embrace.

He felt the last of the stiffness fade away. And then she was leaning into him, as if she were grateful for the warmth, the support.

"You do know it was them, not you, don't you?"

She seemed to move even closer, and he was amazed at how good that felt. Hell, he was amazed at how good it felt that she hadn't taken a swing at him, or even tried to escape. The kind of trust that implied, given what she'd been through, awed him more than a little.

"Gran and Gramps always said that. And I overheard them saying that even if my parents came back, they'd have a fight on their hands if they tried to get me back."

"As well they should. A child isn't a thing you set aside when you get bored or it gets difficult, then pick up again later and expect no damage to be done."

She tilted her head back to look at him. So intently he felt a sudden edginess, as if he'd said something that had upset her. But it had been the truth as he saw it, so he couldn't have said anything else. But when she lowered her head she seemed to snuggle her face against his chest, and he thought she couldn't be that upset.

He, on the other hand, was starting to have a hard time reminding himself that he was trying to comfort her. She was so close now, so warm and alive, and pressed against him from knee to chest. A soft, curved, luscious woman. And one he admired, for what she'd done to protect those she loved.

But she was also a woman who thought she owed him,

and he'd be damned if he'd take advantage of that. Especially when she'd practically expected that, that his required payment for helping her would be sex.

It was the first time he'd put it into so many words even in his mind, and just the thought of sex with her, under any conditions, was enough to send his pulse hammering. Body parts he'd thought arcticly numb came to life in a surge of craving he hadn't felt in years. Maybe ever.

And that scared the hell out of him.

Chapter Twenty

A CHILD ISN'T a thing you set aside when you get bored or it gets difficult, then pick up again later and expect no damage to be done.

Hope heard the words again in her mind as, cheek pressed to his broad chest, she listened to his heart thump. And he would give that strong, steady heart, were he ever to have that child of his own.

That last thought brought a crucial bit of reality crashing back in on her. No matter how good this felt, no matter how much or how often she might imagine exploring the crazy feelings this man roused in her, one immutable fact remained; he would ever and always love his dead wife. Because True Mahan was, as that inscription had said, aptly named. True he was, and true he would ever be.

"Knowing you have someone who'll fight for you means a lot," he said. It took her a moment to put his words back in context, she was so distracted by him rubbing his hand up and down her back. She knew he meant only to comfort, but the longer she stayed in his arms, the more her feelings changed, shifted into something much, much hotter than a simple need for comfort.

"It meant everything."

And yet she'd thrown it away. Charged into that ugly world because she had some crazy idea she could do what Kim's parents hadn't been able to, pull her out of the morass that had sucked her in.

He held her, and she couldn't deny the heat as it expanded through her. Feeling helpless to resist, she leaned into him. It had been so long since she'd felt this. No, that wasn't right, because she'd never really felt anything quite like this. Now that she had, she wanted it to go on. Forever.

And she might as well wish for the moon. So at last she made herself break the embrace, although it tore her up inside to do it. But she had to. Just as she had to do what she'd begun here. For his sake.

She walked back to the bed, stared down at her half-finished packing. He came up behind her. It was a tribute, she supposed, to her trust in him that she didn't feel the urge to run.

Or a tribute to the crazy sensations he caused in her simply by being that close.

"Do you know how amazing you are?"

She went very still as he said it softly, his breath brushing over her ear. Amazing? Her?

"Amazingly stupid."

"For trying to help a friend? And then doing what you thought you had to do to keep the only people who ever stood for you safe? I'd call that admirable, not stupid."

Admirable? He admired her? She almost laughed, it seemed so absurd to her.

"Why is that funny?" he asked, and she realized a small chuckle had escaped.

"I thought I was just one of your rehab projects. Another of the things you want to fix."

He let out a compressed breath. He was so close she could feel it as well as hear it. "In the beginning, maybe. When I thought you were. . .just a scared kid."

She turned, faced him. "Oh, I was scared."

"But not a kid. Thankfully. I was afraid I'd become some kind of pervert."

She went very still. She fought the word that rose to her lips, but lost the battle. "Why?"

"You have to ask?" his tone was wry. "Because I was having some highly inappropriate reactions to somebody I thought was only about fifteen."

She stared up at him. She could barely breathe at the thought that he'd looked at her that way even then. Under any circumstances. Longing bubbled up within her, the same sort of ache she'd fought ever since she'd first seen the man she'd clobbered with that mop handle.

"With some men, that wouldn't make much difference," she finally said.

Something flared in his eyes. "I'm not one of them."

"I know. I may be a lousy judge of people in most areas,

but that one I know."

"Because you ran into a few of them?"

She shrugged because she didn't know what else to say. He was so close, so solid, so warm, making her heart race so she wasn't sure she could find the words even if she did know what to say.

His voice was even quieter when he asked, "Were there any you. . .weren't able to get away from?"

She knew what he was asking. She leaned over and reached into one of the outer pockets of the pack. She pulled out the single thing that had saved her more than once. Held up the carved bone handle, pressed the switch. She could tell by his lack of reaction when the five-inch blade flipped open that he'd known what it was. Then again, it would probably take a lot more than a switchblade to rattle True Mahan.

"No," she said in answer to his question.

"Good." Then he lifted an eyebrow at her. "Why didn't you pull that on me?"

"It's my last resort, not my first." She gave him a crooked smile, somewhat forced. She closed the blade. "And I try not to carve up nice people."

When, after a moment, he spoke again his tone was entirely different. "Is that what I am? Nice?"

"Yes." And she couldn't help herself, she looked him up and down, from boots to thick, dark hair. Nor could she stop the shiver in her voice when she added, "Very nice."

He drew back just slightly, and she thought she saw him

suck in a quick, deep breath. As if he'd heard exactly how she'd meant that last "nice."

"Then why leave?" he asked, acknowledging for the first time that that was what she'd been packing to do.

Her eyes widened. "You can't be that thick. I know you're not."

He blinked. "Thanks. I think."

She shoved the knife back into its pocket. "If you won't worry about yourself, how about me? You've done nothing but help me. How do you think I'd feel if. . .if they. . .if. . ."

He looked startled. "Wait. You're worried they'll come after *me?*"

"Or you'll be collateral damage."

He looked bemused now. "I was born and raised in Texas. That rifle in my truck isn't just décor."

"That only works if you see them coming. And they will come. I'm active in the system now, thanks to what happened."

"But why would an accident here get back to L.A.?"

She sighed. "You think they don't have alerts on me? Add that to your friend poking around. . ."

She forced herself to keep moving, shoving things into the pack. Wondering if she was going to have to leave something behind, because, amazingly, she'd acquired some things here.

"But that's the police," he said.

She gave him a pitying look. "Now who's naïve? You

think they don't own a couple dozen cops?"

"But not all," he said.

"You mean the ones who want to drag me back to testify? Who say they'll protect my grandparents?"

It was a moment before he said softly, "I notice you left protect you out of that."

"They're all that matters."

"Not to me."

Her breath caught in her throat. She imagined she saw a million things in his eyes, promises of things she'd never dared hope for. She knew she was imagining it, because nothing this good ever happened to her, men like him didn't want anything to do with women who had so thoroughly messed up their lives.

"Why?"

God, had she really said it, asked it? Asked him to put it in so many words?

"Do you really not know?"

"Amanda," she whispered.

His jaw tightened slightly. "Yes. I loved her. She will always have a piece of my heart. She taught me a great deal with her quiet sort of courage. Because of her I know a little something about going on when you don't think you can take another step. About going on when you can't even remember why you have to, only that you must."

She stared at him as he described exactly how she felt right now.

"You have that same kid of courage, Hope." He held up a hand when she began to deny that absurdity. "Don't tell me you don't. Amanda never thought she was brave, either. But she was. Braver than I could ever have been."

"No."

"Yes. She deserved a lot better than what life threw at her."

"So do you. And a lot better than what getting tangled up in my mess will throw at you."

"News bulletin. Too late."

Her knees couldn't seem to hold her any longer. She sank down on the edge of the bed. The bed, she realized with a shiver that rippled through her entire body, where she would lie down for him in an instant if he asked just now.

"Then why don't you. . .?" She couldn't finish even the thought, let alone the words; the images that flashed through her mind, of True taking her up on the offer she'd nearly spoken. Of him, that tall lean body naked in her arms, taking her with all the gentle strength she knew was his very core.

He groaned aloud. "Damn, Hope, don't look at me like that, or I will. Right here and now."

In that instant she couldn't think of anything she wanted more. She held out a hand to him, seeing even as she did that it was trembling. After an instant of hesitation, he took it. But he didn't come to her, rather pulled her up to him, into a fierce, hot embrace that was much, much different than the comfort he'd offered earlier. And before she could even begin to put a name to the difference his mouth was on hers, his lips warm and firm against hers. More than her knees went weak, and she finally understood why people talked about melting with love.

Love.

She was such a fool, to even think that word. For so many reasons. Her life was a mess. She was nowhere near good enough for him. And he still loved his dead wife.

But the sweetness of this, the hot, swamping sensation was unlike anything she'd ever known, and she simply didn't have the strength to do what she knew she should. Even though she knew she should be thinking of him, of what it would mean to him when she did what she had to do, run again, she couldn't. All she could think of was that no matter what happened, if she stopped now she would forever regret not grabbing this fire when she could have.

And then it was gone.

Chapter Twenty-One

THAT ONE STEP back he'd taken felt like a mile.

He stared at her as he sucked in a deep breath, wondering where all the oxygen in the room had gone. She stared back, those cinnamon eyes wide, lips—God, those lips—parted. She looked nothing less than he felt.

Stunned.

"You stopped."

She sounded so lost something seemed to shatter inside him. At that instant he couldn't find a coherent word in his head, and doubted he could have gotten it out if he had. He could only shake his head. And finally she lowered her eyes.

"I understand," she said, her voice barely a whisper.

"That makes one of us," he muttered.

"I know you still love your wife."

"I always will," he said; he would never deny what he and Amanda had had together, and that it had made him a better man.

"So, I understand," she said, and it took him a moment to realize they were back to where they'd started.

"Wait. . .you think I stopped because of her?"

"Didn't you?"

He reached out and grabbed her shoulders. "Look at me, Hope. I loved her, deeply. But she's gone. Almost six years, and this is the first time I've felt. . .anything more than a flicker."

Her eyes widened. "Then why—"

"I told you why. You're scared, and you needed help, and I'm not about to cash in on that."

She looked up at him for a long, silent moment. Then, slowly, she shook her head. "This is the first time since I left home that I don't feel scared."

That warmed him in a way he didn't even have words for. But it didn't change the underlying problem. "It won't last, Hope."

She flushed. And said, rather sharply, "I know that. I know you'll never love anyone the way you did her."

The words hit him like the kick of a pile driver. Is that what she wanted? She wanted him to. . .fall in love with her like he had with Amanda? He had to fight down his gut's instant reaction to straighten out his mind.

"I. . .meant not feeling scared."

She went pale, then red. "Oh, God. . ." It came out as a moan, and she buried her face in her hands.

"Hope—"

She threw up her hands and backed away, not looking at him. "I've humiliated myself enough for one day, thanks. I'm sorry. Now if you'll excuse me, I need to finish."

He blinked, snapped out of his confused thoughts and belatedly tuning back in to what she was saying. And he who was usually so with it, who knew what needed to be done, had no clue.

"Finish? You're still. . .leaving?"

She stopped with the pair of jeans she'd mended from the barbed wire tear that day—could it really only have been six days ago?—in her hands. She gave him a smile, but it wasn't happy. "No choice."

"But I thought. . .you said. . .we were. . .almost. . ." He had apparently lost all capacity for coherent speech.

"Almost only counts in horseshoes, isn't that what they say around here?" She shoved the jeans into her pack, then looked back at him. "We almost made a mistake. Or rather, you did."

He frowned. Managed some semblance of sense this time. "I think what we almost did requires two."

"But I'm the one with all the baggage."

"Hope—"

"You made the right decision, all right? It doesn't take a genius to see that." She slapped the flap on the pack shut, then met his gaze head on. She looked both angry and hurt, so much that it was hard to see her eyes. "Do you think I don't know that no one in this town would ever think I'm good enough for you? You think that *I* don't think that?"

He took a deep breath. "How about what I think?"

"Don't," she said, sounding almost desperate now. "You don't want to get any more tangled up in this. You could get hurt, or worse."

"That's my choice, isn't it?"

"Only if I let it be." She held his gaze, and he saw the dull ache of pain there. It twisted something inside him, and he wanted nothing more than to hold her again, get her to believe it would be all right. "I can't take the chance. I can't do that. Not to you."

He wanted to respond to those last three words, to what it seemed like they meant. But he who had had to be sure about so much since he'd come home to see to raising his sister wasn't sure of much just now. So he answered the only thing he was sure about. "So you go back on the run? For how long, Hope? How long do you live like this?"

"I told you—"

"I know. As long as it takes. So you what, stay on the run until they're dead?"

It had been harsh, blunt, but he'd meant it to be. And it hit her hard, she paled. But she only said, "At least they will have lived their lives."

"And every day of it hurting for you, the granddaughter they love."

Nothing less than agony flashed in her eyes then, and he wished he hadn't said it, because it was obvious she already knew he was right. "True, I can't stay here! They'll find out, they'll find me, and if I'm still here, they'll find you, and you don't know how ruthless they are."

He thought about a teenage girl, hiding in terror, and ending up with her best friend's brains and blood spattered on her.

"Let me worry about that."

"I can't stay here just because it feels safe. Because it's not. You were right, it won't last."

"Nothing will, until you deal with it."

"Deal with it?" She stared at him. "You mean. . .what do you mean? Go back? Testify, like the cops want?"

"That would be a start."

She laughed, and it was a harsh, hopeless sound. "I'm not that brave. And even if he ended up in jail, do you really think that would end it? He's just one cog in that organization. I told you, they have connections all over."

"Whiskey River is a small town." He gave her a steady look. "We're pretty aware when strangers show up."

She stared at him. "What are you saying?"

"That Whiskey River takes care of its own."

"But I'm one of those strangers, remember?"

He gave her a crooked smile. "Not anymore."

"I've been here less than a week."

"And you saved Adam's life. If Ginevra Hawkins has her way, you'll have a statue in the square next to Booze."

She colored again, a lighter pink this time. He wondered if there was a correlation between the shade and the source of the embarrassment. Which made him think of how red she'd turned when she'd misunderstood what he'd said and made that comment that betrayed. . .what, exactly?

It won't last, Hope.

I know you'll never love anyone the way you did her. . .

He still didn't know if she was saying she wanted him to feel that way about her. Or had she merely been making sure he understood that she knew it would never be anything more than temporary, whatever this was between them?

He felt the strongest urge to back away. It had been a long time since he'd had to deal with the occasional minefield of female thinking, and he was pretty sure he'd lost the knack. He dealt with Zee fine, but he knew her well, and there was not the extra, added complicated layer of. . .whatever this was.

"You made a deal," he said, wishing it didn't feel desperate. "Two weeks. You've got a week to go."

"True—"

"You can't run without money."

She pulled herself straight, faced him head on. "And what, you won't pay me the rest of what I've earned this week?"

His jaw tightened.

"I know you better than that, True Mahan. You're an honorable person who lives by your values and pays your debts, whatever they may be."

What should have been a compliment instead dug into him like a jagged splinter. "Then why are you in such a hurry to leave?"

The look she gave him then was the saddest thing he'd seen since the day Zee had finally accepted their parents were really gone.

"Because everything you are. . .I'm not."

He studied her for a long, silent moment as she went back to putting her meager belongings into the battered pack. And for the first time in a very long time he remembered what Amanda had told him in the dark hours of the night before she died.

Don't give up on life, True. You're too good a man, you deserve to be happy, and some woman out there will need you.

Need you.

Hope certainly needed someone. But was that all it was? It didn't seem possible. There was surely something alive and crackling between them. So alive he wasn't completely sure he wanted anything to do with it.

But he wanted to know. He had to know. If he was capable of feeling again, he had to know.

"I want that extra week," he said, his voice sounding oddly demanding even to him. "You agreed to it, and I need that job finished. And when it is, I'll take you wherever you want to run."

She stopped fussing with the pack and looked at him. "Careful," she said softly. It was clearly a warning, but he wasn't sure about what.

Or who it was meant for, him. . .or herself.

Chapter Twenty-Two

"I THINK IT would be better if she stayed in your guest room for the duration."

Zee lifted a brow at him and said, her tone a shade too innocent, "Really? And I think Jamie should come home and take care of his aunt's house himself."

True drew back, puzzled. "What's that supposed to mean?"

"That either one of those is about as likely as a blizzard here tomorrow."

He frowned. "I thought you liked her."

"I do. I admit, I was wary at first. Wondered why it had to be her, with whatever her problems are, but then realized it doesn't matter. Besides, then I got to know her a bit. And I do like her."

"Then why—"

"You want a list, brother mine?"

Uh-oh. Those were never good words from his sister. Because it usually meant she had a bullet list of reasons that were likely to be un-dodgeable.

"I—"

"First, how's she going to feel if you suddenly tell her you can't stand to have her in your house anymore?"

"It's not—" He stopped himself, because the only way he could explain that Hope wouldn't mind would have to include why, and he wasn't about to stand here and say "She won't mind because I screwed up the whole situation by making a pass at her." No way he was giving Zee that kind of ammo.

"Second, if you think having her only one wall away will make any difference, you're stupid, and I know you're not."

"Gee, thanks," he said, but he had a sinking feeling she was right about the wall and wrong about him not being stupid.

"Third, I'd hate to think of my big brother as a coward, after all these years."

That made him stiffen. And remember that he never needed to worry about giving his sister ammo, she inevitably had plenty of her own.

"Fourth—" if she was up to four, he knew he was in for it now "—it's fun watching you act like an idiot teenager around her."

"I don't—"

"Fifth, and most important of all," Zee said, her voice going suddenly soft, in that way that told him this was what she'd been aiming for all along, "she's the first woman since Amanda died who's made you nervous. You've been amused, indifferent, irritated, but never, ever nervous."

"You say that like it's a good thing," he muttered.

"I notice you're not denying it."

He turned back to pacing the office, ramming his fingers through hair that had already seen a lot of that action today.

"She's leaving as soon as the job is done." *And not happy at all about staying even that long.*

"You haven't talked her out of that yet?"

More like talked her into it. "She has reasons, Zee. Good ones, in fact."

"Such as?"

"Not mine to tell."

Zee studied him for a moment. "Bad ones? Like in trouble ones?"

He drew in a deep breath. "Yes."

"Her fault?"

"Only in thinking she could help someone who didn't want to be helped."

"Can her situation be helped?"

"That's. . .a matter of opinion, apparently."

"Meaning?"

Suddenly weary he dropped down into the office chair. "Meaning I can see a way out, but she doesn't see it that way."

Zee studied him for a long silent moment. "I know you, brother mine. I'm guessing your way out means facing whatever's dogging her."

He nodded. "But there are. . .other people involved."

Again his sister went silent. He could almost feel her assessing, with that mind that was so logical and yet made intuitive leaps that sometimes startled him. "She's protecting them," she finally said.

Not mine to tell. His own words echoed in his head. But this was Zee, and she would understand that not answering was in fact an answer.

"So why aren't we helping her?" He almost smiled at that. Zee might put on a tough front, but underneath she was a softy.

"Tried."

Again a moment passed. "She's that scared?"

"Yes." His hand went to his head again, fingers burying in his hair, but the heel of his hand stopped against his forehead and he pressed it against the ache that was building there. "Getting her to agree to finish the job here was the best I could do."

"Immune to your charms, is she?"

He glanced at her, then quickly away. He'd thought his expression blank enough, but Zee was right, she knew him. Very well.

"So that's it," she exclaimed. "She's not immune at all. And you're as scared as she is!"

Damn. There was one of those mind leaps again. Feet first into a very cogent assessment. Because he was scared. He hadn't felt anything even close to this in so long he'd thought he was the one who was immune.

And Hope Larson had blasted that to bits with one kiss.

"I don't want you hurt, True," Zee said softly. "God knows you've been through enough. But this is the first time—"

He cut her off with a sharp shake of his head. "Stop it. I know. But that's asking for. . ." *Pain. Heartache.*

"Look, I know you're not the kind of guy for a no-strings fling." Her nose wrinkled in disgust. "That's more Jamie's style. That's why I'm saying—"

"She's leaving in a week, Zee."

"Holy bluebonnets," she said disgustedly. Her use of their father's old phrase both startled him and told him how seriously to take her just now. "If you've gotten from nowhere to here in less than a week, if you can't talk her out of running in another week, I wash my hands of you."

He blinked. He hadn't thought of it quite that way before. Leave it to Zee. But she was right. They had gone from zero to that kiss in the space of six days. And he'd been in Kerrville for nearly three days of that. Surely he could get her to reconsider by then. Couldn't he?

Did he even want to? He felt an inward tug, a suggestion that sliding back into his old life where the only ripples were problems that cropped up on projects, where his biggest worry was getting Deck and Kelsey's pavilion done on time, was what he should be hoping for.

And yet. . .

"It's time to quit hiding, True."

He blinked. "Hiding? I'm not hiding. I'm out there every day, dealing with people. I even went to that damn charity thing last year."

"And spent the whole night dodging that woman up from San Antonio who couldn't keep her eyes—or her hands—off you all night."

He'd forgotten about that. It had been annoying at the time. "You should have been paying attention to your date, not me," he said, trying to turn it back on her.

"She was lovely, rich, and actually fairly nice," Zee said, apparently not to be diverted.

"How would you know?"

"Because I invited her."

He blinked. Stared. "What?"

"You heard me. I met her in Kelly's Boots, and we got to talking. You came up. I showed her that picture of you, working on Kelsey's place."

He groaned aloud. He knew exactly the one she meant. She'd come by one day to pick him up when one of the guys needed his truck. They'd been pushing to finish the hay shelter they were building before a delivery later that day, and he'd happily dumped the clipboard and done some real work. It had been hot enough that they'd all shed shirts before it was done. And then Zee had arrived, phone in hand as usual, and she'd snapped what she laughingly titled the calendar boy shot. She'd teased him unmercifully about the image, how sexy his muscled arms, bare abs and chest were, glistening with sweat.

And he had to admit, even though it was the most irritating kind of sibling jousting from her, and embarrassing, he'd been secretly flattered. And the ego that had been battered into near oblivion by being unable to do a damned thing for Amanda had twitched a little.

"I told her you cleaned up even nicer. She laughed, and agreed to come, and see if she could lure you out of that swamp you were living in."

"You. . .sicced her on me? Why the hell? What were you thinking?"

"I was thinking," she said with brows arched upwards, "it would do you good to get laid."

True felt his jaw actually drop.

"Not necessarily that night, mind you, just eventually," she went on as if she hadn't just blown up the yuck-meter at the idea his little sister had been. . .he couldn't even think of a phrase for it that didn't make it worse. "But she was nice, pretty, and sort of your type."

"My. . .type?"

Zee sighed. "She reminded me of Amanda."

The woman had reminded him, too. "Yes."

"I should have realized that would be a negative, not a positive."

"A negative?"

"I loved her. You know I did. I loved her like the sister

she was to me. But I was getting worried about you."

"I was doing fine."

She gave him a sideways look, one brow lowered. "But I see now where my mistake was."

"You should have butted out?" he suggested.

She dismissed that with an unconcerned wave of her hand. "I didn't think about the possibility that. . .your type might have changed."

He was starting to feel like he was lost at sea in a rowboat with no oars. Sometimes he simply could not fathom his sister's mind.

"I should have realized someone completely different, with a problem, would be better." She didn't say "Like Hope," but the implication was crystal clear.

"How," he asked, hanging onto what patience he had left by a thread, "is somebody having a problem good?"

"You fix things, True," Zee said quietly. "It's what you do."

"This is different," he said. "This isn't some run-down house, or something new to build. It's someone's life."

"Kelsey says you're as much a rescuer as she is, in your own way."

He drew back. "Kelsey said that?"

"She did. And she's right."

He shook his head. "You both have too much faith in me."

Zee's mouth quirked. "Bro, this whole town has faith in

you. I think you could blow up Booze's statue in front of a hundred witnesses, and they'd all wait to see what your reason was. Why do you think everybody opened up to Hope so quickly? They trust your judgment."

"I know," he said, almost wearily. And he did, it was a kind of responsibility he'd never expected to be carrying. Yet another reason to be careful.

"We all know you have to put it behind you. Whiskey River would be as thrilled as I would be to see you happy again."

"I am happy."

"You're not unhappy. Not the same thing."

He'd had about all he could take of female analysis of him for one day. Hell, for a week.

A week. The amount of time Hope had, reluctantly, agreed to stay. A week for him to figure out a way to. . .fix this. He winced inwardly as Zee's words echoed in his head. Okay, so he did fix things. But fixing a house or a barn was a hell of a lot different than fixing a life that had gone astray, good intentions that had had, as they so often did, unintended consequences. And those were the kind of things he stayed away from. Hadn't he proven with Amanda that he wasn't capable of fixing a life?

But apparently that lesson hadn't been learned, because he was still feeling the urge.

"Just keep an eye on her," he said, his tone making clear this discussion was over. He had work—real work—to do.

He headed for the door, then looked back. "And keep an eye out for any. . .strangers hanging around, okay? If you see anyone you don't know or who makes you uneasy, call me."

He'd finally surprised her. He could almost see her mind racing. "That bad?"

"I hope not, she's put it a long distance behind her, but she's still worried."

"I'll watch out," she promised, and he felt a bit better. Zee was smart, and she knew just about everybody in Whiskey River; a stranger with bad intent would have to work to slip by her.

And in the meantime, he'd talk to Jack again. She was already mad at him for that, so what was a little more? Maybe he could find out if the threat was still as acute as Hope thought it was. Maybe things had died down, maybe the murderer had decided he'd run her off for good. Maybe he wasn't even looking any more.

Sure. Maybe a major drug cartel decided to have mercy, just this once. Or maybe a killer just decided to forget about the only witness who could put him away.

Chapter Twenty-Three

"REMEMBER WHEN I sort of warned you off True Mahan?"

Hope looked at the clerk, who seemed to be not looking at her.

"Wasn't much sort of about it, but yes, I remember."

The woman met her gaze then, as she handed her the bag with the new toothbrush and tube of toothpaste she'd bought. Her old one was so worn the bristles were splayed out until they looked like the branch of a dead Christmas tree. And since she was going to be back on the road soon, she'd decided to splurge. Nothing could make the gas station and convenience store bathrooms she had to use much better, but at least her mouth would feel cleaner.

And if the thought of leaving this place, leaving True, made her feel like someone was carving at her with her own knife, that was her own stupid fault.

"—back."

Hope blinked. Tuning out like this was not a good thing. She had to get back in the habit of being hyper aware.

"I'm sorry, what?"

"I said I take it back. Anyone who'd do what you did for young Adam, well they're all right in my book."

"I. . .I'm just glad I was there."

"And knew what to do," the woman pointed out. Then she smiled, and it changed her face, the dour look vanishing. "I should have known. Should have trusted True's judgment."

I'm not sure he should. But all she said was, "Thank you." She couldn't think of anything else. But when she came out of the store and headed back toward Zee's car, parked in front of Riva's Java, she found herself greeted now with smiles and cheery "Hellos" instead of curious looks. A couple of people even paused to express gratitude, and wouldn't accept her rather awkward insistence that any one of them would have done the same.

By the time she got back in the car she was shaking. For once not out of fear, or from vicious memories, but from a longing unlike anything she'd ever felt before. A longing to fit here, to stay in this unlikely little town with the crazy history. To stay and make a place here.

To stay with True.

She found herself laughing at that wish. Mixed with the longing, it was a maelstrom of emotions that was almost overwhelming. Feeling as if she were precariously balanced on the edge of full blown hysteria, she curled her hands into fists and banged them against the steering wheel. Nothing.

Harder. Felt the hurt, but it still wasn't enough. She slammed harder, but nothing seemed able to overcome what was boiling up inside her. She changed the angle, going now for a sharp blow with her knuckles. It hurt even more. Again.

And finally the pain sliced through the swirling cloud and the tightness in her chest began to ease.

But then her gaze came to rest on the tattoo that circled her wrist, the permanent reminder of her own foolishness and mistakes. She stared at it, remembering the moments when it had been splattered with blood and tissue. If her frenzied pounding of a helpless steering wheel didn't prove she was no good for the likes of True Mahan, that permanent reminder did.

"WANT ME TO talk to her?"

True stared at Deck over the soda he was drinking before going back to join the crew working on the foundation for the pavilion. "What?"

The man once known as Crazy Joe, the recluse, shrugged. "I know a bit about being on the run."

True didn't know the whole story, but he knew enough. Enough to realize what a major offer that was. He shook his head in slow wonder. "You've come a long way, my friend."

"Kicking and screaming all the way," Deck said with a lopsided grin. Then, seriously, "She really can't go back?"

"She's afraid to. Not for herself," he added quickly.

He wondered if the concept of wanting to protect someone that much was foreign to Deck. Then he almost laughed; of course it wasn't, he had Kelsey now, and would die to protect her. And if he needed pointers, he had Kelsey's mom, Lisa, to show him the way.

"And if she doesn't?"

True grimaced. "She'll keep running."

Deck studied him for a moment. He had the oddest feeling the man could see way past the surface. True supposed he couldn't be the writer he was without seeing things others didn't.

"I hope you stop some day."

"Stop what? I'm not running."

"Aren't you?"

True blinked.

Deck shrugged. "I just recognize the look. Faced it in the mirror for a lot of years."

True tried to put the words out of his mind as he went back to work. He didn't really need to be here, the crew was entirely capable of handling this, but here he was anyway. He told himself it was part of being thorough, but he had a sneaking suspicion it had something to do with what Deck had just said. Not that he was running, not really. But maybe. . .avoiding?

Yeah, that he had to admit. He was avoiding going home. It had been a long, difficult weekend, at least for him. Not because Hope was there, because she wasn't. She'd worked practically the entire time, coming home only to eat something and sleep. It didn't escape him that she was pushing hard to finish the job, and he had to assume it was so she could get out of here. And she'd been back at it again today, gone before even he had risen to start his day. He'd thought perhaps she'd broken her promise and taken off, but a glance at Zee's place told him the lights in the office were on and she was already working.

He had wondered how Zee felt about that, but she had told him yesterday she hadn't even realized what Hope was doing, she'd been so quiet. And asked him what he'd done to make her push so hard. He'd dodged that, leaving abruptly, and he hoped before Zee read the memory of that kiss in his face. The memory that haunted him, taunted him, and had kept him awake the last two nights with the effort not to get up, walk down the hall, and ask Hope if they could pick up where that had left off and to hell with the consequences.

Damn, Mahan, you're acting like you never kissed a woman before.

He had, in fact. A couple of times since Amanda had died. Just to see. He'd felt nothing but awkward and wrong, as if he were betraying her somehow, even after she was gone. The only good side was that he'd done it on trips out of Whiskey River, not because no one here—Megan Clark, the real estate agent came to mind—caught his eye, but because he was certain the whole town would feel that way. He hadn't lied when he'd said they'd all loved his wife.

They'd be as thrilled as I would be to see you happy

again. . .

"Shit!"

It broke from him as the hammer came down on his left forefinger. He'd been too busy not paying attention to the form they were building for this week's concrete pour and mooning over a woman who clearly didn't want him. At least, not enough to stay.

So you think you're worth her risking her life and her grandparents lives for?

It didn't matter if it was really true or not, because she thought it was. And so she was working sixteen hour days just to get free of Whiskey River. And him.

"Mahan," Chuck Simons, the foreman of the crew, called out with a grin, "you're a menace today."

"Yeah, yeah," he muttered. He shoved the hammer back through the loop on his tool belt, then picked up the belt and slung it over his shoulder. He gave the foreman a rueful smile. "I'm doing more harm than good, so I'll leave you gentlemen to it."

The man's grin widened. "You can trust us alone, honest."

"I know," True said, his voice serious now. Chuck gave him a nod in understanding and thanks.

He drove slowly, not even thinking about passing the delivery truck in front of him as it clung tenaciously to exactly the speed limit. He wondered if word had gotten around about the accident; things like that always rattled people for a while. But the ones not directly involved got over it and went back to old habits, or so it seemed. He'd bet the driver that had hit Adam wouldn't.

He'd bet Hope wouldn't.

The images slammed through his mind again like some jerkily cut movie, the call from Sharon, that moment when he'd walked into the clinic to see her covered in blood, that heart-stopping moment before he'd believed she wasn't hurt.

He'd realized, eventually, that his own reaction in that moment said all there was to say about how he felt about Hope Larson. His entire being had screamed out "No, not again!" with a fierceness that had shaken him.

But her reaction after he'd kissed her—to resolutely continue her packing—said everything about her determination to leave. And he'd be a fool—okay, a bigger fool than he'd already been—to ignore that.

He suddenly realized where he was. In the fog of his thoughts he'd headed home.

Lucky you didn't hit someone, idiot.

He slowed. She wouldn't be there, she'd be next door. It wasn't even five yet, and she'd been working much later than that in her push to get the job done and get out of here. So it was safe to go home.

Safe.

How had the home that had been a haven for him, a quiet, peaceful place, suddenly become someplace he was afraid to go?

Like hell.

Chapter Twenty-Four

THE OBSTINACY HE'D been born with kicked in. True yanked the steering wheel and made the last turn. It was his damned house, and just because it didn't feel like it right now wasn't going to keep him away.

The stubborn is strong with this one. . .

Unbidden the sometimes teasing, sometimes weary words his mother had used flitted through his mind.

Be glad, Margaret. Sometimes that's all that keeps you going.

His father's answer, always steadfast, followed. And he'd been right. Sometimes, after the crash that had ended life as he knew it, that Texas size streak of stubborn had been the only thing that had kept him going. As it would now.

He saw the lights on in Zee's office. He could even see, through the cloth blinds, a figure standing at the table in the back where they'd set up the document scanner. And hated that it gave him a sense of relief as he headed into his half of the house.

Knowing it was empty he wandered from room to room, not certain why. It was not like she'd left her stamp on the place, in fact the opposite, she was very careful not to, with not even a kicked off shoe lying around. Polite? Or maybe she just kept all her things together in case she had to run. That seemed more likely. The only trace she'd ever been here at all was the bookmark that was working its way through Deck's books. She was midway through number three, but with the work hours she was keeping she wouldn't finish before she left. He wondered if that mattered to her. Wondered if she was learning anything from them, because as he'd said, Deck knew a bit about being on the run. She could probably learn a lot from what the not-so-fictional Sam Smith had had to do to survive.

He turned on his heel, still angry at himself, and strode into the kitchen. Hell if he was fixing dinner tonight only to have her not even show up to eat it. He tossed his keys down on the counter. They skidded across the smooth granite, and he had to grab quickly to keep them from going over the edge. That was when he spotted the paper on the floor. It was a piece of paper from the pad he kept handy for notes. He could see from here it was a list of some kind. He picked it up.

A shopping list?

He'd never seen her writing, but he knew it just the same. Strong but choppy, some letters plain, some ending in a flourish.

Socks

Toothbrush and paste. This one was crossed out.

Shoes, if not too much.

Too much. What was too much if you were on the run? How did you choose between eating and keeping your feet from ending up bloody? He wondered if she'd gotten to the part in book three where Sam had stolen a blanket out of a laundromat just to try and survive the freezing nights outside. Had she ever been that desperate?

He dropped the list on the counter of the kitchen island. Stared down at it, this proof of her intention to leave. When the time came, would he see that writing again? Would she avoid saying it at all, and just skulk out some night, leaving a note? Or would she even do that? Maybe one day soon he'd get up and the house would be empty once more, every trace of her fastidiously removed. Except maybe that bookmark.

God, he was flat going insane.

His head dropped wearily. He braced his hands on the counter, widespread, and his shoulders sagged.

He didn't know how long he'd been standing there like that when he heard the inner door. He resisted the urge to look at the clock on the oven; what did it matter to him what time she came home?

Came home. Such a simple phrase.

Yeah, simple like a shotgun shell is simple.

"You found my list."

Her voice was quiet, tentative. She had stopped beside him, but not too close. Or was that not close enough?

"Yeah." His voice was edgy, but he couldn't seem to help

it. "You'd better go shopping, you don't have much time, the way you've been working."

"True, I…"

His head came up then. And for the first time he looked at her. She was standing almost rigidly, her gaze fastened on that list as if she no more wanted to look at him than he did her. He stared at her, at the long, silky fall of her hair, the way the bangs brushed her eyebrows. He wondered inanely if she had a pair of scissors in that pack to trim them, or if she just hacked at them with that knife of hers.

Logistics. She was readying herself to run and he was fixated on logistics.

"The deal was for the two weeks," he said flatly.

"The deal was for the job to be done."

Because what reason could there be to stay once it was?

She put her hands down on the cool granite, as if she needed to steady herself. Or as if she was working up to grabbing that list out from in front of him.

His gaze shifted to her hands, expecting them to move at any moment. His brow furrowed.

"What happened?"

Her fingers curled and she pulled her hands back. He grabbed them, turned them to confirm what he'd seen; reddened knuckles, two with skin scraped off.

She pulled her hands free. "I just. . .scraped them, that's all."

"Funny," he said, "they look a lot like mine did when I

put my fist through a wall."

Her gaze shot to his face. "You put your fist through a wall? I can't imagine that."

"Stick around," he said dryly. She didn't miss the inference, and looked away. "What did you hit?"

She made a small sound that wasn't quite a laugh. "What makes you think it wasn't a who?"

"Was it?"

"No."

"What, then?"

She let out a compressed breath. "Zee's poor steering wheel."

Something stirred inside him, something unwelcome but soft. It echoed in his voice when he said quietly, "I've beaten up an innocent steering wheel a time or two."

He didn't say when, and when she looked at him again he knew he didn't have to.

This time he took her hands gently, slowly, giving her every chance to pull away again. She just looked at him, and the tangle of emotions he saw in her face made him chance it. Maybe, just maybe she wasn't quite as certain about leaving as she thought she was.

He lifted her right hand, looking at the bright red spots across the first two knuckles. Slowly, gently, he lowered his head and kissed the angry places. He heard her suck in a breath. Felt her sudden tension.

But she didn't pull away.

It took him a moment to realize the sound in his ears was his own pulse, picking up, pounding in hot, heavy beats. And when he lifted his head to see her looking at him with a sort of longing he'd never seen in a woman's eyes before, it blasted through carefully constructed walls as if it were the explosives they used to implode a building.

In that moment he knew he couldn't go on like this. He was tired of the dance. He hated the idea of walking away from the only woman who'd made him feel anything since Amanda had died, but he would if he had to.

"Now or never," he whispered, meaning it.

He felt her tremble, but she didn't look away. Her tongue crept out to moisten her lips, and a jolt went through him as if she'd touched it to his skin.

"Now."

There was a quiver in her voice that gave him pause. His body was screaming not to question, but his rules by which he lived his life, the things that this town respected him for, gave him no choice.

"You owe me nothing, Hope. If that's why, I don't want it."

Her chin came up. And her voice was steady now. "I did that once. Second worst mistake of my life."

"I don't want to be the third."

She reached up then, ran a hand over his cheek, traced the line of his jaw. A hand, he noticed, that was steady now. "This doesn't have anything to do with owing. Or obligation. Just. . .wanting."

"That'll do," he said, his voice rough.

The need swamped him then, and he pulled her up into his arms. For a brief moment he realized how light, how little she was, and it amazed him that she was tough enough to get through what she'd been through.

Her arms went around his neck. She shifted, but not to escape. Instead she stretched upward. And kissed him.

Heat blasted through him so fiercely he nearly staggered against the counter. And suddenly he wanted her right there, right now, in the damned kitchen. On the counter she'd be at the perfect height, and. . .wouldn't it be romantic as hell if Zee walked in? With his last shred of control he headed for his bedroom.

And stopped dead in the doorway.

"Hope," he said, sounding as strangled as he suddenly felt, "I don't. . .have anything."

She gave him a puzzled look, as if she were coming out of a daze. "What?"

"Condoms," he said bluntly.

Oddly, she smiled. "That's nice."

He blinked. "What?"

"You didn't plan this. Because True Mahan would never miss something so crucial." He wasn't sure how to take that. Didn't want to even think about trying to quiet his surging body into submission if this was going to come to a screeching halt. "It's all right." She let out a little breath. "My life may be a mess, but I'm not stupid. I stocked up on the pill before I left the west coast, where it's over the counter."

His clamoring body made his mind work a bit longer to realize what she'd meant, that with her life in that mess, she never knew when she might run into that one man she couldn't escape from or fight off.

He let out a sigh of relief.

"And just like that, you believe me," she said, sounding amazed. Surprised, his brow furrowed. "You're an honorable man. Anyone can see that. How do you know this isn't. . .a trap?"

He got it then. "If I'm that wrong about you, then I deserve it," he said gruffly.

They seemed to be the right words, because she smiled. "Thank you."

Somewhere down deep in him resolve grew. Somehow, he would find a way, a way for her to take some kind of normal life back. But right now, with her looking up at him with an echoing heat in her eyes, all he could do was kiss her, long and deep.

Chapter Twenty-Five

HIS BED WAS a tangle of sheets and blanket. He saw the direction of her gaze and grimaced. "Haven't been sleeping much lately."

"Neither have I," she whispered, wanting to ask if she was haunting his dreams, even as she was not quite willing to tell him how he had been haunting hers.

She shivered as he put her on the bed, and the thought flashed through her mind that this was significant somehow, that he'd brought her here, to his bed, when in fact the guest room she was already in was closer. But his steady strength had never faltered, he'd carried her upstairs and to here as if she were no burden at all.

True Mahan would never falter. . .

She knew what she was doing. Knew she was setting her heart up for more pain, that the longing she would take with her when she left would be with her for the rest of her life. But so would the regrets if she didn't seize this one chance she'd ever had for someone who made her feel like this. As much as she didn't want to spend the rest of her life remembering what she'd lost, she wanted even less to never truly taste this, at least once.

And then he came down beside her, his hands, those strong, work-roughened hands moving over her hungrily. Her body arched in response, and she nearly gasped with the wonder of it; if him merely touching her did this, what would taking him inside her do to her?

And suddenly she wanted that so much she couldn't think of anything else, of loss, pain, or regrets. When he tugged at her shirt she simply yanked it off over her head, then used her own shaking fingers to tug at the buttons of his shirt. She wanted that broad, powerful chest naked against her, as soon as she could get it. But then he was cupping her breasts with those hands, and she forgot how to breathe. His thumbs rubbed over her nipples and this time she did gasp as hot, sweet sensation arrowed downward from both peaks to someplace low and deep, and her body fairly rippled, already out of her control.

She became a mindless thing she didn't recognize, half-unaware of tearing at his clothes even as he pulled at hers. And then there was only naked skin against naked skin and she thought she might just burst into flame right here. She'd imagined him, during those dark, sleepless hours, but she knew now that her imagination fell far short; he was more beautiful than she'd ever realized was possible. Lean, muscled, and fully aroused, he took her breath away.

And then his mouth took over where his fingers had

been, his tongue flicking and teasing nipples that were still tight from his touch. His hands kept moving, stroking, lingering here and there, as if she were the most beautiful, precious thing he'd ever held. This man who knew just what needed to be done everywhere else seemed to know it here, too, and her own moans echoed in her ears as she fairly writhed beneath the onslaught.

When his hand slipped downward, probing, reaching flesh already slick and waiting for him, finding that tiny knot of eager nerves and caressing it, she cried out. Helplessly she moved, lifting her hips in an instinctive invitation she couldn't have stopped even if she'd wanted to.

He said her name, in a rough, low voice that sent an echoing shiver up her spine. Her arms tightened around him, then slid down his back. Later, she thought rather wildly, she wanted to trace every taut, muscled line of him, but now, now she wanted one thing more than she'd wanted anything in her life.

"Please," she whispered.

"I want to go slow," he said roughly, "but it's been a long time."

She'd known that, even as she'd thought no one had ever known how to touch her like this. But it had been a long time since she had dared risk this, too. But unlike then, this time was singing in her blood with the rightness of it.

"Yes," she agreed.

"Now?" he whispered.

She had no more words, so answered him in the only way she could think of; she slipped her hands further, to cup that high, tight backside she'd coveted and urge him forward.

Making a strangled sound, he reached for one of her hands and pulled it around between them. For a moment all she could do was register the incredible feel of him, hot silk over rigid flesh. She wanted to stroke, to touch every bit of him, but again her body screamed "later." She guided him, sensation rippling through her at the first blunt probe of him into a body that felt as if it had been waiting for him forever. As perhaps she had.

It was her last coherent thought because then he was inside her, sliding, stretching, filling. She lost herself in the sensations then. It was fast, driving, and a little bit wild, and when the wave swept over her it was consuming, swamping, delirious. In the moment after the fierce clenching of her body began she heard him growl her name in a voice that sent her even higher, and felt the pulsing of his body inside her.

They collapsed together, two souls who had both been lost in different deserts, coming together in an eruption of joyous human pleasure. And in the fading light of day he gathered her to him and just held her.

Much later, when she had satisfied that need to touch, to stroke, Hope cupped his face in both hands, held him so that she could meet his gaze. Very carefully she said, "There was nothing—*nothing*—about this that was a mistake."

He looked startled, then pleased. And she'd meant it, more than almost anything in her life. She had come so close to missing this, to never knowing it could be like this, to never experiencing the most soaring, overpowering sensation in her life. To never knowing the feel of him driving inside her, the power of that strong, lean body, the incredible feel of his skin against hers, the unexpectedly erotic effect of every sound he made, of his very urgency.

She'd never been wanted like this in her life. She'd never wanted like this in her life.

And now she had to walk away.

It nearly broke her right then, the thought of leaving him, of leaving this. She even hated the thought of leaving this town that had somehow grabbed her and woven some kind of spell around her, making her wish she could stay, could have a place here in Whiskey River, with its colorful characters and wild west history.

It didn't matter that, even if she could stay, that he would never love her. Not in the way he had his wife. That kind of love wasn't in the cards for her, she'd messed up too badly. But it didn't matter because now she knew that whatever True could give her, whatever was left of his heart would be more than she'd ever expected to have.

But she had to go. For his sake.

For all his skill, all his decency and goodness, he couldn't fix her life.

"Hope."

Her gaze, which had turned inward as it had so often since she'd landed here, snapped back to his face.

"Stop," he said softly. "Whatever you're thinking, just stop."

"I can't." It nearly choked her to say it. "I want. . .I wish. . ."

He moved then, quickly, covered her with his body. On his elbows, one on each side of her, he looked down at her.

"Listen to me, Hope. I'm only going to say this once." She'd never heard this tone from him before, and there was no mistaking it for anything but deadly serious. She didn't even recognize this True. "I will help you fight this. I will help you do whatever it takes for you to get your life back."

She stared up at him. "Going to find him and kill him for me?"

"Don't think it hasn't crossed my mind."

Her breath caught. He meant it. And suddenly she knew who this was. This was the man who'd made the decision to change his entire life for his sister when their parents had been killed. This was the man who had walked the woman he loved through the valley of the shadow, and come out the other side.

True Mahan would never falter. . .

Even as she'd thought it, she hadn't realized how true it really was.

"You would, wouldn't you?"

"If I thought it would change anything. But it won't. Any more than pounding the steering wheel over Amanda stopped her from dying."

"It would probably make things worse," she admitted. "And. . .it's not worth it. What it would do to your life."

He studied her for a long moment. She was achingly aware of the precious weight of him, the feel of his sleek skin against her, wanted nothing more than for him to make love to her once more and send all these troubling thoughts flying out of her brain. She could feel his response to their closeness, it would take so little for him to slip inside her, she was already slick and ready for him. But this True was intent, determined, and she knew there would be no derailing him. Not even with explosive sex.

She saw his jaw tighten, felt a new tension in his body. He stared down at her.

"You think you're not worth it," he said softly. "Because your parents drilled it into you before they abandoned you."

Again her breath caught as he hit dead center at the heart of her darkest fear, even darker than her fear for her life; her fear that that life wasn't worth fighting for. She couldn't look at him anymore, and turned her gaze away.

He dropped down then, until he was draped over her from shoulder to knee. His mouth next to her ear, he said gently, "Your parents were selfish, self-absorbed fools who should never have had a child. They didn't deserve you."

A shiver went through her.

"Your grandparents, on the other hand, they did. They do."

"True. . ." It was all she could get out.

"I can't give you self worth, Hope. I wish I could. But I can only show you what you're worth to me."

She moaned, low and deep, in the moment before he began to kiss her. He trailed his mouth over her ear, sending delicious shivers through her, shivers of a completely different kind. And then he took her mouth, probing, tasting, as if he'd found treasure there. And she realized he was doing exactly as he'd said, showing her what she was worth to him.

Then he lifted his head, just far enough so that he could look into her eyes. "I will help you, if you want to put an end to this. I won't deny that's what I hope you choose. But it's not my choice to make. It's yours."

"What if. . .I can't?"

What if? Her own words shocked her. When had fighting back even become a possibility? When had she even let it into her thinking?

"I will stand by you if you decide you can't. Keep you as safe as I can. Whiskey River will help. We're a town that pulls together for one of our own."

One of our own. She'd never thought of belonging to a place like that. Not the way True belonged here. But even in the short time she'd been here she knew it was true, this town was his home in a way she'd never known. But True was True, and she was. . .

"I'm not—"

"Stop," he said again. "You're worth what you think you're worth. Your life is worth fighting for. But if you can't, or can't yet, then just. . .stay."

And yet again he took her breath away. Stay? Had he somehow read her mind, did he know that this very wish had brought on that emotional break that had ended up with her hands battered by her own doing?

She felt as if she were drowning. Or had been, and then this man had thrown her a lifeline. And she didn't know what to do. "Oh, God, I wish so much. . ."

"Stop wishing, start doing. This town has lasted over a hundred and twenty-five years on toughness and grit and sheer stubbornness. Learn that from them, Hope."

Something sharp jabbed her deep inside, and she felt the bitterness and self-blame she always carried within her start to drain away. When enough of it had receded to let her think without it coloring every thought, when she was able to look at him and see the man he truly was, not just the man who had thrown her that lifeline, she nearly shook with the wonder that he had asked her to stay.

She didn't kid herself. The love he'd had with Amanda had been perfect, because it had never had a chance to change. It was frozen at that perfect stage, and if it would have someday changed, he would never know.

She couldn't compete with a perfect memory.

But it didn't matter. She might not be sure exactly what

it meant, what, in his mind her staying would entail, but she knew one thing with absolute certainty: it would be more than she'd ever had. More than she'd ever hoped to have.

It would be enough.

Chapter Twenty-Six

"MY SCANNER WAS an hour late this morning," Zee said, looking at her brother over a mug of coffee.

True froze in the act of filling his own mug. His sister had come through the adjoining door this morning with barely a knock, declaring a caffeine emergency.

"She also doesn't seem to be in quite the rush she was to finish the job," she added.

He smiled as he finished pouring.

"And you," she went on casually, "look a bit smug."

He paused in putting the pot back on the coffeemaker. He gave her a disbelieving glance. "Smug?"

"And happy," she added softly. "It's good to see, Bro."

"I. . ." He didn't know what to say.

"About time, too," Zee said with a sudden grin. "I mean come on, I've felt like I was living with a Tesla coil for days, the electricity between you two."

One look at his sister's face told him there was no use dissembling; she knew exactly what had happened last night. Somehow telling Zee about them hadn't popped into his head yet. He didn't even know if Hope wanted anyone to know. At least Zee wouldn't blab. If they wanted all of Whiskey River to know all they had to do was tell Martha and the job would be done before noon.

"And for what it's worth, brother mine, she's also looking rather smug. And. . .content. You haven't lost your touch in bed, if you were worried."

True blinked. Damn near blushed. Zee had never been one to beat around the bush, but that was blunt even for her. And yet something in her eyes removed any snark from it; she truly was happy for him. She'd come to care for Amanda like a sister, but she'd always and ever loved him.

"I was," he answered frankly. Then he gave her the fully smug look she'd teased him about. "But not now. Hope made it pretty clear along about the third time."

Zee coughed on a swallow of coffee. "Okay, we may have strayed into too much information here."

A laugh burst from him; she'd started this, after all. And to his surprise, he saw his sister's eyes glisten with moisture. "Zee?"

"God, True, that's the first real, genuine, from the gut laugh I've heard from you in almost six years." She set down her coffee mug, crossed the six feet between them, and threw her arms around him. "It's a beautiful sound and I've missed it. Remind me to thank her."

He drew back slightly. Looked down at her, although not nearly as far down as with Hope, since his sister was a willowy five-eight. "Does she. . .know you know?"

"I didn't say anything to her, but she'd have to think I was blind not to notice."

"She knows you're not blind. She knows how smart you are, too."

Zee's brows rose. She went back to her coffee before saying, "She does, does she?"

He finally got a sip of his own brew, teasingly waiting before saying, "She said she'd never met a woman who had quite so much of everything in one package, brains, character, energy and looks."

Zee blinked, clearly taken aback. "She said that?"

"She did." He gave her a crooked grin. "In that order, which I'm guessing is order of importance in her mind."

His sister was smiling now. "I knew I liked her."

"Good," True said. More coffee, and he thought he just might make it through the day. Maybe. He hadn't gotten much sleep. Not that he was complaining. Oh, no, not at all.

Zee looked at him once more over the rim of her mug. "Does that mean she's. . .staying?"

And there it was. He set down his mug. Jammed a hand through his hair. Finally spoke. "Yes."

"Uh-huh. That sounded about as convincing as you telling Mom you didn't break that vase of hers. And you always do that hand through your hair thing when you're edgy."

"Staying for now," he amended. "And I do not."

"Well then," Zee said in that overly sweet tone again, "I

guess you just do it to draw attention to that gorgeous hair of yours, huh?"

He scowled at her. "Did she pick up that saccharine tone from you?"

To his surprise Zee laughed. "Did she use it on you? Good for her. Glad to see she's getting a little gumption back."

He hadn't thought of that. He hoped it was true. "But she's still scared."

"Still think she might run? After. . .?"

And that was the thing that had been niggling at him all morning, ever since Hope had given him a last kiss and reluctantly gone next door. If what they'd found together last night couldn't hold her, he wasn't sure anything could.

"I don't know," he admitted. "But she won't do the only thing to end it, which is go back and face it."

His sister took the last drink of her coffee, set down her mug, and looked at him steadily. "I love you, Bro. I love the way you deal with things, and always do what you think is right."

"I sense a but coming. You're never that flattering unless there is."

"It wasn't flattery," she insisted. "I know better than anyone what you're made of, and that not everybody has your kind of nerve and honor and staying power."

He blinked. "Wow. Must be a hell of a but."

She rolled her eyes at him. "Dang, you suck at taking

compliments. I'm just saying that what's right for you, what you would do, may not be right for her. And you can't decide that for her."

"I know that. I told her that."

"But will you hold it against her if she won't or can't do what you would do?"

He opened his mouth to say of course not, but stopped. Would he?

"Just saying, Bro, you're a tough act to follow. And she doesn't think she's strong enough."

He set down his mug. "What do you think?"

"I think she doesn't know how strong she is."

He shook his head in slow wonder as he stared at this woman he'd watched grow up, yet suddenly felt as if he'd missed a huge step somewhere. "When did you get so wise, little sister?"

"Oh, wisdom is easy," she said, pouring herself another mug of coffee, "when it's about somebody else."

Her tone this time had been wry almost to the point of sour, and he frowned. "Something wrong?"

She made it to sour then. "Not with me."

Jamie then. He was the only one who could make her sound like that. "He's been in touch?"

She didn't pretend not to know who he meant. "If you call an email saying 'Tell True to do what's best,' in touch."

"What's best?"

"Your guess is as good as mine what that means."

He suspected her guess was a lot better than his in this case, but this didn't seem to be the time to say so. "I should go back over there. I kind of got. . .distracted the last time."

"Whatever," she said with a negligent shrug. She worked very hard at showing she didn't care a whit what one of Whiskey River's most famous sons did or didn't do. But he knew underneath she probably cared more than anyone. If Jamie ever did deign to come back to his hometown, he was going to have a little talk with him. In fact, maybe he'd have to go to him.

"What's so funny?" Zee asked, sounding a bit offended.

"Just picturing myself showing up at his next concert venue, busting through security to kick his ass."

The affronted expression vanished, to be replaced with his sister's lively grin. "Oh, I'd buy a ticket for that."

True smiled back, glad that he'd cheered her at least.

"I'd better get back to work." She lifted her full mug. "Thanks for the crisis intervention."

"Have you ever considered just setting up an IV?"

"Yes," she said. "But you know I hate needles."

He laughed as he watched her go back through the adjoining door. Resisted the urge to follow her, just to see Hope for a moment. Then remembered he wasn't resisting anymore. No reason he couldn't go out that way, was there? Or would it embarrass her, since he hadn't before? He grimaced inwardly, thinking he'd wandered into an entirely new kind of mine field.

In the end he did go, picking up a blank estimate form he didn't really need since he had a handful in the truck, noticing how Hope went very still standing at the scanner, brushed his lips over the back of her neck as he went by and whispered "Later," against her left ear.

"Please," she whispered back, and suddenly this was the brightest January morning Texas had ever seen.

Chapter Twenty-Seven

HOPE SAT ON the edge of True's bed, the bed she'd made love with him in for the last five nights, each time surprising herself with just how much she could feel with this man. It had been an interlude of joy, of delight, of soaring in ways she had never known possible. All because of him.

And now she had to decide.

She had quit with about an hour's worth of work remaining yesterday. It was silly, but as long as that bit of work remained, she could have this weekend. Two wonderful days. Then. . .

One more hour and the job she'd agreed to do here would be done. One more hour and the reason she'd stayed in the first place would be gone. One hour and the life she'd come to love in such a short time would end.

A shiver went through her. She felt herself weakening, as surely as if she were watching her own blood drain away. That's what it felt like, that if she did what she had to do, she might as well slash an artery and get it over with.

She couldn't weaken.

She listened to the shower running, the image of a naked True, water streaming over that lean, powerful body sending a different kind of shiver through her. The urge to join him, as she had every other morning, was so powerful she thought she might have to grab the bedpost to stop herself. Images of him, of them together as he braced her against the shower wall and slid into her, filling that place inside her that seemed to have been made just for him, raced vividly through her mind. The memory of how his shout of her name had echoed from the tile as he pulsed within her. Even now her body clenched fiercely at just the thought, and she knew if she went to him now she would hit that amazing peak she hadn't even known herself capable of at his first touch. Even when they were apart, it was almost as if she could still feel him.

To have all that, and at the same time a man so solid, so steady, so. . .true, had never been a dream for her, for she'd never believed a man like that existed.

How could she possibly leave him? She would ache for him forever.

You knew before you started how this would end.

Her stern words to herself did little to ease the chaos rolling around inside her. Desperate, she got up to dig into the pack that now sat on the floor here in his bedroom. She'd hesitated bringing it in here at first, until he pointed out it was silly for her to keep running down the hall for everything. He hadn't seemed to mind, even the few female accoutrements she had on his bathroom counter. Nothing she couldn't leave behind if she had to go in a hurry, she'd thought when she'd put them there. Except the toothbrush, she'd have to grab that.

She'd gone from planning on it to trying to think of a way to avoid it. There was none, because the bottom line never changed.

She pulled the worn, dog-eared photograph from its spot in the secure outside zipper pocket of the pack. She sat back down on the edge of the bed, staring at her grandparents. She'd taken the picture, in front of the sign for the local park.

This was the reason, this was why she had no choice. Even if she believed True could take care of himself—and under normal circumstances she would believe that, but she doubted he'd ever had to deal with the likes of Cagan—they could not. The thought of Cagan or his attack dogs going after them turned her to ice. Her grandfather would die to protect her grandmother, and she suspected vice versa. And while they were fit and fairly healthy, they were in their seventies and no match for—

Were they fit and healthy?

She closed her eyes in pain at the grim admission that she didn't know. The last time she'd called, they hadn't answered. That didn't necessarily mean anything, but she hadn't dared risk a call from here when once she decided to stay, not when one look at their caller ID would have told someone exactly where she was. Nor could she borrow a cell phone for the same reason.

"Hey. I missed you in there."

Her eyes snapped open. He was standing there with only a damp towel wrapped around his lean hips. For a moment all she could do was stare. He was so beautifully put together, and there were male models who would probably kill for those abs. But his were earned through work, not workouts, and she admired him all the more for that.

As if she needed any more reason to admire him.

"Hope."

Suddenly he was there, beside her. She moved to put the photo away, but he stayed her hand.

"Your grandparents?" he asked.

It was too late to deny, and she wouldn't lie to him. "Yes."

He studied the image for a moment. "They. . .sparkle."

Her breath caught as he used the word that had often come to her mind looking at this, her favorite picture of them. Her favorite because it had caught just that, the sparkle of life, and of the obvious love between them.

"They used to say it was because of me. I was their sunshine, and they just reflected it." *And look what their sunshine did to them.*

"What are their names?"

"Gordon and Lynn."

"When was the last time you spoke to them?"

"Last summer. I was about to get on a bus out of Lubbock. It was Wednesday afternoon, and I knew Gran would be at her book club meeting. So I called the bookstore and asked to talk to her. I thought that would be safe."

"Good thinking," he said.

"She sounded good. But they're in their seventies."

"And you're worried."

"Always."

He put an arm around her. She leaned against him, grateful that she had bought herself this weekend. He felt so strong, as if for just this moment she could let him help her carry this. Sometimes he even made her feel stronger. As if she might be able to at least try to do what he would do, stand and fight. And if it was only her, maybe. . .but it wasn't.

"I could have Jack have his cousin check on them."

She stiffened. "No. I know they're still watching them, hoping I show up. A cop or anyone connected to a cop…they'll think the cops found me, and came to tell them. They'll go after them to find out." He didn't say anything and she looked up at him. "True, promise me."

"He'd be careful—"

"No. That's how they found the guy I saw them murder. They went after his family. Swear to me."

"I. . .all right. No cops."

His brow was furrowed and she could tell he was thinking. Knowing him, looking for a way to fix this. But this was unfixable, she knew that. She just wasn't sure this man ever accepted anything as unfixable, as long as he was alive to try.

"True. . ."

"I promised," he said. "I don't go back on promises."

"I know."

And then, because she didn't know what else to do, she kissed him. Simply for being who he was.

✪

NOW THAT, TRUE thought, was the way to spend a Saturday morning. He stretched expansively as he listened to the shower. He had missed her joining him as she had the last few days, but she'd more than made up for it when he'd come out. Once they'd gotten past that rough patch about her grandparents, she'd kissed him and it had begun all over again. She had gotten rid of his towel in a hurry, and proceeded to minister to every inch of him with a slow care that had nearly driven him out of his mind. It had felt a little odd, being naked and sprawled before her when she was dressed, but it had also put an edge on the sensations that had his blood surging and his nerves on fire.

And when she'd peeled off her clothes in a rush and straddled him, only the fact that it had happened as fast for her as for him had saved him from embarrassing himself with how quickly he'd lost it.

Saturday.

It suddenly hit him that Saturday was the day Zee allowed herself a visit to the Banner Bakery in town, to indulge in her beloved but calorie-packed cinnamon rolls. And she usually bought the box of four, saying she counted on him to get rid of two for her.

He could do that.

Quickly he got up, pulled his jeans on, and headed out to the connecting door. He wondered if this constituted a caloric emergency, decided Zee wouldn't appreciate the humor and knocked. He heard her call out and opened the door.

He found her in her kitchen, waiting on the coffeemaker, so she'd clearly rectified her caffeine outage. Music was playing softly; she had always preferred the slow stuff in the mornings until she got going. And Saturdays took longer than usual, so it wasn't surprising she was still on the ballads even though it was nearly noon.

The plastic container of rolls sat on the counter, as he'd hoped. But it was a six-pack, not the usual four. Her head came up when he walked in, and she looked him up and down. So intently that he almost wished he'd put a shirt on, too. And suddenly remembered the marks on his back from Hope's nails.

"Sometimes," she said with an odd sort of smile, "because you're my brother and I always focus on how good you are to me, I forget how damn sexy you are."

He blinked. "Are you all right?"

She sighed. "Like I said, you suck at taking compliments."

Not always. The memory of what Hope had whispered to him this morning made a smile flit across his face.

"Well good for her, if she's teaching you," Zee said. As she poured her coffee, she nodded toward the rolls. He could smell them, and his stomach suddenly growled in response. "I got extra. Figured you two need to keep your strength up."

He grinned at her then. "Thanks."

"God, you look like the Cheshire cat with that grin. Take four of those and get out."

There was more than a teasing edge in her voice, and he asked again, "Are you all right?"

She lowered her head, staring at the coffee as if there were some secret to life hidden in the dark liquid.

"Fine. Go eat before you both collapse from exhaustion. I'm going to go change clothes."

She reached out and tapped her phone twice, and the stream of music that was coming from the speaker on the counter stopped abruptly. She shoved the phone into the back pocket of her jeans, turned on her heel and was gone.

True watched her go, frowning. Then, belatedly, he realized what had been playing when she'd shut the music off. The song that had started at the moment her mood had turned. The song written about this place, about the river, about a longing to go back to where you began.

That song always set her off. He'd asked her why once and she'd snapped at him. "It's a lie. If it was true, he'd come home."

He'd never brought it—or Jamie—up again unless it was necessary. Like about his aunt's house. He supposed she had a point, but Jamie was flying high right now. His mouth twisted. He hoped that wasn't a literal description. But expecting the guy to come back to Whiskey River when the band was hitting it big was a little too much. Scorpions On Top—he still laughed at the name, with a smile for Aunt Millie—was hitting big, touring to full houses because Jamie had been an early adapter of every Internet powered way of reaching people. They'd conquered Texas first, then it spread, until they were even hitting places like Nashville and L. A.

They had caught fire in L. A., and had been staying there as a base since—

L. A.

He yanked out his phone, opened the browser. A quick search brought up the flashy website. He worked his way through to the tour schedule. He was almost sure they were ending this tour leg back in L.A. If he wasn't wrong. . .right about now.

He wasn't.

Noon. Ten AM in L. A. After a Friday night show. He didn't know much about that life, but he guessed that might be a bit early. So instead of calling he texted. He'd give Jamie a couple of hours, then he'd call if he hadn't heard back.

He let out a long breath. He couldn't say anything to Hope, in case it didn't work out. Or in case bad news turned up; that's not how he'd want her to learn it.

But at least there was a plan.

And he felt even better as he opened the box, grabbed up two of the luscious smelling cinnamon rolls, and headed back home.

Home.

Yeah, that's what it felt like.

He was whistling Jamie's *River Song* as he closed the door behind him.

Chapter Twenty-Eight

"CINNAMON ROLLS?"

Hope heard the hopeful sound in her own voice, and nearly laughed at herself. She stopped her effort to detangle her wet hair; the heavy, blunt comb she used had lost a few teeth along the way, making it more difficult. She took a step toward the counter where he'd set a plate with the rare treat.

He held another—no plate and a bite missing—in his hand, and rather sheepishly said, "Sorry, couldn't resist."

"Some things you shouldn't even try to resist."

She moved a finger to scrape up a small pool of cream cheese frosting. It reached her mouth at the same moment he said huskily, "I found that out."

The sweetness of his words, his voice, was more than a match for the taste in her mouth. She looked at him, for this moment letting it all show in her face, what she had come to feel for him, what she didn't dare put into words because nothing had changed.

But everything had changed.

"Keep looking at me like that, and we'll end up back in bed."

"Is that a promise? An official, True Mahan, never broken promise?"

She hadn't meant to sound so. . .wistful. She lowered her eyes to the roll, peeling off a strip. She had it in her mouth, savored, chewed and swallowed before he spoke again.

"Outside forces."

"What?" She said as much to his suddenly serious tone as to the words.

"That's the only thing that's ever made me break a promise. Car accident. Broken arm."

His parents, she guessed. The broken arm she didn't know. There was so much she didn't know.

And you won't be here long enough to find out all those things.

The thought was already ripping her to pieces inside. But while she might have stolen these days, these few golden days, nothing had changed about the danger she brought with her.

"Can't do that." Her voice was low, unsteady. "If I go back to bed with wet hair, I'll never get it untangled. It's bad enough now. I should have bought some conditioner."

He frowned. "Sorry. Not something I've got on hand."

She glanced at his thick, dark—and short—hair. "You don't need it."

He finished his roll, wiped his hands on a paper towel,

then reached out to lift a tangled strand. "It must be hard to manage, on the move. I'm surprised you didn't have it cut. Glad, but surprised."

"If I could look like Zee, I would. But I just look like a little boy."

True laughed. "Little, I'll give you. But even at my blindest I never thought you were a boy."

He lifted the strand again. "Let me," he said.

"What?"

"You eat. I'll comb."

"True—"

"My fault I don't have conditioner at hand."

He took the comb from her. If he noticed the gaps from the missing teeth he said nothing. He just started to work, gently, methodically, working his way through the tangles, all the while holding her hair so that it didn't tug on her scalp.

She'd finished half the roll before it hit her. "You've done this before."

"Yes."

"Amanda?"

"Yes."

She hesitated, then said, "It must have been awful."

"It was. For her." He kept combing, but his voice was tight. "We were in an apartment then, kind of small, so toward the end, with Zee there most of the time, and hospice people coming and going, it got to be like a war zone."

"It was a war zone, wasn't it?"

He stopped mid-stroke. The tangles were gone now, but he'd kept combing. She loved the feel of it, so hadn't said anything.

"Yes," he said after a moment. "Yes, it was. And we lost." There was a touch of anger in his voice, even after all this time. She couldn't blame him. "She fought every step of the way, lasted longer than they said she would. But one night she woke me. To say goodbye, because she could feel herself slipping. She died in my arms a few hours later. Peacefully."

Hope didn't dare speak for a long moment, because that he'd shared this painful memory with her meant the world. That it was one more thing for her to carry when she had to leave didn't matter just now.

"That damned disease did not win," she said finally, softly. "It can never, ever take away what you two had."

He went very still. And then he leaned forward and pressed his lips to the top of her head. For a long silent moment he just stood there, silently. She didn't know what to say, didn't want to say anything because somehow this moment seemed crucially important.

And she regretted the moment when his cell phone rang, shattering it.

"MRS. HAWKINS?"

He probably sounded as surprised as he felt; this hadn't been the call he was expecting. Or hoping for at least. And he was still off balance anyway; he'd never told anyone about those ugly last days of Amanda's life. Zee knew, of course, because she'd been there. She'd even offered to do some of the more intimate, female type things, but Amanda had wanted him. The kindly, gentle hospice workers she allowed, but when they were gone, it was him she wanted. And so he did it. Awkwardly more often than not, but she had never complained. And all the while he knew each time could be the last, and so it was never a chore, only a final declaration of love.

"—bring her?"

Belatedly he tuned back in. "Bring her?"

"Yes, to the house. Adam wants to thank her, but the doctors won't let him go outside yet, because you know that boy, he's utterly incapable of not running around at full speed all the time, jumping over this, climbing that, and that's the worst thing for him right now, so if you could bring Hope over since she doesn't have a car, that would be wonderful, we'll have lunch ready and of course you must stay as well, you're the one smart enough to hire her and—"

"I'll ask her," he interjected, marveling as always that the woman never seemed to take a breath.

"Don't ask, just bring her," the woman said breezily, with that imperious confidence that her wishes would be obeyed. And since they usually were, True wasn't sure he could fault her for that. "See you in an hour."

And the flow of words finally stopped, but only because the woman had hung up. Texas tornadoes had nothing on her.

He looked at Hope, his mouth twisting into a wry smile. "Maybe you should have bought a hair dryer."

She drew back slightly. He explained. "Oh, no, I couldn't," she said.

He gave her a sideways look. "One does not simply say no to Ginevra Hawkins."

"But—"

"If you don't show up there, she will show up here and take you in tow. On the other hand, if you go peacefully, she will allow you to escape after a reasonable amount of time."

"And what," she asked, "is a reasonable amount of time?"

Forever.

The word popped into his head unbidden. He quickly shifted his gaze back to his phone, staring at it as if he'd forgotten to do something vital. For some reason his silence seemed to convince her. Maybe he should remember that.

"You'll stay with me?"

He resisted answering with that word; it would likely send her running right now. So he just nodded, figuring that was safe enough.

"All right. I wouldn't mind seeing Adam again."

The ride to the Hawkins's large, just the right side of blatant home was rather silent. He was still wrestling with that word that had shot into his mind, and Hope was not—thank God—a chatterer anyway. Or at least she wasn't now. He wondered if she ever had been, if in her prior life she'd been a gregarious, outgoing, center of attention kind of woman. He wondered if he would ever know.

"Nice house," she said as they arrived.

"Her family's been in Whiskey River practically since Booze." He managed a grin. "And not always on the same side. Her great whatever granddaddy was a preacher."

"Fire, brimstone, and don't drink that whiskey?"

His grin widened, more solid now. "Exactly that."

She shook her head slowly. "This place. . .I grew up in places that weren't towns, they were just expansions of a big city. They had names, but that's all. They were just known by how far they were from L. A. It was all just one big sprawl, practically interchangeable. This place has history. Identity."

"Yes."

"It's. . .amazing." She looked at the house again. "I feel like I should be more dressed up."

Since he knew perfectly well that wasn't an option for her, he just shrugged. "It's Saturday. Casual. She'll live," he said, all the while thinking how much he hated that she had so little. "Besides, Becca, Adam's mom will be there, and she's pretty laid back."

Adam looked good, practically back to himself. And, True guessed, chafing at the bit to get back to his normal, active life. The boy thanked Hope with a nice little speech that was no less sincere for obviously having been practiced. He was followed by his mother, who thanked her fervently for saving her son's life. There were other relatives clustered about who soon surrounded Hope. Followed by friends. She was the center of attention for the moment, and he was certain that was something she hadn't had or wanted since that hot summer night in L.A.

She gave True a nervous glance a couple of times, but it was clear everyone merely wanted to thank her, and she eventually seemed to relax a little. Enough so that when his cell rang and he looked at her before he stepped out of the room to answer, she saw him and nodded that she was okay.

He glanced at the screen. Quashed a moment of hesitation, then answered.

"You're up early," he said.

A familiar, if long unheard voice said, "It's eleven here."

"Early for a rock star after a Friday night show," True amended. And judging by the noise in the background, the party wasn't quite over yet.

"Fuun-ny. How the hell are you, True?"

Well, that could have a variety of answers. "Like your song says, some things never change."

"And like it also says, sometimes that's a good thing."

There was a sudden swell of the background noise, shouting and cheering. True wondered how Jamie could hear at all, but he was probably used to it.

"Look, if this is about Aunt Millie's house—"

"No. We'll deal with that later. Right now. . .I need a favor, Jamie."

There was a split second pause, then he heard, "Hang on, let me get into another room." True heard somebody call Jamie's name, heard him move the phone away and answer, "Later, man, this is important."

True smiled; Jamie Templeton might have left Whiskey River, but he was still a hometown boy at heart, no matter what Zee thought.

A moment later the background noise was gone.

"Shoot, True."

"I need you to do something for me."

"Makes this a red letter day, you being the one asking instead of the other way around."

"It'll be a pain, and you'll have to lose the entourage," he warned.

"Hurt me," Jamie said, and True could almost see his grin.

"Okay, here's the deal," he said. And started in motion something he truly hoped he wouldn't regret.

Chapter Twenty-Nine

"Really, Becca, you've already thanked me more than enough. I'm just glad I was there."

Adam's mother put a hand on her arm. "That boy is everything to us."

"Of course he is." Hope smiled at the woman. "And I can see that you have your hands full with him. He's a sharp one."

"Yes, he is. He takes after his daddy."

"Does he?"

"Yes." Hope didn't ask where he was, or even look around the room, but the woman sighed. "He's in the service, on deployment. Again."

"That's rough. And underappreciated."

"Thank you," Becca said, smiling now, clearly past a moment of weakness.

Hope saw True coming back into the room after his call. He wasn't looking at her, so she let herself watch him, storing up the images of this tall, strong man against the time when she wouldn't be able to look at the real thing.

"You," Becca said, "are a lucky woman."

That was a description she hadn't applied to herself in some time, and her gaze snapped back to Adam's mother.

"Lucky?"

"I haven't seen True like this with anyone since his wife died. And believe me, we all tried."

Hope opened her mouth, then closed it again, thinking what she'd been about to ask would be very wrong. But Becca read her look and smiled ruefully.

"Yes, sadly, I must include myself in that number. I was in the middle of feeling very sorry for myself when my husband's last deployment was extended, and got a little tipsy at Boots and Bangles, our annual charity bash. True was there, for the first time in years, and. . .I made a pass at him. A pretty heavy one."

"Oh." Hope didn't know what else to say, and decided nothing was the wisest option.

"But True is True. An utter gentleman. He told me as appealing as the idea was—which was a total lie, I was so drunk—he could not and would not do that to Reeve. Or Adam. Or me, since he knew how I'd feel when I sobered up. And he took me home. I mean, the man actually put me to bed, and left."

Hope studied the woman in front of her, saw the genuine embarrassment in her eyes.

"I was so humiliated the next morning. I mean, I adore my husband, and I've never felt worse about anything. To this day I haven't had the nerve to face the man. But bless True again, he has never said a word to anyone."

"But you're telling me?"

"True picked you, so you must be trustworthy."

Hope felt her cheeks heat slightly at the words that seemed to be a law in Whiskey River. "Did you ever think," she said quietly to this woman she already liked, "that perhaps that's why, even drunk, out of all the men there you picked True to make a pass at?"

Becca's brow furrowed. "How do you mean?"

"That on some level. . .you knew. That he wouldn't take you up on it, and he wouldn't blab."

Becca's eyes widened. "I. . .never thought of it like that."

She looked suddenly happier, and that made Hope smile.

"Oh, I see why he's with you," Becca said. "You're not just pretty, you're kind, too. I'm glad. He's been alone too long. And that, I know something about."

Hope started to speak, but stopped when she realized she had no idea how to explain that this wasn't permanent. No matter how much she wished it might be. A wish that grew stronger every day. Every minute of those days.

Stay.

You can't. You're not good enough for him anyway.

She glanced at True across the room. As if he'd felt her eyes on him his head turned. She smiled. He turned back and said something to the man he'd been speaking to, an uncle of Adam's, although she wasn't clear on whose brother he was. And then he started toward her. Becca turned as if to go, then stopped. With a glance and a smile at Hope, she stayed. And when he reached them, she smiled up at him.

"I have thanked Hope," she said.

"Endlessly," Hope said with a smile.

"Deservedly so," Becca said. "But I also want to. . .thank you."

True shook his head. "She did it. I wasn't even there."

"She's here because of you," Becca said. "And by the way, I'm glad to see it. She's perfect for you."

Hope's jaw tightened as she bit back the exclamation that she was so far from perfect, for anyone, but especially True. She couldn't look at him, didn't want to see his face as Becca connected them in that way that sounded inevitable and deep.

"But that wasn't what I meant," Becca said. "I've waited much too long, but I wanted to thank you for. . .what you didn't do that night."

He gave Becca one of the gentlest smiles Hope had ever seen. "What night? I have no idea what you're talking about."

Becca looked at Hope. "See?"

She left them there and went back to her son, who was holding court to visitors from his spot on the couch, wrapped in a blanket under his grandmother's fiercely watchful eye.

"She. . .told you?"

"Yes. You're quite something, Mr. Mahan."

He shrugged. "Doesn't take much of a man to pass up something that wasn't really meant and would hurt so many, including friends."

She wondered if he realized just how many there were who would never pass up such an offer. Surely he did, he was hardly naïve, he'd been through the worst life could throw at a person. Perhaps it was just that that kind of man wasn't worth his time or thought.

"You know," he said, clearly leaving the topic behind, "I think with a little nudge they'd throw you a parade."

She nearly laughed aloud at the idea.

"You could have a place here, Hope," he said softly.

That longing she'd quashed welled up in her again, to have that place, to belong here, in this place with the quirky history and the tightly knit community. She felt like a child reaching for a treat that was teasingly just out of reach.

Your life is worth fighting for.

We're a town that pulls together for one of our own.

She had to look away before he saw the tears welling up in her eyes.

✪

SHE WANTED TO stay.

He'd been quiet all the way home, but he'd seen her fighting tears. And when they got there he couldn't stop himself from reaching for her. He meant to be gentle, coaxing, knowing Hope was in a fragile place. She wanted to stay, he could see it in her eyes, her face, but she was afraid. And he was so weary of that damned, hideous emotion. He'd seen too much of it, and he hated seeing it in her.

And suddenly it triggered something deep within him; maybe she couldn't fight, but he could. He hadn't been able to save Amanda, but he'd be damned if he'd let Hope suffer. As if he could burn it out of her with the heat they struck together he didn't just slip the leash, he threw it away. He wanted that fear in her turned to ash, he wanted the only things in her mind to be him, them, and the amazing thing they'd found.

He had them naked so fast she sounded a little breathless. He wanted more of that, he wanted those moans from her, the rippling of her body against his, and he wanted to hear her cry out his name while he was buried deep inside her. He wanted her thinking of nothing but how much she wanted time after time of this, of how hot, how explosive they were together.

Together.

He wanted that so welded into her mind that there was no longer anything of him or her but only them, more together than either was apart. He wanted to imprint himself on her so deeply she simply couldn't walk away. Maybe it wasn't the best way, but it was the only way he knew right now.

He took her hard and fast and deep, and gloried in her

wild response. He savored the slick, hot feel of her, and even the sting as her nails dug into his back. He drove harder, his mouth moving over every inch of silken skin he could reach, his tongue circling her nipples, his hand slipping between them so his finger could duplicate the caress over that tight knot of nerves that would send her flying. And when it happened, when he got that fierce, awed cry of his name he let himself follow, and in the end he wasn't sure which of them was quivering more with the aftershocks of a pleasure unlike any he'd ever felt.

Much later, as the day faded, he opened his eyes to the gleam of her eyes, open and watching him in the faint light remaining. He hadn't meant to doze off, but wasn't surprised given how utterly relaxed he felt.

"Getting dark," he said carefully. There was something in her eyes, something different, and until he knew what it was he couldn't quash the feeling he needed to tread carefully.

"Yes."

He half wished she would reach for him, start that incredible dance again. He would never forget how it made him feel, the first time she had initiated it, knowing how tentatively she felt about. . .everything. But that change in her made him wary. Instead he said, "I didn't realize that was going to turn into a party today, or I would have warned you."

She smiled, but it looked somewhat half-hearted, acknowledging his words but as if she were focused elsewhere.

The wariness kicked up another notch, and he wondered if there was a guy on the planet who could wake up to his woman studying him like that and not be nervous about what she was thinking. In his case he was nervous enough to just keep his mouth shut.

Finally she spoke. "It was. . .nice. Especially to meet Adam's family."

"They're good people. His grandmother may be overbearing, but she loves every one of them, and has made sure Adam and Becca have everything they need while Reeve is deployed."

"She has to feel so alone sometimes, missing him, watching Adam grow and change without his father. It must be awful for her."

"Awful enough that she made a pass she didn't mean at all," he said, trying to gauge how she felt about what Becca had told her. "She's crazy about Reeve."

For a long moment then she just looked at him. When she spoke again, her words startled him.

"Is it different?" she asked.

He hoped everything was different now. But was vaguely afraid it was a bit too male of him to think a decadent afternoon of incredible sex would fix everything. And he had a feeling that wasn't what she meant anyway.

"What?" he asked, carefully.

"Sex with someone you love and with someone you don't."

He felt as if a jackhammer had slipped and nailed him in the chest. His heart seemed to stutter for a moment, then race to make it up. For an instant a vision of Amanda flashed through his mind, and in it she was smiling, nodding.

Don't give up on life, True. . .you deserve to be happy.

The words echoed in his head. He knew she had meant them.

But how do I convince a woman who doesn't seem to think she deserves to be happy?

He didn't know. But he lifted up on his elbow, met her gaze and gave her the only answer he could. An honest one.

"I don't know."

Chapter Thirty

IT WAS A moment before Hope could process what he'd said. Before it sunk in what he'd meant. Inanely, her first thought was what a True way to say it. Her second was that she'd clearly misunderstood. Her brain, filled to overflowing with wishful thinking of late, had taken a casual "I don't know" and turned it into a declaration he'd had no intention of making.

"Don't run from it, Hope," he said softly. "You don't have to return it, or even accept it, but don't run."

"I—"

"I meant it. I know all the reasons it's crazy, I know you never wanted this—"

"No."

It was all she could get out, but she could see by the way his jaw tightened what he thought she was saying. She had to find the words, the right words, because she could not bear him to think what he was thinking. But neither could she say it back to him, no matter how much she wanted to, no matter how true it was. How could it not be? He was the best, the finest man she'd ever met, the kind she'd been half convinced didn't really exist. Any woman would fall in love with him.

It wasn't cold in the room, but she shivered anyway.

"You're wrong," she got out, although her voice was a low, broken thing. "I want it. Too much. I can't. . . It can't. . .You know why."

The last words came out in a desperate sort of rush. Because she knew what it would mean, if she told him the truth, if she said she loved him, too. Because she knew as surely as she knew the dawning would grow lighter that True would fight for the people he loved.

She felt the burning in her eyes, knew she was on the edge of tears. And then the edge crumbled, and she dashed at them as they began to flow down her cheeks. Useless, pointless things accomplishing nothing. She'd sworn off crying; it was a sign of weakness she could ill afford in what her life had become. And yet she had cried more here, in this place, than she could ever remember.

And then True reached for her, pulled her into his arms. He didn't speak, just held her. His warmth seeped into her, vanquishing the sudden chill that had swept her. In that moment she wanted more than anything to just hand it all over to him, to let his strength be hers.

I will help you fight this. I will help you do whatever it takes for you to get your life back. . .

But this was not his battle to fight, it was hers, and the

fact that he would do it for her only made her more certain she could not let him. And even though he had also said he would stand by her if she decided she couldn't fight, she could not help believing that she would be less than she could be in his eyes if she chose that course. And that thought was almost unbearable.

Because he loved her.

She shivered again, not from a chill but from the wonder of it. It was a moment before she realized he must have felt it, for he was stroking her back, long, steady strokes that somehow calmed her. She had a sudden vision of Kelsey Blaine stroking her frightened horse, and wondered if it was some instinctive thing these Texans knew.

But she couldn't deny the comfort it gave, she couldn't. . .couldn't. . .

Oh, there was such a long list of things she couldn't. And a very short list of things she wanted. And with fate's wicked sense of twisted humor, the one made the other impossible. But for the first time her mind crept into a dark corner she'd kept blocked off since that night Kim had died, so hideously, right in front of her. Not the memory of that, and of the boy who had also died that night, those images she revisited far too often, against her will.

No, in this corner were the images of what it would be like if she went back, if she went to the cops, if she did what True would do, stood up, stood strong. And for the first time she didn't reject the idea instantly. If there was a way to keep Gran and Gramps safe, if she could—

His phone rang, with an intricate guitar riff she realized she'd heard before. Often. It was from one of the songs on the playlist Zee usually had going in the office.

He went very still.

"True?"

"Do you trust me?"

She thought about asking why he thought she was naked in bed with him if she didn't, but something about the way he was acting told her this was not the time for jokes.

"Yes," she said simply.

He sat up abruptly. Simultaneously grabbed his phone and the nearest shirt, which happened to be his. He tossed the latter to her.

"You might want to put that on for a minute."

And then he answered the phone.

"Jamie?" A pause. And then he was smiling. Widely. Anything that made him smile like that couldn't be bad, could it? "Thanks, my friend."

He glanced at her then. Drew in a breath like a man about to plunge off a cliff. "It's safe, Hope."

Her brow furrowed. "What is?"

"Nobody will ever, *ever* be able to connect the guy who owns the phone on the other end to you."

"True, what are you talking about?"

"Video chat," he said.

She blinked. "What? Me? Now?" Instinctively her hand

went to hair tousled by his hands. “I don’t think—”

“Don’t think. And they won’t care.”

“They?”

He handed her the phone. She hesitated, but something in the way he was looking at her made her take it. It was still a moment before she looked down at the screen.

She was looking at the face of a total stranger. Male, True’s age or maybe a bit younger. Sandy blond hair, a little long, with a couple of lighter strands kicking forward over his forehead. Green eyes, so vivid they gleamed even on the phone screen. In fact all of him seemed vivid, in a way she couldn’t quite put her finger on.

“Hi, Hope. We’ll meet later, but in the meantime there are some folks who’d really like to see you.”

The image blurred as the phone moved, she saw a sign but couldn’t read it. Yet it seemed familiar somehow. Hope’s eyebrows lowered in bewilderment. And then the image stilled again. A tiny sound escaped her, nothing less than a whimper.

“Gran? Gramps?”

Her voice was barely a whisper, but her grandmother’s voice was louder as she cried out, “Hope! Oh my God honey, it’s really you.”

“We were afraid you were dead, squirt,” her grandfather said, a quaver in his usually steady, deep voice.

“No, no, I’m fine, I’m good, really, I. . .” She stopped, her throat too tight to get out another word as she stared down at the two beloved faces she'd feared she would never see again. She was aware that True had left the room to give her privacy, but she wished he had stayed. She felt so wobbly right now she could use his solid strength. "Are you all right?" she finally managed.

"We're better now," her grandfather said. "We've been mighty worried about you, girl."

"I know, and I'm sorry, but you don't—"

"We know, Hope," her grandmother said. "It wasn't hard to figure out when the police came looking for a witness to those awful murders."

She sucked in a breath. She should have known; her grandparents were as sharp as ever.

"Come home, honey," her grandmother said urgently. "It's all right."

"I. . .can't," she said, in the weakest declaration of it she'd ever made.

"You can," her grandfather said. "We know why you went, to protect us, and we love you for it, but it's all right. You can come home."

"I can't. You'll never be safe."

"Don't write us off so easily. I remember a few things about fighting, and that gang isn't what it used to be," her grandfather said stoutly. "They've cleared a lot of them out over the last couple of years. And the feds are chipping away at the cartel from the other end. Haven't put the ringleader away yet, but they will someday. But they're getting close on the guy here, who killed Kim."

Close. He didn't say it, he never would, but it seemed to be glowing in neon in her mind. *They could put him away now if you testified.*

"He can still give orders from jail. You're only safe there if he knows you don't know where I am." She didn't want to waste this precious time on this. "Are you all right? Both of you?"

"Missing our girl, but we're fine, Hope," her grandmother said. "It's been hard, searching for you for so long—"

"You're still searching?"

Her grandfather snorted. "Of course we are! You think we're a couple of old fuddy-duddies who'd just let you vanish like that without doing a thing?"

Her mind was racing. She should have known. Neither one of these feisty septuagenarians would have just let her go and stayed home worrying. They would have done something.

Did you not learn anything from them at all?

"This boy here, he says you're in a safe place," her grandmother said.

"I. . .yes."

"Seems nice, under all that scruff and messy hair," her grandfather put in.

Since she had no idea who the guy they were referring to was, she couldn't say much about that.

"He also says the man who set this up is the best, most

honest, decent and honorable man he's ever known."

True. In the shock and joy of seeing them she'd almost forgotten about the engineer of it all. But the feelings came flooding back now, amplified by the small miracle he'd wrought. For her.

"He is," she whispered. "He is all of that. And more."

She was sure everything she was feeling was showing in her face, but she didn't care.

"I told you you'd find him, someday," her grandmother said, sounding inordinately pleased, "the man who could make you feel like that."

Someday you'll find a man who will make you feel the way your grandfather makes me feel, Hope. When you do, you grab him and hold on.

Hold on.

And for the first time since the night her life had dissolved into an ugly, bloody mess, she felt a rush of the emotion she'd not allowed herself to feel since.

The emotion she was named for.

Hope.

Chapter Thirty-One

SHE HEARD THE faintest sound at the door and looked up from the now blank phone screen. True was peeking in, and she guessed he'd judged from her silence that the call was over.

"You mad?" he asked, sounding wary.

She shook her head, not sure she could trust her voice yet. True took it as a sign it was safe to come back in. In a moment he was sitting beside her on the bed.

"You look great in my shirt," he said.

"It smells good. Like you."

He blinked. "I. . .okay."

"Who is he? The guy with the phone?"

"Jamie. Jamie Templeton. He's from here."

Templeton. The people who were killed with his parents? She thought so, but didn't want to bring it up now. "I gathered," she said. "He had good things to say about here. . .and you."

True shrugged. "We've been friends a long time. And," he said with a slightly wry expression, "that was his aunt's house you were squatting in."

She felt her cheeks heat. "Oh. I should have apologized."

"No need. At least, not yet. I didn't tell him. He's a bit touchy about that house because Zee nags him about it."

"Why is he in Los Angeles?"

He smiled then. "Ever heard of Scorpions On Top?"

She nodded. "They were the hottest thing when I left L.A. They're really good." Another realization hit. "Your ring tone, that was from that song of theirs, about the river."

He nodded. "They're playing L.A. this weekend."

"Your friend went to see them?"

True grinned. "Honey, Jamie *is* them. Lead singer, songwriter, and guitarist."

She blinked. All the music that had been the background for her work these past weeks ran through her head, all the driving rock, the intricate arrangements, the beautiful lyrics. . .and that voice.

She stared at True. "So you called the lead singer of one of the hottest bands in the country and. . .had him run an errand for you?"

"You can take the boy out of Whiskey River," he said, ending with a shrug.

The last thing Jamie said to her, as her grandparents had handed back his phone, played back in her mind. *Can't wait to meet the woman who finally brought True back to the living. In the meantime, thanks.*

"When their music comes on Zee always seems—" she

began, but stopped when he put up his hands.

"No, thanks. Not my pool to swim in."

So there was something there. She hadn't just imagined those brief moments of stillness whenever a song featuring that voice had come up in the stream.

"How. . .did you. . .did he find them?"

"You told me their names. I took a shot that they lived near the park in your picture, and near the accounting office. Jamie's pretty Internet search savvy, and he found them from that."

That would have given her chills, how easy it had been, had she not been so stunned.

"They made the call from the park, so it would look even more random," he said, as if he'd sensed her thought.

She looked at him then, saw by his watchful expression that he was letting her ramble, talking about everything but what was obviously the most important.

"I don't know what to say to you." Her voice was low, quavered slightly, but she didn't try to hide it. He deserved to hear the emotion, the wonder she was feeling. "What you did was. . .the best thing anybody's ever done for me."

She saw him let out a long breath. "I was afraid you'd be angry."

"I might have been, but there, at the park, with him making the call, on his phone. . .you're right, there's no way on earth anyone would connect him to me."

"Although they might be wondering about your grandparents' taste in music."

She laughed. Actually laughed. "Gramps is more of an oldies guy, but Gran loves keeping up. Says it tickles her to hear what's old become new again. And if I know her, she'll be tracking down his music the minute they get home."

"They sound amazing, Hope."

"They are."

She waited, staring down at the silent phone still in her hands. She knew what she expected him to say. That she should go home to them, that she should never have left them, or even that he'd like to meet them. He said none of it. And finally she looked up at him. What she saw in his face, in his eyes, had their exchange ringing in her head.

I will help you fight this. I will help you do whatever it takes for you to get your life back.

Going to find him and kill him for me?

Don't think it hasn't crossed my mind.

He wouldn't, she knew that bone deep. But that he would even consider it meant. . .she wasn't sure there was a word for the scope of what that meant to her.

I will stand by you if you decide you can't.

She had no doubt anymore of that, either. He would stand by her, live with her decision.

The only doubt she had left was one she thought she had quashed long ago: Could she live with it?

In the space of one phone call everything had changed. And she realized her biggest decision was no longer going back and facing what she'd run from, but accepting what she'd found here.

Someday you'll find a man who will make you feel the way your grandfather makes me feel, Hope. When you do, you grab him and hold on.

Grab him and hold on.

She dropped the phone on the bed. And did just that.

She poured everything she was feeling into every touch, every stroke, every caress. She had them both back to naked in seconds. She was all over him, heedless of the wild thing she had become. She heard him swear once, low and harsh.

"Stop?" she asked.

"God, no," he said reverently, pressing himself against hands that were tracing every line of him. Especially the part she wanted back inside her as soon as she could have it. Which, judging by his already rigid state, would be as soon as she wanted.

She rode him until he was groaning with the pleasure of it, until he was arching upward to drive himself even deeper. She saw the sweat beading up on his skin, that glorious, wonderful skin, saw he was biting his lip. Holding back, she realized. And with a joyous laugh she leaned forward and kissed that lip.

"No holding back," she whispered. "Not for you."

He pulled her down to him then, and arched upward one last time. In that same moment he still thought of her, slipped his hand between them and stroked her just above where they were joined. One touch was all it took and she was with him, crying out his name as his cock surged within her and he echoed her with a guttural, explosive shout of hers.

It was much later, in the quiet hours before dawn, when she felt him wake up beside her, that she raised herself up on one elbow and met his gaze.

"That question I asked you? About whether it's different having sex with someone you love?"

He went very still.

"I know the answer now," she said softly.

Chapter Thirty-Two

Hope watched Kelsey work with the little black horse. The difference between the time she had first met the animal and now seemed astounding. He seemed more than willing as Kelsey rode him in ever tightening circles in the corral. She wondered if riding him bareback was part of her method, maybe establishing a more personal contact between horse and rider. Or maybe he didn't like being saddled and she was working up to it.

Hope leaned forward, resting her arms on the top rail of the fence. The sun was glorious today, after three days of clouds and rains, and she felt as if she were back in California where it was also breaking seventy degrees in January. Even the horse seemed to be enjoying it. Or perhaps he just enjoyed Kelsey's gentle touch.

When the circle got so small the horse was nearly turning in place Kelsey stopped him, laughing, and leaned down to throw her arms around his dark neck.

"Well done, my little Shadow!"

Hope couldn't help but smile as Kelsey rode him toward

her; the horse was practically prancing under her praise.

"If you can do this in just a few days," Hope said, more than a little awe in her tone, "you'll have him doing pirouettes by tomorrow."

Kelsey laughed as she reined in at the fence near where Hope stood. The horse gave a little snort and reached out his nose to her. She patted it, then stroked the velvety muzzle.

"You've come just about as far," Kelsey said as she slid off the animal's bare back.

Hope gave her a startled look. Just how well tuned was the grapevine in this town, anyway?

"I meant with the horses," Kelsey said.

"Oh." Embarrassed, Hope ducked her head.

"Although," Kelsey added, "I hear things have progressed in other areas, too." When Hope didn't—couldn't—meet her gaze, Kelsey went on very softly. "If it helps any, I don't think there's a person in Whiskey River who isn't glad to see it. We all adore True, so we're all thankful to you."

"I. . .thank you."

"You love him, don't you."

Hope's head came up then. It hadn't really been a question, but she answered as if it had been. "Yes. I do." *I don't deserve him, but I do.*

"So you'll be staying?"

Hope looked into the warm expression on the other woman's face. She instinctively liked and trusted her, and fought not to envy her the simplicity of her life. The man she loved had shadows, yes, but they were in the past now, and he'd risen above them. They were building a great life here together, and in the way of good people were trying to help others build one too.

"I—"

"I was just thinking, Zee mentioned the job you were doing for them is pretty much done."

"Yes."

Kelsey smiled. "And done well, she said. Anybody who can earn that from Zee Mahan has proven herself."

The words pleased her immensely; she was still a little wary of True's formidable sister. "Thank you."

"So I was thinking you might be looking for something else to do."

Hope drew back a little, startled. Glanced at the black horse, who then nudged her hand as if looking for something.

Kelsey laughed and dug into her pocket. "Sugar. He's gotten quite spoiled, I'm afraid. Deck is down here sneaking it to him all the time."

"Speaking of people who have come a long way," Hope said as she took the two sugar cubes Kelsey offered her.

"Oh, yes," Kelsey said rather fervently. "He's made great strides. More every day. I'm in awe of him almost as much as I love him." Hope smiled at the soft feel of the horse's muzzle on her palm as he gently took the offered treat. "But that's where you come in."

Hope blinked. Shifted her gaze back to the woman with the blonde ponytail. "What?"

"You know we're developing the outreach program. The kids who come to interest meetings really relate to him, because he's been through a lot of what they have and they instinctively know it. And when we actually start the equine program, bring kids here to interact with the horses, it's going to really get time consuming. And it's already taking up time he needs to spend writing. He's getting behind."

"Well, that can't be allowed," Hope said. "I'm halfway through the third book and already nervous about running out of Sam Smith."

Kelsey laughed delightedly, and Hope couldn't even put a name to the kind of feeling it gave her, to have done that. She felt as if she was groping blindly half the time, trying to find her way even in welcoming Whiskey River. It had been so long since she'd tried to live. . .normally that sometimes she was certain she'd completely lost the knack.

"You're not alone, and the fans are getting restless. So we were thinking. . .maybe you could get involved."

Hope blinked. "What?"

"Look, I don't know exactly what you've been through, but I know it's a lot and it's been rough. Kids can sense when somebody's for real or not. I don't even try, because they can sense I don't have a clue what it's really like to live through what they have."

Hope looked at her curiously. "Happy childhood?"

"The best."

"But your father. . ."

"Yes. But while I had him, he was the best. I've known loss, heartbreak and grief, but that's not in the same universe as having the people you should be able to trust most abandon you, or turn on you. The kids we're trying to help would get that you're not just blowing smoke. You've been there."

"I. . .maybe."

"It's not going to make you rich, but it'll keep you in clothes and sugar cubes," she said with a grin.

A job. It finally got through. Kelsey was offering her a job. A way to stay in Whiskey River without feeling like True was always and ever paying her way.

"I. . .thank you, Kelsey."

"We won't really get started until summer," Kelsey cautioned, "but we'll need a program in place. Zee said you're good at organizing."

She wasn't sure how she felt about being a topic, but was flattered at the assessment at the same time. "But. . .horses," she said. "You know I know nothing."

"You can learn that. In fact, it might even help, if you were learning along with the kids. Besides," Kelsey added as she patted the black horse on the shoulder, "you've already got Shadow's approval. And that's no small feat. And True's," she added, looking over Hope's shoulder, "and you know that's platinum around here."

She didn't need to look to know he was coming up behind her. She'd swear she could feel him, sense him, anytime he was anywhere close. And when he was there she was quivering inside even before he leaned down and pressed his lips to the nape of her neck. It was quick, nothing blatant, but it was a claim as clear as the Texas sky was today.

"Kelsey," True said.

The other woman smiled at him. "I just offered her a job. Convince her to take it, will you? She's perfect for it."

"I'm not much of a replacement for a world-famous author."

"I think those kids care more right now that you'd know where they're coming from," Kelsey said. "Besides, Deck will still be doing the readings out at the house."

Hope looked at her curiously. "Don't you worry about that? Having people at your home, knowing where you live, given he's so famous?"

Kelsey smiled at her. "I might. If we lived in L.A."

For an instant Hope wondered if Kelsey had meant that as a jab. Just as quickly she discarded the idea; Kelsey wasn't the type.

As soon as she thought it she went very still inside. That was twice in a matter of a few minutes that she had discarded the kind of thoughts that had been her constant companion on the run. Twice that she had had those hard-learned warnings pop into her mind and dismissed them as unnecessary here.

Twice she had traded suspicion for trust.

"Speaking of L.A.," Kelsey said, glancing at True, who seemed to hesitate, then nodded. So he knew what Kelsey was going to say. "My mom is an attorney out there. She's not on the criminal side, but she's kind of a big deal at her firm. And they do have criminal attorneys."

Hope's brow furrowed.

"And Lisa Blaine is a force to be reckoned with," True said.

Hope's gaze flicked from him back to Kelsey, who smiled. "I'm just saying, if and if and if, you'd need someone to stand for you, to advise you and protect your interests."

If and if and if.

If you go back.

Her gaze shot to True. He held hers steadily.

"He only told me there was some trouble back there, which I'd already guessed," Kelsey said quickly. "I'm not telling you what to do, only saying that if you decide to go back, my mom's people can help."

Hope took a deep breath, trying to steady herself. Shadow nickered, as if bored now with all the human discussion. With a nod to Hope, Kelsey turned to the horse and swung up—Hope didn't quite see how—onto Shadow's back and headed the horse toward the second corral that held the other rescue horses.

"Does everybody in this town know I'm in trouble?" she muttered.

"They know you have trouble," True corrected. "And as you can see, they want to help."

She wasn't sure how much of it was wanting to help her and how much was simply his standing in Whiskey River, but either way she was the beneficiary. And it was almost overwhelming after all the time spent on the run, suspicious of everyone and everything.

They were back in his truck before he asked, "You going to take the job?"

"I don't know. I need to think." *About a lot of things.*

She was doing just that when she realized they had gone past the turn to the house. In fact, they'd left the entire neighborhood behind and were out in more rural country. Off to the right she could see the glint of sunlight on water, and guessed they must be paralleling the river. And then, on a dirt track she never would have seen had he not turned on it, they were headed toward the river.

He stopped, and she realized they were parked at a bend in the river, a place where the flow slowed to a lazy meander before picking up again further down, over the shelves of limestone. It was a peaceful place, quiet, even the river silent here.

"This is where I come to think," he said quietly.

"I can see why."

"Come on. There's a place to sit down by the water, under the trees."

She'd noticed the stand of trees providing shade. "They

still have leaves."

He nodded. "Anacua. Most people call them knockaway trees. They don't shed leaves until spring."

"They smell wonderful."

"Wait until they flower in a couple of months."

Spring. Would she still be here?

"They don't need to be this close to water, they're pretty drought tolerant," he said. "But they sure seem to like it here."

She came to a halt when she saw the bench under the largest of the multi-trunked trees. She'd seen its twin, under a tree at Kelsey's rescue.

"You built it, didn't you?" He merely shrugged. "Do you dismiss all the amazing things you do as if they were nothing special?"

He gave her a startled look. "I. . ."

"The answer is yes, you do."

"It's just a bench," he said.

"I wasn't," she said quietly, "talking about the bench."

He started to answer, stopped. Gave a shake of his head. She sat down. He sat beside her. She was thankful that he didn't speak as she stared out at the river, fattened by last week's rain, this section looking cool and lazy. There was something about it that did help her think, go through all the tangled thoughts that had piled up in her mind.

She didn't know how long she'd been sitting there when she finally drew a long, deep breath. For a moment she closed her eyes. The image of her grandparents, seen for the first time in so long. . .

Don't write us off so easily. I remember a few things about fighting.

Gramps. He had fought overseas in an Asian war, although he didn't talk about it much, so she tended to forget that sometimes. Had she shortchanged him? Even insulted him by implying he couldn't take care of himself and Gran?

She heard them again, urging her to come home, that wonderful image forming in her mind so clearly she couldn't help but smile. True had given her that, in a way that endangered no one. He'd sent a freaking rock star to do it. And the guy had done it, apparently no questions asked. For True.

I will help you fight this.

And he would. She knew that. But she finally faced what was wrong with that.

When she opened her eyes again she turned to him, saw he'd been watching her. And for a moment she marveled at the steadiness she saw in him, the quiet strength that had been hard won, and had earned him the respect and liking of this entire town.

And he loved her. She felt as if she'd been given some great honor, some award she'd never expected.

In a way, she had.

So now, belatedly, she would earn it. Because the inevitability had finally sunk in.

It was true that this was not his battle to fight.

And yet it was a battle that had to be fought.

There was only one person who could do it. And if she was to ever feel she deserved this life, deserved him, the kind of man he was, she had to at least try. She had to do what he would do.

She had to go back.

Chapter Thirty-Three

SHE WAS GONE.

True stood listening to the silent house that confirmed what he'd known from the moment after he'd awakened to the full light of morning to find himself alone, and had realized all her things, and her worn backpack, were gone.

Still he checked the guest room. He even tried to joke with himself, that maybe he'd started snoring last night and she'd had to retreat.

Nothing. No sign she'd ever been here at all.

It was the thought that had haunted him come to life. He remembered the day when he'd found her shopping list, and had wondered if one day he'd get up and find the house empty, had wondered if she'd even leave a note.

The damned house practically echoed with the emptiness. She'd run again. Nothing he'd done or said had made any difference. What they could have built here, what they already had, hadn't been enough.

He suppressed a shiver. He'd sensed something different

about her since the time they'd spent on the bench by the river. And last night she had been a wild thing, driving him raving mad with her hands, her mouth, her body. She had begged him to take her, then taken him in turn with a passion that had been more consuming than anything he'd ever felt in his life. She'd kindled a blaze that became an inferno, again and again, until he'd at last slipped into an exhausted sleep sometime after midnight.

And now he knew what she'd been doing was saying goodbye.

He'd made how he felt as clear as he could. He'd told her he would stand by her, whatever she decided. Whiskey River had welcomed her, he knew mostly on his say so—which he doubted now would ever be quite so solid. She'd had their love, a chance at a life, even a job thanks to Kelsey's generosity. And it still hadn't been enough to keep her from running.

He hadn't been enough. Just as he hadn't been enough to beat back the evil that had taken Amanda.

He sank down on the guest room bed. Rubbed a hand over his eyes. He couldn't do this again. He felt as he had in those exhausting last days of Amanda's illness, as if he couldn't possibly take another step. And suddenly he was the one who wanted to run. Except that he knew no matter how far he went, there would be no escape.

He didn't have the strength anyway. He barely had the energy to go downstairs. And once he was down, he wanted nothing more than to go back up, because the first thing he saw was the door to Zee's place.

He'd have to tell her. Her, and Kelsey, and. . .everyone. And he didn't know how to do it. He didn't—

He saw something out of the corner of his eye. Turned his head. A note, on the granite of the kitchen counter. Right where she'd left that shopping list on that day he'd just been thinking about.

It took everything he had in him to cross those few feet of kitchen floor. He reached for the note—he could see the writing, knew it was hers—and then yanked his hand back.

Not looking won't change it. And it won't bring her back.

Thinking he already knew what it would say, he finally picked it up.

True—

I love you.

What I did was the only path I could see, and I've never slowed down long enough to search for another. I've stayed that terrified teenager, doing the only thing she thought she could to protect the only people who had ever loved her. Run. And keep running.

You've given me a taste of a life I never, ever hoped to have. But being with you, seeing who you are, has taught me one thing above all else: the only way to deal with a nightmare is to face it in the light of day. Like you do, every day of your life. And for that lesson I will be forever thankful. Just please, please be aware and stay safe, just in case. I could not bear anything happening to you because of me.

I love you more than I can express. And I am humbled that you love me. But I can't live with this feeling that I don't deserve a man like you if I can't face my own life. But maybe, someday. . .

I will dare to believe in my name, thanks to you.

Hope

For a long moment he just stared at the page. What the hell did she mean? What was she going to do?

He was sitting there at the counter an hour later when Zee knocked on the inside door. He'd made coffee, going through the motions by rote, thinking maybe the caffeine would jolt him out of this fog. So far, it hadn't.

"Hey," his sister's voice came from the doorway as, getting no answer, she pushed it open. Came in a few steps. "Are you up? I've been—"

She stopped suddenly.

"Dear God," he heard her whisper, and then she was beside him, looking up into his face in shocked concern.

He gave his head a sharp shake. "Let me guess. I look like hell."

"Worse," she said. "What happened?"

He couldn't even begin to tell her, so he just handed her Hope's note. She read it quickly, then looked back at him.

"She's. . .gone?"

He nodded.

"All her things?"

He repeated the motion.

"Where?"

He shifted his gaze to the note, the damned note he'd read a dozen times already. "You know what I know. I woke up to that."

Zee looked back at the paper. "Face it," she murmured. "She talks about facing it. . ."

"And that she can't face her own life."

"But maybe she means—"

"Stop, Zee. Do you think I haven't turned that thing inside out, looking for all the possibilities? The bottom line never changes. She's gone."

"No."

He blinked. "The bottom line," his sister said firmly, "is that she loves you."

"I believed that."

Zee straightened, put her hands on his shoulders, making him look at her. "Just stay here. I'm going to make some calls."

He couldn't see the point. "To who? Why?"

"Because it's what I do. Don't go anywhere."

When she'd gone he got up, then couldn't remember why. So he wandered into the living room. And a moment later he was sitting in the spot Hope had claimed—and where she'd left Deck's last book.

The bookmark was about halfway through. She'd never finished it. And suddenly that seemed symbolic of the whole damned thing. He groaned, and let his head loll back.

He had no idea how much time had passed, but Zee was back.

"Wake up, Bro!"

"Not asleep." He might never sleep again.

"I know where she went."

His eyes snapped open. "What?"

"Charlie gave her a ride. Said he ran into her in town early this morning, just as he was leaving to make a delivery out to Cedar Valley. She asked for a ride."

"What the hell is in Cedar Valley?"

Zee waved him off. "Doesn't matter. Because he said he took her a little further when he found out she was going to hitchhike."

His stomach knotted. He was sitting up straight now. "How much further?"

"The wildflower center. He dropped her off where the buses come in."

"Did he freaking bother to ask her why she was leaving?" True snapped.

"He did. She wouldn't say anything except that it was for the best."

"For the best," he muttered. "That's just—"

His cell rang. He nearly jumped for it, even knowing Hope didn't have a phone. Maybe she borrowed one, maybe—

It was Jack.

"True?"

"Yeah."

"Nice job."

He knew he'd been a step behind all morning, but now it seemed the distance was widening. "What?"

"Talking your girl into testifying."

For a moment he couldn't even breathe, let alone speak. "What?" he finally managed.

"My cousin just called, saying the D.A.'s office is scrambling like mad. She completely bowled them over, calling like that and telling them to come get her, she'd testify."

He only realized he hadn't responded when Jack said, with some concern, "True? You okay?"

"I. . .will be."

"You didn't know, did you."

It wasn't really a question. But then Jack Ducane was a sharp guy.

"No." Then, as if a switch had been flipped, his brain snapped back on. "Where are they supposed to pick her up? When?"

"Well, that's the other reason I called. My cousin heard them panicking about getting somebody to her quickly, at the airport in Austin, before she vanished again. They want her under watch until they can get people assigned and a flight arranged, but Austin PD is working a situation and their ETA would be over an hour. So he told them I could be there in fifteen minutes. They didn't like it, but they agreed."

True realized he was on his feet. Zee was staring at him.

"Do, it Jack. Please. I'll be on my way."

"I was thinking I should make a couple of calls, about who should be going where, under the circumstances."

"Thanks," True said, meaning it. "And call your cousin. Make sure there's a watch on her grandparents."

"Already in place. That was her first condition, my cousin said. That if anything happened to them the deal was off."

True was smiling now. *Good girl!*

"Anything else?" The amusement in Jack's voice told him he'd been giving orders like it was his right. But damn it, when it came to Hope, he claimed the right.

"Go easy on her," he said, his voice rough. "This took every bit of nerve she's got."

"I'll treat her like a spring lamb."

"And. . .tell her I love her."

There was a moment's pause before Jack said, in a clearly heartfelt tone, "Now that will be a pleasure, my friend."

They ended the call. Zee was staring at him. "She's going back, isn't she?" she whispered. "To testify?"

He nodded.

Zee's smile was brilliant. "Good for her!"

"No more running," True said, still processing.

"And now this makes sense," Zee said, holding up the note.

"What?"

"Don't you get it, Bro? Why she's going back to do what

she knows you would do?" His brow furrowed. Zee shook her head at him, but she was still smiling. "She's doing it so she can come back knowing she deserves you."

He stared at her. "You got that out of—" he gestured at the note "—that?"

She rolled her eyes at him. "Holy bluebonnets, for a smart guy you can be thick. I'll explain later. We need to hit the road."

✪

HOPE SAT NEAR a coffee kiosk on the public side of the airport check in counters. Once she'd made the call to Los Angeles, she felt. . .stranger than she'd ever felt in her life. Terrified, yes. But also lighter. Freer.

She had a magazine in her hands, one that someone had abandoned. It gave her something to look at, so she wasn't constantly scanning the crowd like some sort of paranoid person. Besides, she was likely going to be here for several more hours. From the monitors it was clear it was a three hour flight from L.A., and they likely wouldn't have it all together even now, an hour after she'd called.

A tall, rangy man in a cowboy hat pulled a chair from the table next to hers and swung it around to sit next to her. Her heart slammed into her chest. Could they really have found her that quickly? The DA's office had assured her she would be safe, that no one had any idea where she was.

Until you just told them. And now—

"I'm Jack Ducane, Hope," the man said in a low key, very pleasant voice. "And True Mahan sent me to tell you he loves you."

✪

THINGS WERE CHANGING so fast Hope was nearly dizzy with it. But Jack Ducane was a steady, calming presence, and when he said he was here in part to make sure she was treated right, because "sometimes those L.A. folks forget their manners," she actually smiled.

He explained to her what would likely happen now, that there would be detailed interviews, further delay while an arrest warrant was prepared and executed, and once a trial date was set she was looking at some long days of trial preparation before she actually had to testify.

He also explained there had been a change of plans. "You're a very high value witness to those West Coast people. As such, you hold all the cards. And I don't think you need to be going back there just yet. They can come here to do the prep work."

"Will they?"

"They saw the wisdom of keeping you under wraps here, once it was explained to them. If you go flying into the media pit of L.A., there's no way they can keep you secret. Not these days."

One look at the man's steady gray eyes told her who had likely done the explaining.

"And the longer I'm under wraps, the safer my grandparents are?"

"Yes. I know you want to see them—"

"I want them safe," she interrupted.

He nodded, as if he'd expected nothing less. Then he gave her a nod and a smile. "It takes guts, to do what you're doing."

"It took me too long to find those guts," she said regretfully. Then, softly she added, knowing he knew True, "But I've had a stellar example the last few weeks."

"Yes. One of the best. And speaking of the man, I think it would be nice if you said hello."

She blinked. Then realized Jack was looking past her, over her shoulder. She turned.

True. Moving toward her with that long-limbed easy grace, focused on her as if she were the only person in this busy place.

And then she was in his arms, and he was whispering to her.

"I'm so proud of you, Hope."

"I needed to. . ." She wasn't sure what to say.

"I understand. And you did the hard part. You made the decision and you followed through. But you don't have to do the rest alone."

And her topsy-turvy world suddenly righted itself.

Chapter Thirty-Four

"HAPPY ST. PATRICK'S Day," True said, gesturing ahead as he maneuvered around the corner of a large, metal building.

Hope smiled at him before she looked; she'd been smiling a lot in the last two months. And even the sometimes brutal preparation for the trial hadn't taken that away from her. But now she looked where he'd indicated.

Hope stared at the sleek little jet parked some yards away. She hadn't even realized Whiskey River had an airfield, although True had explained it wasn't the city's per se, it was a private field outside the city limits, but it was used by any locals who had the need, and several private planes were hangared here. He'd also explained the name by pointing out the rock formation visible from the end of the runway; it was quite clear how the place had come to be named Devil's Rock Airfield.

"So it showed up," Zee said from the back seat, staring at the little jet.

"He said he'd get it here," True answered mildly as he

slowed down.

"He also said this was home, that Whiskey River would always be in his blood."

"I'm not sure song lyrics are for literal interpretation."

Hope's breath caught. True had said they had a sweet ride, but. . .did that mean this indeed sweet little jet was Jamie's? And he'd had it flown all the way here to pick them up? She opened her mouth to ask but stopped when she saw Zee giving her brother a sour look.

True drove past a spot where some construction was going on, then stopped and parked near the nearest hangar. They got out and walked to the back of the vehicle for their bags. And once more Hope looked at Zee.

"I really appreciate you coming," she said.

"Start as you mean to go on," Zee said. Hope gave her a puzzled look. In turn Zee gave her a beautiful smile. "You're going to be around. Besides, True loves you. I'd do it just for that, but as it happens I like you quite a bit myself."

"I. . .thank you." She managed a smile. "I think I'd like you even more than I do if I wasn't in such awe."

Zee laughed, her sour mood obviously forgotten. "You'll get over it."

"I don't know. I'm pretty much in awe of both Mahans."

True came up behind her, slipped his arms around her. "You know what I can't wait for? The first day you get screaming mad at me, and let it out. Then I'll know you feel safe."

Hope's breath caught at the words. She looked at Zee, who was smiling now, a soft, happy sort of smile, aimed at her brother. She shifted her gaze back to True.

"I rest my case," she said softly. "Awe is definitely the word."

"Hey, guys!"

Hope turned to see Kelsey waving from the window of the pickup that had just pulled in behind them. The battered red truck was hardly what she would have expected the fiancée of a world-famous writer to drive, but Kelsey had told her that truck had a special place in both their hearts, and they would keep it forever. Startled, she waved back. To her further surprise, Deck was in the passenger seat. And he laughed when he saw Hope's expression.

"She does most of the driving. I tend to get lost in my head and have to double back a lot."

Hope laughed. "I was just surprised to see you."

"Thought we were going to be late?" Kelsey asked as she came over and put her arm around Hope's shoulders in a half hug.

Only then did she realize Deck was unloading two bags from the back of their truck. She stared at Kelsey. "You're coming with us?"

"Absolutely. My mom's going to meet us on the other end, with one of her law partners. She swears he's the best, he'll be your buffer, deal with the media, all that."

Hope swallowed. "Media?" She'd kind of forgotten

about that aspect of this whole trial of the year thing.

Deck came up beside Kelsey. "Mom says you're the story of the moment out there. Runaway witness to gang executions, with cartel connections, makes for great copy."

Hope knew just enough of Deck's history now to know what a small miracle his easy use of the term "Mom" was. But it wasn't enough to distract her from what he'd said; this she hadn't expected either. She'd gotten to know both of this pair well enough to know going public still wasn't easy for him.

Kelsey grinned. "Deck's going as a distraction. Once they get wind he's there on your side, Mom says the whole tenor will change."

Hope was still gaping as Deck gave her a hug as well. "You'll get through it," he said.

She pulled back and looked at him. "Don't think I don't know this is a big deal for you."

Deck gave her the smile she'd seen more often as he'd gotten to know her. "I'm just glad they took the guy down easily."

"He got cocky," Zee said. "Thought he'd skated."

Because the prosecution couldn't find their only witness, Hope thought, still having a bit of trouble accepting that it was all going to come to an end one way or another.

Another car arrived. Hope recognized this one.

"Jack is coming, too?" she asked, her shock growing.

"He's your official escort. He got it cleared yesterday,

since he's back on full duty." True smiled. "Took some selling to L. A., but he's a pretty persuasive guy when he needs to be, plus it saved them two or three plane tickets. And he figured a Texas Ranger in uniform on your side couldn't hurt. *One riot, one Ranger* isn't just a motto."

She watched the tall, broad shouldered man with the gray eyes that looked as if they were used to looking out over long distances, get out of the truck. He was indeed in the traditional non-uniform, including a tan cowboy hat, and the circled star on his chest, images from legend.

She was glad he was fully recovered; he was the kind of law enforcement the world needed. She had spent a lot of time with him since the court date had been set, and, with the LAPD detective and assistant district attorney that had flown out, they'd worked hard toward this day. Jack had made sure they handled her politely, even as they came at her as hard as the defense likely would. By the time they were done, they had a full picture and a plan.

"They've put at least half of that gang away," Jack had told her, "and they think taking out this guy will break the back of the cartel's local operation, at least for a while. They'll have to rebuild, with new people, and with him already in prison they won't have the time or the dedication or care enough to come after you."

"I'm glad it's you," she said now, rather fervently.

He smiled at her. It was a good smile, not tight with pain as it had once been, and she was glad of that. "I want a word with this clownhat anyway," Jack told her. "The Rangers have a lot of pull even outside of Texas. I want it clear to him I can make his life even more miserable on the inside if he so much as sends you a birthday card."

"Helps to be part of a legend," True said with a grin.

Hope was just realizing she was going to lose the battle against the tears welling up when the door to the jet opened. Or hatch. Whatever they called it. A lean, lithe figure appeared, grabbed the stair rails and slid down, foregoing the steps altogether. The motion lifted his sandy blond hair, already tousled, and put a grin on his face.

She heard Zee gasp.

"Well, now," True drawled. "I didn't expect him to come with it."

Hope recognized him then. The face from the phone. The rock star who ran errands for an old friend.

He ran toward them, slammed into True full tilt.

"Still solid, I see," he said with a laugh as he bounced back and True barely swayed.

"As a rock," Hope whispered.

The man looked at her then. "Ah. Hope." He gave her one of the most amazing smiles she'd ever seen. And his eyes really were that vivid. "Good to meet you in the flesh."

"You, too. That call, I can't thank you enough, Mr. Templeton—"

"Jamie. It's gonna be a long flight if you insist on that mister stuff," he said with a laugh. "Besides, I really like your gran. She fed me cookies."

Charm, she thought, rather numbly. It fairly oozed from the guy. Along with that charisma. No wonder a small town like Whiskey River couldn't hold him. She wasn't sure even L.A. could hold him.

Only then did he look at Zee. But by then she was busily organizing everyone's bags and barely spared him a glance.

"She's still ticked at me I see," Jamie said.

"Do not," True said firmly, "even try to get me to the edge of that event horizon."

"Yeah. Well."

"Meet Kelsey Blaine, our horse rescuer. And her fiancé, Declan Kilcoyne."

He was leaving it to them whether to reveal Deck's alter ego, Hope realized.

"I talked to your mom, told her where to meet the jet," Jamie said to Kelsey. "She's really something."

Kelsey grinned. "And then some."

"She seems to think me hanging in the background couldn't hurt, so here I am."

"She recruited you, too, huh?" Kelsey glanced at Deck, her grin widening. "The both of you? That ought to do it."

Deck gave a wry shake of his head. "Let's hope. For Hope's sake."

Kelsey turned back to Jamie, whose brow was furrowed with curiosity. "My fiancé has a pen name," she said.

"Oh?"

"Declan Bolt," Deck said with a shrug.

Jamie's eyes widened. "Whoa." And then he grinned. It was obviously genuine, yet lacked none of the charm—or charisma—of the more practiced one. "Wow. I love your stuff."

Deck grinned, too. "Back at you."

And suddenly it was all too much for Hope. She'd been surprised enough that Zee was coming, but now she was about to get on a private jet owned by a rock star, accompanied by a woman who had called in her powerful attorney mother for help, a world-famous author, a Texas Ranger, and above all the man she loved so completely it sometimes frightened her. And when they arrived in L. A. they all planned to stand beside her as she faced down what she'd run from so long ago.

She was overwhelmed. True, being True, sensed it immediately and ushered her aboard the small plane. She was barely aware of what happened then, of their luggage being loaded below, and the others boarding and chatting as they looked around the slick little craft.

It was arranged more like a cozy den than an airplane interior, and even as dumfounded as she was she didn't miss the three guitars on a rack on a back wall. Or bulkhead. Whatever it was on a plane. But there were no signs of what else she might have expected on a rock band's plane, no trashed furnishings or drug debris or whatever else her wild imaginings could conjure up. So either it had been cleaned up, or Jamie ran a tight ship. But not nearly as tight as Zee's expression as she carefully avoided him, clearly not caring if it was obvious.

Hope ended up sitting with True on one side of her, Jack Ducane on the other.

"Those two still as friendly as a pair of rattlesnakes I see," Jack said.

True rolled his eyes. Hope looked at him, and he gave her a wry grimace. "Not my story to tell."

"And that," Jack said to Hope with a laugh, "is why everybody in Whiskey River and beyond trusts him."

She smiled. "I certainly do."

True said nothing, but he reached for her hand, she knew he'd understood the full depth of her words. She had come a long way in the last two months, but she thought she'd come even further in that first two weeks.

Hope had never flown on a plane like this, and the takeoff was enough to distract her for the moment from the chaos in her mind. But once they'd leveled off—far above the maximum altitude of commercial flights, Jamie told them—it all came flooding back. She couldn't quite believe she was really doing this, the thing she'd run so hard and far to avoid. She didn't realize she'd tightened her grip on True's hand until he squeezed it back.

"It will be all right," he said softly in her ear. "And if it's not, we'll deal. And if it ever comes back on you, we'll deal with that, too. Together."

She looked up at him. “I love you, Truett Mahan.”

The smile he gave her then did more to clear her turmoil than anything else could. “I love you, too.”

“I think you just said that already.”

And then he kissed her, not caring there was a plane full of people. And the moment his mouth came down on hers, she didn’t care either.

Chapter Thirty-Five

"WOW. NICE."

Hope could not argue with Zee's assessment as the big black SUV with the dark tinted windows made the turn toward an obviously multi-star hotel.

She had liked their driver, Lisa Blaine, from the moment she had introduced herself as Kelsey—and Deck's—mom rather than the high-power attorney she was. She had glanced from her to Kelsey and back; the resemblance was profound.

"Lucky guy, aren't I?" Deck had whispered in her ear, then climbed into the very back seat, along with Zee, so that Kelsey could sit with her mom up front. That left her and True and Jamie the middle seats since Jack had taken himself off to check in with the locals as a matter of protocol, and would meet them at the hotel later.

They pulled to a stop in front of the building. The phalanx of police, uniformed and not, startled Hope.

"You're worth the case to them," Lisa said. "And that," she added when Hope focused on a tall, dark-haired man in a perfectly cut dark-blue suit, "is the guy who will make sure they treat you properly."

Hope didn't doubt it. He had the look of power and control. Handsome, but more. Regal, she thought.

"Diego Culhane," Jamie said in obvious surprise.

Lisa glanced at him. "Yes. You know him?"

Jamie gave her a wry smile, and his head turned slightly, as if he were flicking a glance at the back seat before he answered. "Afraid so."

Zee didn't make a sound, but Hope could almost feel her react. As if she weren't at all surprised that Jamie had needed the services of the man Lisa said was one of the best and most sought out criminal defense attorneys in the city.

"Who's paying for him?" Hope asked ruefully.

"No one," Lisa said cheerfully. "He owes me."

That had to be a story, Hope thought as True got out of the vehicle and waited for her. The next few minutes were a blur as she was hustled inside. Not to the registration desk but straight to the elevators. There wasn't even time for Jamie or Deck to be recognized, although the rocker got a few glances as they swept through the lobby.

The ride ended on the fifteenth floor, the walk at the double doors to a suite labeled 1500. She'd never even set foot in a place like this, and now she was going to stay here? She'd had in her mind she'd be at her grandparents' house, at least until Jack Ducane had pointed out that might not be the safest for all concerned until this was over. That had brought all her fears flowing back. But she'd decided to take her life back, and she wasn't going to wobble at the first hint it wasn't going to be easy.

So she had agreed to let the experts handle it, but she had never expected anything like this. But then every other part of her life had been turned around, why not this? She was beyond anxious to see Gran and Gramps, but this was a heck of a distraction.

At the doors, Culhane again spoke to their escort, who nodded and took up positions outside and back by the elevators. It made Hope shiver.

"Sorry," she muttered when Culhane noticed. "I'm the one who decided to do this, so I have no right to gripe now."

"Oh, but you have every right," Culhane said. "And advantage. Without you, there is no case and they know it."

"And right now," Lisa said with a wide smile, "this is much, much more important."

She tapped on the door, then stepped back. Hope realized she was letting whoever was in the room see her through the peephole. She frowned, she hadn't realized there would be police already inside. She told herself to get used to it, this would be her life for the next few days.

The door was pulled open.

Not by the police.

Her grandparents.

TRUE THOUGHT HE'D never seen anything quite like the transformation that had come over Hope when she'd opened that door. As much as he'd known, he realized now he'd never fully understood how the life she'd undertaken to protect these two had drained her. In the past couple of months she'd been so much happier—since the night they'd given in to the attraction between them, in fact, and if that was a bit full of male smugness so be it, he thought. But now she was joyous, and it fairly glowed from her.

Gordon and Lynn Larson seemed to take the entourage in stride. They already knew Kelsey's mom, who was every bit the powerhouse Kelsey had said she was and had organized everything on this end. Although he did wonder if she was maybe twelve when she'd had Kelsey.

They also greeted Jamie like family, still thanking him for that phone call. And Lynn teased him that they'd looked up his music and were now probably his oldest fans.

"You mean our most honored fans," Jamie corrected with a smile. And even Zee smiled at that.

Zee herself got hugs and thanks for her help. And True thought she'd overheard when Culhane had looked Jamie up and down and asked, "Staying out of trouble?" and Jamie had answered, very respectfully and seriously, "Yes, sir."

For a moment, after Jamie had excused himself for a meeting with a venue owner, True had thought Zee might corner the man and ask what he'd represented him for, but then realized she wouldn't because she probably already knew. For one who said she'd washed her hands of her one-time crush, she certainly kept tabs on him.

There was a break in the buzz of introductions when Jack arrived, announcing he'd successfully convinced LAPD he would be Ms. Larson's personal escort here, and that while welcome, they were to leave the final decisions about her welfare to him. Such was the weight of the Texas Ranger reputation that they hadn't quibbled much. And both Hope's grandparents took in the imposing man—and that famous star on his chest—with obvious approval.

And then, inevitably, they turned to True. Saving the grilling for last? He didn't blame them. In fact not only expected it, but would have been disappointed had they not.

"I don't have to ask who you are," Lynn said. "You're just as Hope described you."

Her grandfather studied him for a long moment before speaking. "I'm told your name suits you. And that if not for you, our girl would still be running."

"Not to mention he was able to put together—" Hope gestured at the people in the living room of what was clearly a large suite "—all this, because somewhere along the line he's helped almost every one of them."

"You called in the troops for our girl?"

True took a deep breath. He knew what this was, that he was being judged by the only people who had truly loved Hope.

"Yes," he said simply. "And I'll do it again, and more, if

necessary."

He saw approval and, he thought, relief in the older man's eyes. But he only nodded and said rather gruffly, "Good."

He noticed that Zee, after a whispered chat with Lisa Blaine, had disappeared for a few minutes. That was explained a short while later when room service arrived with a table full of various things to sample. The whole thing took on the atmosphere of a party, for which he was very thankful. For the moment Hope's worries were vanquished, and he couldn't help watching her practically every minute, savoring the change in her, the new lightness. It filled him with a sort of satisfaction he wasn't sure he'd ever felt before, to know that he'd had a big part in that.

The reason they were here came up only briefly. Hope had finally asked, and Lisa had explained. "You'll need to meet with the D.A., and go over your testimony a final time. And I'll take you by the courtroom later, after hours, so it won't be totally strange to you when they call you."

Lisa Blaine looked over at Diego Culhane, who had unbent enough to be chatting amiably with her grandfather. "He will be there every step of the way for you. There's no one better at being a barricade than he is. He's withstood the worst, more than even this case will throw at you. And he came up on those streets, he's known, respected, and if he's seen on your side it will mean something to those gangsters."

Hope was staring at the man, and True guessed she was

comparing the elegant, polished attorney to the people she'd, for that brief time, risked her life with. After a moment she slowly shook her head.

"All of you," she whispered. "I don't know what to say."

"You don't need to say anything," True told her.

"But I got myself into this—"

"Trying to help someone else," Lisa said briskly. "And that's something a lot of us in this room understand completely."

True could have kissed Kelsey's mom for that. And a while later, after he'd heard Hope laugh, the sound of it echoing with the joy that shone in her face as she sat between her grandparents, he did.

✪

HOPE NOW KNEW the true meaning of the phrase "media circus," and from the inside. It had been horrifying the first day, but now, after a week, it was actually amusing.

"Insects," she had muttered that first day outside the courtroom when they'd encountered a seeming wall of them. "Swarming."

"Cockroaches in particular," True suggested.

But now it was almost fun to watch them try to decide who to focus on. They'd had no luck getting past Diego Culhane, so they'd almost given up on her. But she suspected they weren't trying as hard as they normally would once they realized her entourage—she'd nearly broken down in hysterical laughter the first time she'd heard that word used—included the front man from Scorpions On Top, and world-famous but rarely seen outside of Texas children's author Declan Bolt.

"They're in a quandary," Jamie said as they headed in today. "They want to think I'm here promoting a tour, except we don't go back out for another two months. They want to think Deck's promoting a book, except his newest is two months old and he doesn't, anyway."

"All of which keeps them off me, and I can't thank you enough for that," she said.

Deck and Jamie linked arms and grinned at her. "That's us, the united front."

Hope smiled back; the two men she would have said could not be more different had hit it off. Perhaps it was the brotherhood of fame. Whatever the reason she was glad, because she spotted Kelsey watching them with tears in her eyes.

She made her way over to her. "It's wonderful to see how much joy watching them brings you."

Kelsey nodded, and her mother, standing beside her, put an arm around her. Lisa Blaine was everything Kelsey had said and more, but where once she would have felt envious, now her own lack of that kind of parental bond meant less than nothing. Because she had so much more now. Including her grandparents back.

She felt a little bit like the eye of a hurricane, with the wind of the others' passage swirling around her. Kelsey and Deck went home with Lisa at night, and she was glad her situation had given them that time to be together. Jamie only dropped in to see how things were going, but promised he would be there the day she had to face the lions, as he put it. And Diego presented himself promptly every morning, ready to answer any questions or, if she wanted to venture out, to accompany her and fend off any media outside the hotel. The presence of her supporters had, he said, made this even higher profile than it would have been, but in the long run it would likely put the seal on her and her family's safety, so best to accept and deal. And of course True was ever and always there, her bulwark, her guardian, her support.

And that night he made love to her with such exquisite care she melted, feeling utterly boneless. And in the morning, when she awoke feeling nervous because today was the day, he nibbled on her ear and suggested she take out those nerves on him. The words, and the way he stroked his hands over her body sparked a wild need in her, and she practically attacked him.

In the moment before she hit the peak, that soaring peak she'd only ever known with him, he'd whispered, "Think of this today. Only this."

By the time it was time to go, she was sated, calm, and confident. She didn't fear the moment when she would be called as the prosecution's star witness. Diego had warned her of what they would throw at her, things the D.A.'s office likely hadn't even thought of, trying to discredit her. But somehow making the decision to face it had wiped away the fear. She was tense, but not afraid. And when it happened in the courtroom she hadn't been surprised, or even angry. She had a small army of sorts at her back, who all thought she was worthy of their support, and who she would do anything for in return.

And she had the love of a steady, straight-arrow, impossibly strong man, who was an excellent judge of character and had seen something in her she hadn't even known existed. And from that place deep inside she found the courage and determination to get through her testimony.

The district attorney was a brusque, take-no-nonsense woman who obviously knew her stuff. In a way she reminded Hope of Diego, and when she had seen the two deep in conversation before things started, she had asked Lisa, "Isn't that sort of like consorting with the enemy for him?"

Kelsey's mom laughed. "For both of them. But they respect each other. And she knows no one is better than Diego Culhane at making a witness appear a certain way in front of a jury, so if she's as smart as I think she is, she'll listen."

And in the end, it all came together. Her testimony was simple but resolute, and thanks to them all, unshakeable.

I tried to help a friend. I made a poor decision on how to do it. And because of that I was there to witness two brutal crimes, including the murder of my best friend. Two cold-blooded executions committed by the defendant. Who then tried to kill me, too.

That was the bottom line, and no matter how the opposition tried, it never changed. She couldn't help the emotions that showed through, and Diego had told her that was a good thing. But she did not break down as she'd feared. She took everything she'd learned—not just from Jack and Diego and Lisa Blaine, but from True, and she stood her ground.

Even the story of how—and especially why—she had run played to her credit, with her grandparents sitting there in the courtroom, doing their best to look fragile and helpless when in fact they were anything but. They were surrounded by the rest of the entourage, and Hope knew Lisa Blaine had been exactly right; this case had become so high-profile because of Deck and Jamie that the police agreed what was left of the gang would never dare to strike at her or her family.

When the guilty verdict came back, she felt the last of a dark cloud lifting, and a lightness that fairly made her giddy. The night vanished into a swirl of celebration and laughter, and she was practically bubbling over with love for all these people who had banded together like a small army to help her through this.

Because of True. The one she loved most of all, in a way she'd never thought possible, never thought she would ever experience. She tried to show it to him that night, using words and hands and mouth and body until he lay, exhausted, but smiling.

"Darlin' if you're trying to kill me, you sure picked the way I'd want to go," he drawled into the darkness just before dawn.

"I'm trying to say I love you."

"Believe me, I got that a while back." He reached for her, pulled her close. "You know I love you, don't you?"

She couldn't stop her grin. "Believe me, I got that a while back."

She felt his laugh, that wonderful laugh, rumbling up from his chest before she heard it. She settled against him, listening to the strong, steady beat of that heart that she knew was as constant as his name.

Later, after they'd slept for a while and the room was beginning to lighten, she sighed. "I can't believe I wasted all that time running when I didn't really have to."

True went very still beside her. "I'm glad you did. If you hadn't, we'd have never met."

She hadn't thought of that. But then that's what True did, made her think of things differently. She lifted up on one elbow to look at him.

"You're right."

"I'd say you ran just far enough."

She sighed again, but it was a happy one this time. And she put her head back on his chest. "And I can't wait to get back."

It was a moment before True said, "You mean that?"

She gave him a puzzled look. "Of course."

"I just. . .we haven't really talked about what happens now. What you want to do."

"Go home," she said simply.

He let out a long breath that sounded relieved. "I'm glad it's home to you."

She raised up once more, glad that it was light enough now that he could not mistake her expression. "Home to me," she said seriously, "is wherever you are."

He grabbed her then, held her so tight she could barely breathe, but she didn't care. Then words tumbled out of him so rapidly she knew he'd been carrying them for a while.

"Marry me, Hope. Not right now, if you don't want, I know this isn't the best time, you need to settle after all this, and get caught up with your grandparents, and get used to not being afraid anymore, but later—"

She cut off the flow with a finger to his lips. "You said you would help me take my life back. You have. So it's mine again. And now. . .I give it to you."

Epilogue

TRUE WAS NOT sorry to leave the circus behind. It had died down after the trial had ended, although it had taken a couple of days, but it seemed everyone wanted Hope's story. True understood why, it was an emotional, dramatic tale, and the addition of Jamie and Deck made it irresistible. But he'd been relieved when she'd said she wanted to get away from it.

They'd spent a couple of days at her grandparents' tidy suburban home, because he'd wanted to see where she'd grown up. And, he'd told her, talk to her grandfather. When she'd realized what he'd meant, she'd smiled broadly.

"Oh, he'll love that. He's kind of old school."

"I got that idea, when it comes to you. So I'll ask his permission."

"It's beyond corny, but so sweet I can hardly stand it," she'd said.

"Not," he said pointedly, "that I'm going to take no for an answer."

"He won't say no," Hope said with a smile bordering on

smug. "Gran won't let him. She thinks you're too hot to pass up."

He grinned. She sighed happily. She'd been doing a lot of that lately, and every time it made him feel good inside in a way he couldn't put words to.

Gramps hadn't said no, had only smiled widely and said, "Well, son, that's the smallest surprise I've ever heard. But thanks for humoring an old man."

He'd glanced at Hope, then said impulsively, "Come back with us now. You should see where she'll be."

"Do come," Hope chimed in, "I want you to see why." She grinned before adding, "Besides, when will you get a chance to fly on a private jet again?"

And so, after a few days where Hope went off on various errands, sometimes with Zee, sometimes with Kelsey and Lisa, sometimes the four of them together, and one semi-mysterious one alone, reclaiming her life, here they were, finally headed home. And after showing her slightly nervous grandparents around the jet, she settled in beside him for the flight.

He watched the older couple, smiling as they looked excitedly out the window of the jet as they took off. He reached for Hope's hand, noticed again the edge of the bandage on her wrist. The mysterious errand she hadn't been able to keep secret because of the care it would take afterward; she had, she'd said, done something about the tattoo. He wouldn't have minded if she'd kept it, in a way it reminded him of what she'd gone through to protect this loving couple. But it was her wrist, not his, and her decision.

"I think it's great, how Deck and Jamie hit it off," she said.

Since Kelsey and Deck had decided to stay with her mom a bit longer and Jamie was based here, the two men had been spending a lot of time together to escape the copious wedding shopping.

"I'm not sure if being seen hanging out together will destroy Deck's reputation or improve Jamie's," True said dryly.

She laughed. Genuine, carefree. He couldn't think of anything to say, his heart was suddenly too full of the love he felt for this woman. And then Jack saved him, getting up now that they'd leveled off and coming to sit opposite them.

"They're good people," he said, nodding toward her grandparents.

"The best," Hope said.

"They did right by you," he said.

"I would have been totally lost without them. I made my mistakes—" she paused and glanced at True "—I know, I'm putting it behind me, but it still matters that none of it was their fault."

"In a way it was," True said. Hope drew back, startled. He squeezed her hand as he went on. "They're the ones who taught you how to care enough about a friend to even try to help."

She smiled, closed her eyes for a moment, as if in

memory. "Yes," she said softly. "Yes, they did." Her gaze shifted to the couple at the jet's window. "I have the best parents and grandparents in the world."

"Yes," True said, then gave her a wink. "I hope you'll share, though."

"With you? Anything. Everything."

"And I," Jack said with an exaggerated cough next to them, "will go back to my magazine and pretend I can't see you two making out. Again."

True would have laughed, but he was too busy doing exactly that.

AT LAST THEY were home. Zee had announced that breakfast was at her place in the morning, before heading through the connecting door. Her grandparents were settled in the guest room that had once been hers, admittedly weary after not just the trip and the welcome but the trial, ready to rest before venturing out to see the town that had accepted Hope so warmly.

In the quiet aftermath, Hope paused before the photograph of Amanda Mahan. And instead of feeling wistful, she smiled at the image. "I understand now, how you felt. I will be good to him, I promise."

And then Hope found herself standing in True's bedroom—their bedroom now—a little at a loss. He came up behind her and slipped his arms around her.

"It's all right," he said. "The next few days you'll be busy, catching up with them, showing them around. It's after that the crash will come, when you finally realize it's really all over."

"It is, isn't it?"

"Yes."

She sighed, leaned into him. Her wrist, still slightly tender, signaled that fact as the cuff of her shirt rubbed over it. And she realized there was one last thing to do before it was really ended.

She stepped away from him, turned to face him. He gave her a puzzled look. She shoved her sleeve up, and peeled at the protective cover around her wrist. It came away easily enough; she'd given it enough time. The skin was still slightly reddened, but that would fade.

"I love you, True Mahan," she said solemnly, and held her wrist out for him to see.

His brow furrowed as he looked down. He stared for a moment, and she saw the moment when he realized what she'd done. His gaze shot back to her face.

"Hope. . ."

"I thought of getting rid of it, but this seemed. . .better. I don't ever want to forget how close I came to losing everything. And who gave it all back to me."

"I gave you nothing. You fought for it, and you won."

"I never would have, if not for you."

He looked about to speak, then stopped. Instead he slowly lifted her hand, then bent to press his lips to her wrist where the once rather harsh black lines had been softened by a string of blue and green that were easily discernable as the initials T and H entwined.

When he lifted his head, those blue eyes looked into hers and he said softly, "Welcome home."

She smiled, and repeated what she'd told him before, and meant now more than ever. "My home is wherever you are. But Whiskey River will do nicely."

"I love you, Hope."

"And that," she said, "makes me the luckiest girl in the world."

She spent the rest of the night showing him she meant it. And in the morning, her new, golden life began.

The End

The Whiskey River Series

Book 1: *Whiskey River Rescue*

Book 2: *Whiskey River Runaway*

Book 3: Coming soon

Available now at your favorite online retailer!

Love the town of Whiskey River, Texas? Stay awhile. Where the women are feisty, the men are sexy and the romance is hotter than ever.

The Brothers of Whiskey River Series

If you enjoyed **Whiskey River Runaway**, you'll love the other Whiskey River stories!

Book 1: **Texas Heirs** by Eve Gaddy and Katherine Garbera

Book 2: **Texas Cowboy** by Eve Gaddy

Book 3: **Texas Tycoon** by Katherine Garbera

Book 4: **Texas Rebel** by Eve Gaddy

Book 5: **Texas Lover** by Katherine Garbera

Book 6: **Texas Bachelor** by Eve Gaddy and Katherine Garbera

Available now at your favorite online retailer!

About the Author

Author of more than 70 books, (she sold her first ten in less than two years) Justine Davis is a five time winner of the coveted RWA RITA Award, including for being inducted into the RWA Hall of Fame. A fifteen time nominee for RT Book Review awards, she has won four times, received three of their lifetime achievement awards, and had four titles on the magazine's 200 Best of all Time list. Her books have appeared on national best seller lists, including USA Today. She has been featured on CNN, taught at several national and international conferences, and at the UCLA writer's program.

After years of working in law enforcement, and more years doing both, Justine now writes full time. She lives near beautiful Puget Sound in Washington State, peacefully coexisting with deer, bears, a pair of bald eagles, a tailless raccoon, and her beloved '67 Corvette roadster. When she's not writing, taking photographs, or driving said roadster (and yes, it goes very fast) she tends to her knitting. Literally.

Visit Justine at her website at JustineDavis.com

Thank you for reading

Whiskey River Runaway

If you enjoyed this book, you can find more from all our great authors at TulePublishing.com, or from your favorite online retailer.

TULE
PUBLISHING

Printed in Great Britain
by Amazon

55205583R00199